C

It's Always Raining in Noir City
A Murderous Ink Press Anthology

****

Murderous–Ink Press

CRIMEUCOPIA

It's Always Raining in Noir City
First published by
Murderous-Ink Press
Crowland
LINCOLNSHIRE
England
www.murderousinkpress.co.uk

Editorial Copyright © Murderous Ink Press 2021
Base Cover artwork © Filip Mroz (www.unsplash.com)
Cover treatment and lettering © Willie Chob-Chob 2021
All rights are retained by the respective
authors & artists on publication
Paperback Edition ISBN: 9781909498341
eBook Edition ISBN: 9781909498358

Acknowledgements

To those writers and artists who helped make this anthology what it is, I can only say a heartfelt Thank You!

And to Den, as always.

Contents

I Smiled, But It Wasn't My Nice One...
(An Editorial of Sorts)

So what is Noir fiction?

Is it what draws the line between the Detective – hard or soft boiled – and the Anti-Hero? Can they sometimes be one and the same?

Some believe that the genre stems from Woolrich's six 'Black' novels, written between 1940 and 1948 – a lucrative period, given that Jim Thompson and David Goodis were also coming through various publishers.

But, for me, it goes much further back, to the likes of George C. Sims (aka Peter Ruric and Paul Cain), James M. Cain and Horace McCoy – though with a very agreeable nod to Patricia Highsmith's 1955 *The Talented Mr. Ripley.*

And thankfully it's getting something of a revival through authors such as Cathi Unsworth, Christina Faust, and Joolz Denby, the punk poet turned novel writer.

However, one thing this collection proves is that Noir really can be served sunny side up – and **Laurence Raphael Brothers** not only supplied the title for this anthology, but also only the second piece of flash fiction to appear in CRIMEUCOPIA.

From there we open with the more traditional in **Shannon Hollinger**'s **Money Talks**, and then shift into the 21st Century with **Lillie Franks**, who puts a twist to cyber stalking, in **Yours, The Repairman.**

H. E. Vogl's *It's Only a Cannoli* and *Allison Whittenberg*'s *Killing in Periot* take us to another part of Noir City, where the P.I.s don't usually go, before *Bruce Harris* gives us *The Seventh Round* – a classic mix of Noir and Sport.

Robert J. Mendenhall and *Shawn Kobb* drop us back into law and disorder with their *No Way Out*, and *We'll Take a Cup of Kindness Yet*, respectively – while the late *Dan Meyers* flips to the other side of the coin with *Oliver, Marty and Me*.

James Roth then presents us with what must be the most traditional Noir piece in this collection, and his *Black Market MPs* is close on the heels of *Jesse Aaron*'s curiously twisted *The Leaky Faucet*.

Julian Grant takes us to Noir City's edges with his *Baby Mamma Blues*, and *E. James Wilson* (when not wrangling alpacas) gives us a portion of *#27 – The House Special*.

I Tried to Warn You from *Brandon Barrows* puts us back on the Detective side of the Noir fence once more with his period piece, before *Hollis Miller* offers to take us for a ride as he tells us all about *The Li Fonti Job*.

And that just leaves *Joe Giordano* to close us out with his amusingly off-beat *Voice Over*.

As with all of these anthologies, we hope you'll find something that you immediately like, as well as something that takes you out of your comfort zone – and puts you into a new one.

In other words, in the spirit of the *Murderous Ink Press* motto:

You never know what you like until you read it.

It's Always Raining
in Noir City
Laurence Raphael Brothers

It's always raining in Noir City, or at least it seems that way. There's a glum, steady downpour when I'm sitting around the office playing chess against the cat, waiting for someone, anyone to show up and give me something to do for a hundred bucks a day plus expenses. Could be a blonde or a brunette, a missing heiress, or a gambling debt gone bad. I'm not picky.

A light, prickling mist raises my spirits when a case is fresh and new. No one's betrayed me yet and I haven't even heard my first lie. I know an answer's out there, occult meaning hidden in the obscuring clouds waiting to emerge if I can only choose the right direction to follow. But then I get lost in that damn fog, and somehow it all goes wrong.

Thunder and lightning accompanies the gunsel lying in wait for me when I return to my office. The sour stench of wet rot lingers with the pair of corrupt cops who bust up my office and scare the cat, while the relentless sound of the drops drumming against the pane tells me I'm running out of time.

Then there's the deadly drizzle that comes down when forensics carry off the corpse and the police inspector pretends to commiserate me for my bad decisions. It's the body of someone I failed to protect, but maybe could have saved if I'd just been a little quicker, a little smarter, a little more understanding.

Worst of all is the lull when the case is finally wrapped up and it almost seems like the sun might emerge. But then the client tells me it's not going to work out, not this time and not ever. And with one last caress she walks away, leaving me destroyed as rain streaks the window, a cig burning down to nothing in my fingers and the bitter taste of another failure in my mouth.

But dismal as they are during the rain-sodden days, the streets are beautiful at night in Noir City, with garish neon and taillights gleaming off the slick black pavement and that rich wet-earth scent rising all around me. The chilly trickle down the back of my neck is like the city's own cool, perverted kiss. Sometimes when the last case was a really bad one, I think about going somewhere else, anywhere else, but the realization that I'd be leaving those streets behind changes my mind. When that happens, I hunch down into the collar of my trench coat and light another cigarette, and it tastes good for a change. Then I turn and walk into the nearest dive of a bar and order a double, straight up. I slam it back, and the fire burns down my gut and makes me strong again. I go home to my cat, and I set up the pieces for another game.

Money Talks
Shannon Hollinger
1

I can't believe it's come to this. Believe me, I'm sick about it. But he's got what I need. The green stuff that spends. Money. And lots of it.

The rent on this dingy closet office is two months past due. I'm three months passed on my dingier studio apartment, and my landlady's started giving me hungry smiles, tangerine lipstick bleeding from the deep creases of her puckered lips, tarnished smokers' teeth bared in a predatory leer while she imagines me working it off. I've taken to sneaking things out every time I leave. I can sleep in my office if I have to. I can't run a professional service without a place to conduct business.

Most of my clients are walk-ins. People just marching through the steps of life until something about my faded sign (Devin Dudley, Private Investigations, with a magnifying glass next to my name) stirs them into action. Occasionally, I get word of mouth business due to my innate ability to be discreet. That's what's brought in the guy I'm talking to today.

He's a bulbous, walrus of a man, all bulk and meat and muscle. Sprawled in the chair across from mine like we're old friends. Scratching the ample gut that hides his belt (if he's wearing one) as he laughs at his own jokes.

"Shouldn't be that hard. She's not that smart," he says, then slaps his knee and guffaws like he just said something hilarious. Beneath the thick layer of insulation, his face grows serious. "But she is up to something. Or maybe I should say someone." He rubs his ample chins, his palm rasping against stubble like he's sanding wood.

"That's why I'm here. I need a man of your…" he looks around at the little slice of slum I call my own. "Discretion. I want proof, of course. My ideal exit strategy involves not having to pay her a dime, and an affair will make the prenup worth squat. But no one else can find out. A mouse like that trying to pull the wool over on a man like me? Well, let's just say there'll be a nice little bonus in it for you if what you find stays between us."

I want to ask just how little the bonus would be. Instead, I say, "I don't think that will be a problem."

"Good. Now, Jonesie said it's $500 a week plus expenses."

"I worked for your friend Jonesie several years ago. My rates have gone up since then. Inflation, you know?"

He stares at me like I've sprouted coconuts out my ears.

"But I guess for a friend of Jonesie's I can make an exception."

He nods, breaking out into a grey toothed grin, and we shake on it. His palm is moist and sticky. It's like squeezing a garden slug. Takes everything I've got not to wipe my hand on my pants while I slide the retainer form across the desk, wait for him to sign and push it back to me along with the check I desperately need, and walk him to the door.

Five minutes later, I'm Clorox wiping my hand and taking a picture of the check illegibly signed by Mr. Horace Wallace for mobile deposit. I've got a generic gig (prove an affair) for a

4

client I dislike (detest is more like it) for crap pay (I could have gotten more if Jonesie had kept his fat mouth shut). It's official. This Private Detective is back in business.

2

Sweat rolls down my face. Trickles down my neck. Floods down from my armpits, soaking my shirt. Bottom line is, it's summer in Florida - every part of me is oozing.

I shift on the bench, pants stuck uncomfortably deep into my skin from the wooden slats, a couple of vertebrae complaining. Turn the page on the newspaper I'm pretending to read in case anyone's paying attention. Keep my eye on the faded green door of the motel room that Wallace's wife entered twenty minutes ago.

I got a look at the wife, Loraine, while she walked from the car to the lobby and then from the lobby to the room. Pale, petite, plain, with a slight, fragile build and hair some shadeless color between blonde and brown. With brows knit together over lips pressed tight into a stern looking frown, she bears the expression of grumpy cat, personified. She doesn't look like an apt match for Wallace. I can't imagine how the hell that happened. She doesn't look like the kind to cheat, either, but I'm sitting outside the motel room that she just went into, so, yeah.

Can't complain too much, though – she's making it easy on me. First day on the job and I've already got her where I want her. She left the house in an awful lime green VW that was impossible to lose in traffic and came directly here, to a one-story dive with hourly rates and all the doors facing the exterior perimeter. No lurking in hallways, peeking round corners or bribing desk clerks here. Just a hard bench in the hot shade, which isn't that bad, considering some of the things I've had to do in the past.

The door cracks open. I peel one leg off the bench, cross it over the other, shifting my weight forward. Behind the newspaper, I bring my phone to life and zoom the camera in, waiting for the money shot. Dare I hope it's that simple?

My limbs twitch. My foot taps an erratic pattern on the pavement. I'm ready to jump, run, hop behind the wheel of my car, whatever the situation calls for. I'm ready. And . . . I'm waiting.

The door remains about six inches open. I can imagine an endless parade of events taking place on the other side of that metal slab, all of which I'd love to get a picture of so I can call it a day, go home and pop a beer. My mind spins different scenarios, trying to keep my adrenaline up, my responses ready. I keep my eyes focused on the door, not the squirrel on my left inching closer to the bench or the smoking hot redhead whose skirt just caught the wind.

Damn.

And, of course, now the door opens the rest of the way. A man exits, closing the door behind him. Aiming the camera, I take several close-ups of his face before panning out for full body shots. He's short, slender, the polar opposite of Wallace. She either doesn't have a type, or her husband ain't it.

He heads for the sidewalk, loafers kicking beneath khakis, a glimpse of white undershirt visible at the neck of a long sleeve button-down. He, and I'm going to call him Samuel because that's what comes to mind, must be crazy, wearing layers in this heat. Either that, or he's trying to make himself look thicker than a pencil.

Standing, I tuck my newspaper under my arm and follow in his direction. At the corner, he pulls out a pair of eyeglasses, slips them on, then crosses to my side of the street. I trail him as he meanders past the strip of shops (a deli, a coffee house, boutiques, a bakery that I'm going to stop at on my way home because the cinnamon buns they just pulled from the oven smell like my next meal).

Fake Samuel stares at the display behind each pane of glass, window shopping, but doesn't actually go into any of the stores. It's maddening. I pass him, go into a shop full of dog clothes, one entire wall a display case of gourmet treats decorated so fancy they make my mouth water, and watch him dawdle past.

At the corner, he turns around. I duck out of the (make your doggie a doll) store, keeping my distance as he heads back up the street, crosses the road, and returns to the motel. I cross, too, watching him through the slats of the fence behind the 7-11. Ten minutes after he gets back, Wallace's wife exits the room, stops by the lobby, slips behind the wheel of her VW lime-mobile, and takes off.

I'm not going to lie - my curiosity is piqued. This has got to be one of the most boring affairs I've ever been witness to. But the past hour has been a solid day's work, and it's time for that beer. I'll pick up the trail again tomorrow. Right now, priorities. I've got to go see a baker about some buns.

3

"Duds."

My last name is Dudley. People who call me Duds just suck.

That's a fact, not an opinion. I swallow my contempt (and my pride).

"You got an update for me, my man?"

I hear high pitched giggling in the background. Someone cooing to Horace to come back to bed. I wonder how he'd like it if I called him Hore. Sounds like it would be fitting enough.

"Nothing concrete, not yet."

"Duds, Duds, Duds, what am I paying you for?"

Right now, I'm thinking it's to not reach through the phone and punch him in his fat throat, but I swallow again, take a deep breath. "I've followed her to three different motels around the city this past week, Mr. Wallace. She met the same guy at each of them, but I haven't seen them together once yet, so no proof for your lawyer."

"That's not good. You've got to work harder, Duds."

"I'm trying, Mr. Wallace." Said between gritted teeth. "They don't seem that interested in spending much time together."

"Ha! I don't doubt that. That woman's the biggest bore I ever met."

I don't doubt it. If her IQ's over 60, I'm sure they have nothing in common. There's a question I'm reluctant to ask, something that may put an end to the case, but I can't shake the niggling feeling that what I'm spying on isn't an affair.

"I don't suppose she has a brother, does she?"

Wallace snorts on the other end of the line. "Not likely. Her parents did the world a favor and stopped after they had her. Figured bringing one oddball into this world was enough, I guess."

I swallow again, this time my spit getting stuck on the phlegmy ball of disgust lodged in my throat.

"How'd you two end up together, anyways?"

"What she lacked in looks, talent and personality, she made up for in capital."

"So, the money's hers?" Part of me wants to track his blubbery butt down and take the sure to be easy to capture pictures for Mrs. Wallace and her lawyer. The other part of me, the logical part, wants to pursue what's sure to get me paid.

"Was hers. Loraine was kind enough to invest in my company when it was starting up. A gift. She hasn't made a penny since we've been married. Just me." The chuckle that carries through the phone is pure slime ball. I feel dirty just listening to it. And while I'm sure his nice little bedtime story helps him sleep well at night, he wouldn't have hired me if he was confident that it would hold up in court.

"I see. Well, Mr. Wallace, she's just come out of the house now. Maybe today will be our day."

"You better hope it is."

I stare at the phone in my hand, not believing that he just vaguely threatened me before hanging up. The guy's a real piece of work. But he's paying real money. And I need it real bad.

4

This time, it's a three story Econolodge, the rooms entered by an interior hallway. I try to intercept her before she makes her way into the building, but I'm too late. She's moving with

9

purpose today, almost like she knows this situation is quickly coming to a head. By the time I reach the entrance, it's clicked shut behind her. It's just my luck that this is the first exterior motel door that requires a swipe from a room key card I've ever encountered that actually works.

I retreat to my car, which I've boldly parked next to her neon peon. At this point, I can either try bribing the front desk clerk or wait for fake Samuel to make his appearance and accost him. I choose the latter since it's free.

True to form, twenty minutes later, fake Samuel emerges from the motel. Slipping on his glasses, he keeps his head down as he crosses to the back of the lot, vanishing behind a dumpster.

I trot to catch up with him, but he's gone. It takes me a minute to locate the hole in the chain link fence that runs along the back perimeter of the parking lot. Another two to thread my way through the gap and burrow through the thick shrubs on the other side.

I find myself in another parking lot, this one behind a fancy hotel. Spying fake Samuel heading towards the building, I dash along the mulched curb fronting the parked cars, keeping low. It looks like he's heading towards the black metal gate that leads to the pool. I cut diagonally over the blacktop and through the outdoor seating area of the hotel restaurant to intercept him, jogging the last few steps so we reach the fence at the same time.

Placing my hand firmly on the gate, I hold it in place. "Hey. Listen, I'm sorry to bother you, but we've gotta talk."

His eyes go wide. Up close, I'm struck by the delicate

structure of his face, high cheekbones, thick lashes, expertly arched eyebrows.

"I, um, this is awkward, but I was hired by Mrs. Wallace's husband. He wants proof of an affair to negate the prenup in a divorce settlement. And I hate to be like this, but I've gotta get paid by someone, you know? But it doesn't have to be him. The guy's a total tool. He's fooling around, I know I can get the proof. Do you suppose you could get Mrs. Wallace to listen to me for a few minutes? Get her to give me a chance and hear me out?"

"Oh, I know the pig's cheating."

My jaw hits. The. Floor.

Mrs. Wallace straightens her back, pulls at the collar of her shirt. Behind fake Samuel's glasses, tears glitter in her eyes.

"It's. You're."

"Yes."

"But."

"How much is my husband paying you? Never mind, he's a cheap toad, you probably wouldn't be talking to me right now if he wasn't."

"Actually, I can't stand the guy. I think he's a complete blowtard and he deserves a lot worse than he's gotten with you."

She smiles. Even dressed as a man, hair tucked up under what is now an obvious rug, I'm struck by how pretty she looks. During all my time watching her, I don't think I ever saw her smile before.

"I like the sound of your proposition."

I wrack my brain, trying to remember what I proposed, hoping it wasn't too dirty. But since she's into it, maybe I should hope it was.

"And I think you're right. We should strike a deal of our own."

I arch an eyebrow, give her the lopsided grin I reserve for sport (the girls at the bar), because I still can't get over what a difference a smile makes. There's nothing plain about her at all.

"My husband is here right now, entertaining one of his lady friends. Same room as always, first floor, poolside, fourth from the right. They usually leave the curtains open. Get me some incriminating photos and I'll be in your office first thing tomorrow morning to pay for them. Five thousand, cash. Does that work?"

"Well, yeah, sure."

"Do you have a card?"

Reaching to my back pocket, I grab my wallet and withdraw one of the few business cards I possess. Her tapered fingertips brush my hand as she takes it, oval nails neatly filed, unpolished. Skin smooth and soft. A light smattering of freckles dance across a porcelain canvas.

I wish I had invested in better cardstock, something thicker, something that would make a gal think, *this guy's got class*. Or at least not, *this guy's so broke he paid for the xerox with a quarter he picked up off a public bathroom's floor*. I hold my breath as she inspects the piece of paper with my name and number on it, watching for her reaction. Her head tips forward for a closer look. The glasses slide off her nose, tumbling to the ground.

I swoop low and snatch them up, holding them by the left lens as I offer them to her. I know I'm probably marking them up with my greasy fingerprints, but they're wireless, lightweight, the arms thin and fragile like a piece of uncooked spaghetti, and I don't want to break them. She smiles gratefully, cupping the edges between her pretty pink palms as she takes them from me and slides them back on.

"Thank you. I'll see you tomorrow then, Mr. Dudley."

"I'll be there, Mrs. Wallace."

"I can't wait until you can call me something different."

It feels like a pinball's been released inside my chest, the bright metal orb careening off every surface, lighting up bonuses. I hold her eyes as I pass through the pool gate and during my first several steps backwards, not wanting to look away. Or leave. But eventually I do, both so I don't trip and make a fool of myself, and because I finally have a case I'm actually excited about.

Pulling the camera app up on my phone and rounding the pool, I realize I forgot to ask her why she does it. Dress up like fake Samuel. Guess it'll have to wait until we meet again. Luckily, I only have to wait the night.

5

The next day, I'm running late. It's more than just the Monday lag – I got sidetracked by a story on the morning news. Burned my omelet so bad I probably ruined the pan. Forgot to pour myself a sip of coffee, even though I feel like I drank the whole pot. Now, running up the stairs to my office, I notice that I didn't even manage to match my shoes.

As I reach the landing, I see I have bigger problems. The detective who was leaning against (and possibly listening at) my office door straightens up at my approach. I try to smile, but can feel my face is too tense, lips drawn too tight. I probably look like a chimp.

"Mr. Dudley?" The detective looks down at my shoes, one brown and one black, his face pursing like he's biting back a snarky comment. Either that or sucking on a lemon's butt – your pick. He extends his hand to me, amusement shining in his eyes, and we both know he has my number. I'm a nervous, flustered, hack.

"That's me," I say.

"Detective Kline. Orange County Sheriff's Office."

I take his hand, pump it like I'm shaking a can of spray paint, face still frozen in my best ape impersonation. (And this is me trying to play it smooth.)

"I think we both know why I'm here."

(Do we? I sure as hell hope not.) I gulp so loud that the psychic down the hall must have heard. If she hurries, she can come tell me I'm nervous and get something right for a change. I don't intend to give her the chance.

"Why don't we discuss this in my office?" I unlock the door and gesture for him to enter. Ignoring the way his nose wrinkles as he looks around, I hurry to the far side of the desk, eager to put space and a large block of wood between us.

"I'm here because Mr. Horace Wallace is dead."

I nod. "I heard something about it on the news this morning."

He sharpens his gaze, eyes boring into mine like he's

14

scanning the images I've seen over the last twenty-four hours. I fight the urge to squirm. Bite my tongue so I don't break the silence. His head tilts ever so slightly to the side and his eyes return to normal, releasing me from the creepy cyborg stare but still watching me closely.

"He was shot yesterday afternoon, right around the time hotel security has footage of you on the property. And here's another interesting tidbit for you. We also noticed that Mr. Wallace wrote you a check last week. I don't suppose you'd care to enlighten me on any of this?"

I clear my throat, searching for my voice. I find it hidden beneath my sour stomach. "Mr. Wallace hired me to follow his wife. He suspected she was cheating."

"And was she?"

I shake my head. "No. She wasn't."

"And you were at the hotel yesterday because?"

"I, um." In my mind I see a single, exquisite smile, like a rare orchid that blooms only one night a year. My wheels spin so fast I'm afraid I'm going to have a blowout. I keep speeding ahead before I have a chance to get stuck in the mud. "I was also doing a little surveillance on Wallace himself. He was planning on using proof of his wife's affair to void the pre-nup. I was concerned that he'd decide not to pay me the rest of my fee when I gave him the disappointing news."

Detective Kline's left eyebrow arches almost to his hairline. "Is that so?"

Another nod. I stop only when I start to feel like a bobblehead.

"And what did you find?"

I rub a hand down my face, rubbing my jaw. "Well, Detective, it appears that Mr. Wallace was the one having an affair."

"Did he know that you knew?"

"No, sir. Not yet."

I sneak a peek at my watch.

"Are you in a rush, Mr. Dudley?"

(Apparently, it wasn't as discreet as I thought.)

"No, just expecting a client soon." And hoping Mrs. Wallace doesn't show while the detective is here. Not that I'm so sure she'll come at all anymore. (I've got a nasty suspicion that this has all been a set-up.)

"Then I'll try to make this fast." He reaches inside his suit jacket. I'm sure he's going for his handcuffs, maybe even his gun. Instead, his thickly furred hand withdraws holding a folded paper. He opens it, revealing a picture of me talking to Loraine as fake Samuel by the pool gate. "Do you know this man?"

"I don't."

He raises his eyebrows, looks at me from the tops of his eyes. "Looks like you're pretty chummy to me."

"It's supposed to."

"Care to explain?"

"I wasn't a guest at the hotel. I had no right to be there, especially not to spy on a paying customer. I figured if I chatted up someone who *was* staying there, it would look like I belonged. In case any staff members were watching."

"Is that so?"

"You learn all kinds of helpful tricks when you don't have

16

a badge to back you up."

His head dips from side to side, like he's considering the merit of my words. "What can you tell me about him?"

"Who? The guy in the picture?"

"Yes."

"Why?"

"Satisfy my curiosity and maybe I'll indulge yours."

I shrug. "He didn't know if smoking was allowed on the pool deck. Or where we could get pool towels."

"Conversation seemed a bit longer than that."

"He'd never stayed there before. Didn't catch where he was from, but he had a soft voice."

"It appears as if you didn't want to turn your back on him. Why was that?"

I think for a moment, decide to go with the truth. "He had a nice smile."

"Did he, now?"

The detective gives me a knowing smirk. Was that a wink? What a douche.

"Anything else?" he asks.

"He seemed kind of nervous. I figured maybe he just wasn't the chatty type, but since you're asking about him, I'm guessing there's a little more to it than that."

He looks around my office, says, "It's no wonder you get paid the big bucks."

"Eh. I know it doesn't look like much, but overhead's low, I'm my own boss and I make my own hours." I give him the grin I reserve for play (slightly sheepish, like when I'm about to lose my shirt at the poker table.) "So. What gives?"

"He matches the description of the gunman given to us by Mr. Wallace's, er, companion. It's too soon to say anything for sure, but he's definitely a person of interest and we'd like the chance to speak with him."

"Wow."

"You seem surprised."

"I guess I just wouldn't have taken him for the type. Guess that's why you get paid the big bucks." I grin and lean back in my cheap office chair.

"We suspect the shooter had an accomplice," he says.

The grin slides right off my face, down all the way into the gutter outside on the street. I lick my lips, mouth suddenly drier than the Sahara during a drought. "Why'd you think that?"

"According to the eyewitness, the assassin was pretty awkward. Forgot to take the safety off the gun at first, dropped their glasses at the scene, didn't even bother to pick them up. A real amateur."

I snort, even though I'm worried that Loraine might have gotten herself into some real trouble. "Sounds like a winner, alright."

"It does indeed," he says, giving me an odd look. I wonder if the snort was overdoing it. "Probably an amateur doing someone else's dirty work. Shouldn't take long to wrap this one up." A niggling feeling scratches at the back of my mind, like I'm forgetting something. I wonder if I forgot to lock the front door when I left this morning. The detective stands, purses his lips and scratches his nose. (It was totally a pick.) "Well, I guess I'll leave you to it. Just one more question."

"Shoot."

"How do you like this gig? Really."

"There's nothing else I'd rather do."

"That's great. Real great. Because I don't believe in coincidences, Mr. Dudley. I have a feeling when we find this guy, something's going to lead me straight back to you. So, do us both a favor and don't leave town."

I watch the door close behind him, then release the sigh I've been holding. I've got to stop getting myself into these situations. Still – I run my hands over my hair and pop a breath mint – just in case Loraine actually does show up. Who knows? She might decide I'm a good friend to have. The strong, silent type.

Am I a liar? I don't think so. It's all about knowing which questions to ask. Detective Kline asked me if Wallace's wife was cheating, and if I knew who some guy who didn't exist was. He never asked if I knew who committed the murder.

So, maybe I stretched the truth a bit. But reality is, I don't really know what happened, do I? I didn't witness a thing. I did what I was paid to do. Be discreet. After all, didn't Wallace say he wanted to keep what his wife was up to between us? And maybe there's still a way to wrangle that bonus after all – I have a sneaking suspicion that if I send a bill to Wallace's estate, it'll get paid. Money talks, but for the right price, I won't.

Yours, the Repairman

Lillie Franks

Excerpt from the 𝕹𝖊𝖜 𝖄𝖔𝖗𝖐 𝕮𝖑𝖆𝖗𝖎𝖔𝖓, September 21

CEO, philanthropist and tabloid regular Richard Scott was found dead in his penthouse office after apparently taking his own life with a gun he kept in his desk.

"It was the most horrifying thing I've ever seen," said attorney Ellen Bishop, who entered his office at 3 p.m. for what she thought would be a normal meeting only to discover the 76 year old businessman dead in his chair, with the gun he'd shot himself with still in his hand. He had been seen alive just twenty minutes earlier, when his secretary, Madeline Green, watched him say goodbye to a client at the end of a routine meeting.

"I can't help thinking if I'd have been there, it might have meant something," Ms. Green said. She was called away by her administrative responsibilities during the twenty minutes in which the tragic suicide took place. "It just goes to show how you never know what someone's facing."

For the moment, control of the Guardian Law Corporation has passed to junior executive Louis Hughes. "There's no need to worry about the business," he reassured investors. "The day to day running of affairs is all provided for. If there's one thing I learnt from Rick, it's to prepare for everything."

When asked for his personal feelings, Hughes said. "Rick was a mentor and an idol to me. I simply can't describe what it was like to get out of a concert and be met with such tragic news. Rick had confided some dark feelings to me, but I had no idea it went that far."

As well as founding the highly successful Guardian Law firm, Richard Scott will be known to many New Yorkers as...

From: The Repairman [the_repairman@x_ray-mail.com]
To: Louis Hughes [lhughes@glco.com]
Date: September 22, 4:31 PM
Subject: A Proposition

Dear Louis Hughes,

I hope this e-mail finds you well. At your earliest convenience, I would like to speak with you regarding the recent death of Richard Scott at your hands.

Please confirm that this is the most convenient e-mail address for you and feel free to ask any questions you have, although I will answer only at my own discretion.

If you contact the police, I will obviously do the same.

Yours,

The Repairman

From: Louis Hughes [lhughes@glco.com]
To: The Repairman [the_repairman@x_ray-mail.com]
Date: September 22, 5:33 PM
Subject: RE: A Proposition

I don't know who you are or what game you think you're playing, but I'm giving you just one warning that I don't take this kind of accusation lightly. Rick Scott killed himself, and throwing around accusations like this is not only trivializing to the suffering he went through, but libelous and defaming.

If I hear from you again, I will instigate disciplinary actions.

In other words, fuck off while you still can.

From: The Repairman [the_repairman@x_ray-mail.com]
To: Louis Hughes [lhughes@glco.com]
Date: September 23, 10:12 AM
Subject: RE: A Proposition

Dear Mr. Hughes,

I will assume this e-mail address is fine to use going forward.

If I don't receive an answer to my initial e-mail by 3:00 PM today, I will tell the police about Damian Mitchell.

Yours,

The Repairman

From: Louis Hughes [lhughes@glco.com]
To: The Repairman [the_repairman@x_ray-mail.com]
Date: September 23, 2:59 PM
Subject: RE: A Proposition

What do you want?

From: The Repairman [the_repairman@x_ray-mail.com]
To: Louis Hughes [lhughes@glco.com]
Date: September 23, 5:43 PM
Subject: RE: A Proposition

Dear Mr. Hughes,

I'm so glad to see you're already adjusting your approach.
While I certainly understand your initial defensiveness, please
realize I am not interested in harming you, and I believe that
together we can forge a powerful and mutually beneficial
relationship.

As for what I want? You're probably expecting me to name
some amount of money. In fact, while financial investment
will be a part of our work together, money is not my primary
goal. Murderers, you must understand, are something of an
interest for me. When I read about Mr. Scott's death in the
New York Clarion, I immediately suspected you, a suspicion
that a small amount of investigation quickly confirmed. I
asked myself what exactly was to be done about a person like
you. Would throwing you in prison, assuming the trial went
as it should, really represent justice? Hardly. What does sitting

in a prison have to do with taking a life?

And so, I've formulated my own program, a sort of rehabilitative regimen that I believe will offer you both justice and the chance to improve. While it may not be one you listen to, you know as well as I do some piece of you wants what I'm offering.

Simply put, I will fix you.

Yours,

The Repairman

From: Louis Hughes [lhughes@glco.com]
To: The Repairman [the_repairman@x_ray-mail.com]
Date: September 23, 7:15 PM
Subject: RE: A Proposition

You can drop the bullshit.

There's only one person in the world who would read that article and suspect me, and that's Damian himself.

So as you're alias has been exposed, you can stop all this pseudo-subterfuge. I don't admit to anything, but we can at least talk this out, face to face. We are friends, after all. I hope you don't think I was just using you.

How about tomorrow at 12:30? The cafe across from my building. It's plenty public, if you don't trust me, though I assure you, I'm not the kind of person you're taking me for. We'll talk. It'll be just like we were back at the old cafeteria.

Trust me. You want me as a friend, not whatever this is trying to make me into.

From: The Repairman [the_repairman@x_ray-mail.com]
To: Louis Hughes [lhughes@glco.com]
Date: September 24, 10:26 AM
Subject: RE: A Proposition

Dear Mr. Hughes,

Don't bother going to the cafe. You won't find either Damian or myself there.

As for your insistence that only Damien could possibly suspect you of murder based on the newspaper article I mentioned, I'm afraid you aren't as subtle as you think you are. Simply put, you act like a murderer. It's a more distinctive type than you may realize.

In my opinion, there is nothing quite as revealing of a man's character as their plans. In your murder, you showed both what you believe are your strengths, that is, careful timing and control, and what you most fear, namely, suspicion and uncertainty. You put yourself on display for anyone willing to interpret you.

I am simply the one who happened to do that.

If you harm or attempt to harm Mr. Mitchell, I will be forced to take retaliatory action. I assure you, neither of us want that.

Yours,

The Repairman

From: Louis Hughes [lhughes@glco.com]
To: Damian Mitchell [dmitchell@glco.com]
Date: September 24, 10:57 AM
Subject: Sorry for the silence

Damian,

I hope you enjoyed that concert we went to together. Sorry for not having got in touch since then, but there's been a lot going on at work. You might even have heard about it in the papers.

I was wondering if you wanted to hang out again. We didn't get to talk much during the concert, so maybe something a little more one on one. You could come by my house and I could show you my swimming pool!

Would Saturday work?

Thanks,

Lou

From: Damian Mitchell [dmitchell@glco.com]
To: Louis Hughes [lhughes@glco.com]
Date: September 24, 6:02 PM
Subject: RE: Sorry for the silence

Yeah, sounds great! Address and time? Also, what's been going on? I don't follow news too much, lmao.

From: The Repairman [the_repairman@x_ray-mail.com]
To: Louis Hughes [lhughes@glco.com]
Date: September 25: 10:35AM
Subject: RE: A Proposition

I know you've been in contact with him.

Yours,

The Repairman

From: Louis Hughes [lhughes@glco.com]
To: The Repairman [the_repairman@x_ray-mail.com]
Date: September 25, 3:18 PM
Subject: RE: A Proposition

Got visited by the police today. They said they'd received an anonymous tip. I assume it's your idea of trying to put pressure on me. I explained exactly what happened. At 2:45 PM, I left my office, took the elevator and got into a limousine to the concert, where I stayed until 6:00. My secretary, the driver, and multiple people who were at the concert can all attest to it.

They left muttering about crackpot phone calls and the press.

Looking forward to you coming over tomorrow! Unless you're as much of a coward as I think you are, of course.

From: The Repairman [the_repairman@x_ray-mail.com]
To: Louis Hughes [lhughes@glco.com]
Date: September 26, 5:29 PM
Subject: RE: A Proposition

Mr. Hughes,

May I remind you, whatever quarrel you think you have is with me, not him.

If you believe that harming Mr. Mitchell will defang me of the ability to expose you, I can assure you it won't. I have concrete documentation which will incriminate you to any investigative eye. I would not have mentioned Mr. Mitchell's name if he were my only assurance.

Yours,

The Repairman

From: Louis Hughes [lhughes@glco.com]
To: The Repairman [the_repairman@x_ray-mail.com]
Date: September 26, 6:46 AM
Subject: RE: A Proposition

You don't have documentation because there is no documentation. Even if it did happen.

There's not much sport in bluffing over the internet.

Since you're so interested in plans, why don't I tell you what I would do if you came to my house tomorrow at 4 p.m and I really were the kind of person you think I am. We'd share some drinks in my studio. I'd have less alcohol in mine than you in yours, but I'd play it up so you didn't notice. After about an hour, I'd be pretty sure you were drunk. Then, we'd head out to the pool. Only a few minutes later, some papers that I didn't quite fill out correctly today would be filed and rejected, meaning I would get a phone call from the office asking me to sign and fax new copies. When I came back down to the pool, you would be floating there, face down, having blacked out and drowned while I was working in my office.

What does that tell you about me?

TXT MSG

From: The Repairman //Burner Phone Number Withheld//

To: Louis Hughes //Private Phone Number Withheld//

September 26, 7:01 AM

12:00. The Red Eye cafe at 25 N Lake Drive. The table by the window.

Deal with me, not him.

Yours,

The Repairman

TXT MSG

From: Louis Hughes //Private Phone Number Withheld//

To: The Repairman //Burner Phone Number Withheld//

September 27, 12:08 PM

Should have expected you wouldn't be here. I take it Mitchell gave you this number?

TXT MSG
From: The Repairman //Burner Phone Number Withheld//
To: Louis Hughes //Private Phone Number Withheld//
September 27, 12:09 PM
Don't move.

TXT MSG
From: Louis Hughes //Private Phone Number Withheld//
To: The Repairman //Burner Phone Number Withheld//
September 27, 12:10 PM
Now what?

TXT MSG
From: The Repairman //Burner Phone Number Withheld//
To: Louis Hughes //Private Phone Number Withheld//
September 27, 12:11 PM
Stay in view and wait for my next email.

From: The Repairman [the_repairman@x_ray-mail.com]
To: Louis Hughes [lhughes@glco.com]
Date: September 27, 12: 32 PM
Subject: RE: A Proposition

Dear Mr. Hughes,

Thank you for your patience.

I regret to announce that I am canceling my offer for a
rehabilitative partnership. This is because I am, unfortunately,

unable to meet your needs at this time. I wish you luck going forward, and will provide a short summary of my reasons for terminating our relationship.

You repeatedly expressed skepticism that my awareness of your crime came, at least initially, from reading a newspaper article. Nevertheless, it is true. The first detail that struck me as suspicious was the window of time. Suicides normally occur in long periods of solitude. This happened within a specific twenty minute period. This told me not only that it was likely a murder, but that whoever the murderer was, it was important to them that time of death be fixed within a twenty minute window, and that, in fact, this was so important to them that they were willing to sacrifice plausibility in order to achieve it.

In your interview in the same article, you took time from discussing your own emotions and the future of the business to establish that you were at a concert when he died. That fact, in other words, was more important than any of the other matters you mentioned.

Put simply, you were playing innocent, which is the farthest thing from acting innocent.

A casual contact with your secretary was enough to establish both your alibi, the limousine that took you to the concert, and that you had recently revived an old friendship with a high school comrade, Damian Mitchell. The limousine ride was obviously the alibi because, unlike the concert, it required the precision of time that had characterized the murder. And knowing all that, it was no great mystery what you had done. You had told Damian Mitchell to pretend to be you in order to enjoy a limousine ride to the concert, while you took that time to murder Mr. Scott and meet him by train. Thanks to a very careful choice of time and concert venue, you were able to make it comfortably.

From this came my initial assessment. You value careful timing and control. You fear uncertainty and the suspicion of others.

It was thanks to this assessment that I discovered the documentation you didn't think I had. I theorized that someone as partial to planning as you wouldn't leave the presence of Mr. Scott's secretary to chance. Sure enough, I found the papers you misfiled in order to get her to leave her office at the precise time of the murder. It might pass for an accident if you hadn't specifically added a note to submit them at 2:00;

As you can see, I was well prepared to work with you. Unfortunately, you threatened Mr. Mitchell and myself.

I wasn't shaken by the threat to me, thanks to my lengthy career rehabilitating murderers before you. Mr. Mitchell, however, had none of the protections I do, and I don't have the resources to reliably protect him myself. Any attempt I made would only provoke your fear of uncertainty and need for precise control of your situation, leading to more unpredictable behavior. For this reason, I was forced to admit I couldn't ensure a safe environment for you to grow in.

You may remember the death, almost a year ago, of Florence Cliffe in an automobile accident. If you don't, suffice it to say I was similarly unable to maintain a safe environment for her husband, Mr. Cliffe. In a recent e-mail, I agreed to meet Mr. Cliffe in this same table at this same cafe.

Based on my understanding of Mr. Cliffe and the way he

plans, I don't believe you'll make it home alive. He is less thorough than you, but more violent. If you do, thank for your help in dealing with Mr. Cliffe, and both Damian and the police have received messages including the document mentioned above.

I regret our partnership must end on such a sour note. Let me assure you, I feel no malice towards you.

Yours,

The Repairman

It's Only a Cannoli
H. E. Vogl

Alawishus Danker was a collector. A collector of bad debts. He traveled up and down the Florida coast, freelancing for any loan shark in need of his services. Knuckles, as he was known in the trade, discovered his special talent the day he knocked out his eighth-grade history teacher with a hard right. Destined to pursue an alternative career path, he stepped out onto the streets where he used his God given ability to beat the crap out of anyone foolish to get behind on their loan payments.

Knuckles pulled his black Escalade off I-95 and coasted into the rest area to hit the can and check on the location of his afternoon appointment. He drove around to the back of the building and parked in a shaded spot. Then he leaned against the wheel to pull his wallet out of his back pocket and came up empty.

"Must have fallen out," he muttered.

He bent down and ran his right hand, swollen from the morning's work, along the floor mat. Nothing. Of course, he left it at the bakery where he stopped before the morning run to Jacksonville. Relieved, he jumped back on 95 and headed to

Leonardo's.

When he got downtown, he pulled into a diagonal slot near the bakery. He grabbed the doorframe to extract himself from the caddy. Then he rummaged through his pocket for a quarter and slipped it into the parking meter. No sense in asking for trouble, he thought.

The bakery, a renovated brick building, sat on the beachfront strip, sandwiched between a bookstore and a lawyer's office. Two bistro tables guided customers inside and down a narrow hallway. Against the wall five hightops sat opposite a glass case lined with baked goods. The owner, a small bespectacled man named Clarence, was a lifelong friend. Knuckles stopped to see him every week. But he frequented the bakery for another reason, Clarence made the best cannoli in town.

The front doorbell rang, and a long shadow slid along the hardwood floor.

"Gone already. Keep eating like that and you won't fit through the door," Clarence said.

"The cannoli are still alive. I left my wallet here and came back to pick it up."

Clarence took off his glasses and squinted a puzzled look.

"Didn't see no wallet."

"You sure? I left it on top of the case."

"Nothing there."

"Dam. Somebody must have run off with it. Who was in here?"

"Lots of people since you left."

"Like who?"

"Don't know," Clarence said. "Tell you what, I'll tack a note to the bulletin board. Everybody looks at it when they come in."

"If somebody took my wallet, they're in trouble."

Clarence pulled a large index card from under the register and started writing.

"You want to do a reward?"

Yeah, fifty," Knuckles thought for a moment and said, "No, make it a hundred."

Clarence dropped the marker and pinned the card to the board.

"Hope you get it back," he said.

Back on 95, Knuckles did his best to envision the contents of the wallet. He wasn't worried about the money. Only a couple thousand. And his credit cards and license could be replaced. But the wallet had sentimental value. His late father gave it to him. He pictured its soft brown leather embossed with the outline of an old bull's head on one side and its rear end on the other. Over the bull's head were the words, Fuck'em all. The Caddy's steering wheel flexed as he imagined what he'd do to the guy who took it.

*****

The following week Knuckles stepped into Leonardo's and ordered his usual, two cannoli.

When he pulled out his wallet Clarence said, "See you got everything back."

"Everything except my wallet. If I ever catch the bastard

who took it, he's going to die."

Clarence nodded as Knuckles armed with his dose of pastry disappeared through the door.

Today would be busy. A regular was delinquent, and his creditor wanted Knuckles to not only collect the back money, but to make sure he understood that a loan represented a serious obligation. As he was about to get in his car, another vehicle pulled up alongside. A thin, nervous looking man, draped in a lizard green jacket, slid out and started to feed the meter.

"I've still got ten on this one if you want to pull up after I leave," Knuckles said.

The man uttered a stammering thank you and stuffed his wallet back into his pocket.

On the way to his next appointment, Knuckles hummed along to Freebird on the radio. As the song picked up tempo his hum dropped to a murmur. The wallet the guy in the green jacket pulled out, resembled his. A coincidence, he thought. There must be a million brown wallets, and he didn't get a good look at the design.

*****

It was a busy afternoon. And even with the air turned up full, sweat rolled down his cheeks. Fortunately, he was finished for the day. Knuckles checked his watch and saw he still had an hour before Judge Judy. Enough time to detour to Leonardo's. He pulled into an open parking spot and started to lift himself out. Parked two down the nervous stranger with the green jacket. Knuckles took his hand off the frame and slid down into the seat. He watched behind the tinted glass as green jacket reached around for his wallet. It might be his, but he couldn't be sure. Five minutes later, green jacket reappeared with a small bag and drove away.

Knuckles went inside and rapped his keys on the counter.

Clarence came out of the backroom wiping his hands on his apron.

"Who's the guy that just left?"

"Huh?"

"The guy, tall thin, green jacket, Adam's apple sticking out like he swallowed a golf ball."

Clarence rubbed his chin, "Name's Frank I think. Comes in here once and awhile."

"Call me next time he comes in. You got my number.

*****

On Monday, Knuckles got the call.

"The guy you asked about came back. Said he wanted a birthday cake for a friend. He's going to pick it up on tomorrow."

"What time?"

"One."

"Thanks, I owe you," And he slammed the phone down.

Knuckles cancelled his Tuesday afternoon appointment and waited in front of Leonardo's.

"Dam, I should have got some cannoli to keep me company. Maybe I still got—"

Too late. There he was. Knuckles watched in the side mirror as green jacket went into the bakery. When the front door swung shut, he pulled himself out of the caddy. He went inside and pretended to examine the notes on the bulletin board. Green jacket stood at the counter drumming his fingers as if he was late for an appointment. A minute later Clarence came out of the backroom with a small white box. Tucked under the crisscross of string was an envelope. Green jacket took out his wallet, folded the envelope, and slipped it inside. Knuckles saw the outline of a bull's head. He took a step toward the counter intending to twist the neck off of the green jacket, then stopped. He didn't want to cause a scene in his friend's bakery.

Knuckles waited until green jacket left. Then he got in his car and followed him down the street. His temples pounded like a drum as he kept the car in sight. Down Washington, a right on Minnesota, and finally a turn onto a deserted side street. He sped up and closed the distance. When they neared a stop sign, he hit the gas and rammed the car, putting a good crease in the trunk. He waited as green jacket got out to inspect the damage. Finally, he opened the door and donned his best embarrassed smile.

"I'm really sorry. I guess I wasn't paying attention. Let me give you my info."

He stepped closer and jammed his knee into green jacket's crotch and followed up with an elbow to the chin. Then he grabbed him by the hair and used his head to add a new pothole to the road. Knuckles looked down at the crumpled mass on the asphalt and realized he might have overdone it. He reached into the green jacket's back pocket and took out his wallet. Knuckles smiled as he ran his thumb over the bull's backside. He scanned the street to make sure no one saw and drove off.

The rain slowed him down. But that didn't matter because his last appointment had been easier than expected. The guy shook so bad when he handed over the money, Knuckles thought he'd have to call 911. He pulled in front of Leonardo's thinking only of cannoli. At the counter he ordered the usual and pulled out his wallet.

"See you found it," Clarence said.

"Yeah. Funny thing, it was on my dresser all the time."

Clarence smiled as Knuckles lumbered out the door.

After he left, Clarence went to the backroom and called his wife.

He cupped his hand over the speaker and said, "It's done."

"How do you know?" she said.

"I saw the wallet. He has it back."

Clarence collapsed on a chair and wiped his forehead with his apron.

Two weeks ago, he was at wit's end. Every Tuesday Frank would drift in sporting his green jacket and roll a pair of dice for a jelly doughnut. Then Clarence would open the cash drawer and hand him an envelope. At first, he made the payments, but as time went on, he couldn't scrape the money together for the following week let alone the next thirty he owed.

Clarence looked at the clock. Frank would be in shortly to collect a payment he didn't have. He'd spent years planning to open the bakery. Only to end up like this. Mindlessly, he wiped the countertop. That's when he spied the wallet, stuffed with bills, laying on the counter. Desperate, he pulled out five one hundred dollar bills and hid the wallet behind the cash register. When Frank arrived, he handed him the money. Safe this week, but what about the next? Clarence sat behind the counter nibbling on a leftover croissant, and slowly an idea took form.

The following Tuesday Frank strode in and said, "Hey pal. Seven says I get a jelly doughnut."

A pair of red dice tinkled along the counter and he came up empty.

He handed Frank the money and said, "Sorry, no doughnut, but I got an offer for you." Clarence licked his lips and said, "I found this," and he took the wallet out from behind the register. "You roll seven and it's yours. Maybe give me a break next week."

Frank took the wallet and turned it over. When he saw the bull's head his eyes lit up like a cat who bit into a lamp cord.

"Okay pal. You got a deal."

He reached into his pocket and took out a pair of green dice. The cubes bounced on the counter and settled on five and two.

"Looks like the wallet's mine."

Clarence smiled as Frank's green jacket slithered out the door, Sooner or later he would cross paths with his old friend and the debt would be cancelled. He removed his glasses and massaged the bridge of his nose. His worries were over.

*****

The trip to the gulf coast kept Knuckles busy, and he was looking forward to some toes in the sand and beer in the hand time off. He eased off I-95 onto the exit when the message popped up on his dash screen. One of his clients had an emergency. He needed Knuckles to resolve a past due account because his regular collector had suddenly retired. The delinquent took the collector's absence as an indication that the debt had been cancelled, and he refused to make any more payments. Knuckles scrolled down the screen. When he saw the address, a tear ran down his cheek. He'd miss those cannoli.

Killing in Periot

Allison Whittenberg

I wasn't just Solly's brother; I was his protector. Over the years, I had done a pretty good job of it considering what I was up against. Nick was my stepfather. He was Solly's real father. He was our main adversary. Everyone else, I could handle.

It all came to a crossroad late that fall when I was fifteen, nearly sixteen, and Solly was younger than that. We both upped our ages so we could work long hours at shit jobs because that was what Nick told us to do. Nick pimped us out to honest jobs since his own illegal exploits were going slow. Between Solly and me, we pulled an all-right grip; the only hitch was Nick took it all.

Now, I was no dummy, so for quite a while, I'd been holding back, in one-way or another. You know, deep pocketing some of the money, most of the time I'd leave some pinned to the inside of my shirt then when I got inside I stashed in the fraying fabric of a chair in our room. That evening, I was careless.

"Empty your pockets," Nick demanded. He would not let Solly or me pass him to get inside of the house where it was warm.

"I did," I said.

"You're coming up short," he insisted. I could tell his ire had already formed. Like a bull in a ring preparing to charge, his nostrils flared. "You two worked forty hours between you two. This doesn't add."

I maintained a poker face while I lied, "It's all there."

He looked from me to Solly. "What do you know about this?"

Solly wore a blank look. He said, "I don't know anything."

In disgust, Nick shook his head. "You can say that again."

"Look," I told him. "You got your money."

Nick shot a look over to me that could split rock, but I held myself together. As he advanced toward me, his gaze switched like a light bulb going on. He pushed me down.

"Hey –" Solly began.

"Shut up," Nick said as he raised his hand to him. I hated when he did that. That was worse than the slap itself. I couldn't tell if Solly flinched from my vantage point. I turned over and sought to get back to my feet.

That's when he grabbed me again. He had me by the foot and wrestled my right sneaker off, then my left sneaker. It was there he grabbed the funds.

For a moment, his anger turned to laughter. He kicked his head back as if it were all good fun.

He paid me a back-handed compliment. "You know, Boy, you're pretty smart."

He got like that with me. My name was Jonah; how hard could it be for him to call me that? When he referred to me as 'boy', I knew he wasn't just highlighting my age, it was his way of never letting me forget that I wasn't all the way white.

After Nick quit laughing, he pocketed the money, leaving out one bill, a twenty, which he tore into pieces.

When I stood up, he spat on me to further his spite.

I felt a shiver go up my spine.

What was I going to do?

I swallowed hard.

What could I do?

Nick was a big man, a least a few inches over six feet. Not heavy at all, he was muscular and picked Solly and me up like we were babies. He had both of us by the back of the neck, throttling us; then he crammed our faces way down deep into the snow.

Before I knew what was what, Solly's whole head was so deep into the white it was drowning him. Solly was gasping for air and chunks of the freeze were coughed up each time his father let him up for air.

I was fainting worse because not only was it impossible for me to breathe, but since I had a slimmer neck, Nick could get a tighter grip on me. Kneeling in the chest high snow, Nick bore down with his might. Nick swept up a hand full of snowy gravel and slammed it down into my face. He braced me still and worked the wet and cold rocks into my eyelids, cheeks, and lips — grinding them against my teeth.

I hollered and spat and squirmed, but I could not escape his clutches. Each new fist full of gravel brought a fresh array of scrapping. My flesh tore and seared and stung and all I could do was yelp and buck like a wild horse. I could hear Solly close by his coughing and coughing, it sounded like a lung was coming up.

I wished for a weapon, anything. If only a large rock or fallen branch within grabbing distance, I wouldn't have been so helpless. A few minutes passed, I didn't have the strength to struggle free; I was looking for the stamina to just stay conscious. I did stay alert, barely. After my stepfather let me go, I saw that Solly was in the same bad shape I was.

Like me, he couldn't even make a crawl for it.

Nick strutted in front of the moaning lump of torn meat, which was better known as me and said, "Tell me was that worth it?"

I didn't answer. This already was way past being a bad movie. What was the point?

Then he walked over to Solly and gave him a series of kicks right to his ribs. "And you, Oink, I'm your father. You're barely related to him. Don't you ever side with him over me."

"He didn't know," I managed to get out.

"Shut the fuck up, unless I wanted some more," he told me.

So I shut the fuck up, and there was an end to it.

He walked away, leaving us to our wounds.

In the past after such attacks, I always thought about Solly first, since I was his protector and all, but I admit right then I wasn't thinking about how Solly was doing and then suddenly didn't even care. I was concerned about me. At the very moment when I regained my bearings, I got myself vertical, and I didn't concern myself with helping Solly up.

I just ran.

I ran and ran.

By this time, barely within earshot, I could hear Solly calling after me, asking me where I was going. But, as I ran, I could only hear this faintly and then more faint still till my brother's voice all but disappeared.

*****

In Periot, Wisconsin, the houses were spread out like sailboats along a shoreline. You had to go from one to another. I went heading for the Leland's. I wanted to talk to the man of the house; I needed to borrow something.

Knocking on the door, I nearly collided with Mr. Leland's granddaughter, Lori. Our eyes hooked. She had extraordinary irises of emerald green, intense and searching. She had some books in her mittened hands, and she was all suited up in a coat and scarf as if she was just about to run an errand. She asked me what happened.

"Nothing happened. I'm alright. I'm just here to see your grandpa."

Lori said my face looked like a used razor blade.

"I'm fine," I repeated.

"Sure, you are," she frowned. "Come on, I'll get you something for your cuts," she said, taking my arm.

I pushed her away. "No, I want to see your grandpa."

She knitted her brows together and told me Mr. Leland was around the back in the shed.

I walked around to the back, slowly, with measured steps. It was hitting me now. I felt so queasy in the core of my stomach. My fear bubbled. I kept waiting for a pop. *How in the Hell was I going to ask for this?*

I approached Mr. Leland's bent figure. Over a sanding

board, he was just filing away. He didn't notice me till I was right up on him. He was a funny looking old man. Stocky as a bulldog, he wore his graying blond hair in a ponytail. He straightened up when he saw me and put his hand to his lower back. He shook his head in a pitying manner.

"Why don't you just stay out of his way?" he asked me.

"It's not so easy, Mr. Leland."

He tilted his head to the side and told me, "You don't have to make it this hard."

"You think I asked for this?"

"All I'm saying is you gotta do what he says. Everything he says. Maybe you've heard that old saying: the life you save may be your own."

"I've heard it," I said.

Pause. Then more silence as he peered into me more deeply.

"Where's your other half? Where's Solly?"

"I left him," I said, taking a visual sweep of the room. "It's all right though. The storm is over."

He nodded and frowned. "Why don't you go inside? My wife will clean you up. She's in there making a pie. You can stay --"

"I didn't come all the way over here for pie, Mr. Leland. Or to get cleaned up."

He nodded again, this time more slowly. "Well, then, what did you come here for?"

"I came here for a loan."

"Sure, sure. Take what you want. You know, I promised

you many years ago I'd always been here for you and your brother. What do you want?"

I didn't hesitate for an instant.

"That," I said and pointed to his gun rack.

He turned and looked behind him. "That?"

"Yep."

"Well, this is a fine time to think about that? You want to hunt, now? When I took you boys out last month --"

"I ain't hunting."

"Say what? Are you crazy? You want a rifle, but you don't want to hunt with it? What are you talking about? That man must have hit you too hard in the head."

I smirked. It was funny because if anything the sense had finally gotten knocked into me, not the other way around. At last after many episodes, I was going to move from a defensive posture to an offensive one.

This is why I picked Mr. Leland. He was an old soldier, Vietnam and all that, so he knew all about shooting and shot positions. Since Lori had little interest and he didn't have a grandson, he had shown Solly and me everything about how to wield a rifle, even how to fire from a prone position. I guess it was only natural of me to turn to him at a time like this.

"I'm thinking clearly, Mr. Leland, I need a gun for protection. I'm not going to get beat like this ever again."

More silence followed. I shattered it by telling him that I'd been thinking of this for a good long time.

Mr. Leland's color rose but his smallish, green eyes didn't tell me anything. He shook his head. "You don't want what you're asking for. You're fixing on doing something you're going to be sorry for."

I nodded. "I'm just going to have to be sorry then."

"Wait a minute. Have you thought this through? I mean really thought this through. This ain't the way. This ain't you, Jonah. You don't go around doing rash things."

"Mr. Leland, I have thought this through --"

He talked over me, speaking quickly using wild hand gestures. "Jonah, I've been mad. I've been crazy mad, but you have to believe me that sometimes the smartest thing to do is to hold your fire."

"Mr. Leland, I don't have any fire. That's what I'm here about."

"Look, you and Solly, I know you have had it rough, but this ain't no way. You're about to blow this thing sky high... You two made it this far; just keep doing what you're doing. Don't do this, I'm begging you."

I shook my head. "Don't beg, Mr. Leland."

"I will beg you. I will. I am begging you."

"You're begging me and my brother to wait –"

"Yes, wait."

"With all due respect," I said as I eyed the rack of weapons, again. "But it's gotten past waiting. Who knows what's going to happen next? I don't want to get hurt or worse and I don't want to see my brother hurt or worse and that's it. End of story."

"But it's not the end. You do this, and it's only the beginning."

"My mind is made up. It's set. If you don't want to help me, don't. I'll get it from someplace else. This is Peroit; everyone has a gun, except for the people who need one."

I was prepared to leave right then when he again said, "Don't do it."

My brown eyes met his green ones, which were just like Lori's emerald, searching. I wished he'd cut it with all the grave concern. All it did was add another layer to things that were already deep enough.

"All right, I won't take it," I said to him but that was a lie. A big one. As soon as Mr. Leland turned his back to go inside, I knew I had only a short period of time to get what I'd come for.

In every bad situation, there's always time to act but only a second or two before the cliché comes true, bad goes to worse.

I walked toward a side cupboard. The floorboards creaked beneath my footsteps. I opened a drawer and pulled out a short heavy revolver. They call this type of weapon with its snub nose. It's also called a belly gun because it's just right to shove against someone's stomach. And sure there was nothing brave or noble about anything I was doing – stealing, plotting a murder, etc. But I wasn't aiming for those descriptions. What's the use of honor? I'd rather be safe.

Maybe this would work out for the best because a small weapon is more portable and I figured Mr. Leland won't notice it missing for a while since as far as he knew my interest was in his rifle.

I took the gun and slipped out with it.

It felt good to be out in the air.

Out of the corner of my eye, I saw the large white clouds floating across the sky. I caught my breath. Though I had secured what I'd come for, I knew this was just the start of things. Mr. Leland sure got that part right.

I came in like a cat burglar. I clawed at the pane until I was able to squeeze through. Solly walked by, just as I fell to the floor. In surprise, he nearly dropped the large can of ravioli he was finishing.

Solly and I had the exact opposite way of diffusing stress. He ate, and I didn't. At least so far, he hadn't turned into a blimp, and I hadn't gone full manorexic.

"What's wrong with the front door?" he asked.

"I saw his pick-up. I thought he'd come back."

"Naw, he ain't here," Solly told me in between shoveling down spoonfuls. You'd think he'd grown up in a great big family where you have to stake your claim early. His habit of eating fast was so that barely even pausing to breathe was his way of keeping the food warm. "Where did you go?" he asked.

"I went over to Mr. Leland's."

"Did you see Lori?"

"Yeah."

Solly smirked.

"What are you smirking about?"

"Nothing… She likes you."

I didn't answer his lead. I went into the bathroom and got my first look at the damage. My lip busted pink and purple. My whole pan was bloody with lacerations.

"Did you hear what I said?" Solly called after me.

"Yes, I did." I wet a small towel, so I could use it as a warm compress.

From the other room, I could hear Solly still on the same topic. "Lori's not bad looking. She talks too much, but she has pretty eyes."

"I don't have time for girls; I've got too many problems," I told him flatly, but in a muffled voice on the count of I was holding the cloth to my mouth. "Besides she'd be better paired with you," I said, thinking of her wide mouth and dizzily curling blond hair.

"Don't push her off on me. I got just as many problems as you have."

And we were silent again.

I came back to the room and sat on the bed. I felt a little more composed. I was at least breathing steady. "Let me see your ribs," I said to him. That was the last thing I recalled from the attack, his father kicking him there.

Solly came closer to me and lifted his tee shirt. What I saw was definite, half-moon shaped bruises made from his father's boots —tip and the heel.

"How does it feel? Sore?"

Solly nodded. "How does it look? Do you see any swelling?"

Solly was a husky kid, so the words: "No more than usual," slipped out of my mouth though I didn't mean it the flip way it sounded. If his ribs felt anything like my face, it didn't matter how meaty he was built, he must be in real pain. I laid my hand against the skin there to see if I could feel any heat. Pain draws heat, and there was radiating heat coming off his skin. I began to worry.

"Maybe we should swing by the hospital?'

"That's too much waiting. We'd be there half the night."

"But, I can't tell. I ain't a doctor. Maybe there is really something wrong. Remember before – "

"Of course, I remember before. How could I forget when I had to wear that thing for two months?"

"Solly, maybe you have some broken ribs or something."

"They can't put a cast on my ribs, can they?"

"No."

"Then how do they fix it?"

"I think they tape it."

Solly put his hand up as if to say he didn't want to hear it. "Skip it. I don't want to be taped."

He pulled his shirt down and ate the last of the ravioli.

"Solly…" I began to whine. I hated to whine, but I was so tired and achy and cold and pissed off. I just wanted some cooperation from him. I only wanted to help. I laid back on the bed totally forgetting that it was there I had hidden the gun. It was between my waistband and the back of my jeans.

I quickly sat bolt upright. I removed the weapon I had secured to my lower back.

Still not noticing, Solly chucked the empty can in the trash. Its clank made a violent sound.

I held up the weapon for him to plainly see it. "I got this."

"That's a gun," he said after a double take.

I nodded.

"Is it loaded?"

"Not yet."

He motioned to me to let him hold it.

I did without reminding him to treat it like it was armed even though it wasn't because I knew he already knew that.

Solly held it for a while, examining it. He checked the chamber and said to me, "It's cute."

"Cute?" I asked. Of all the adjectives in the world, how did that one pop into his mind to describe a weapon?

I gave it a deeper look.

"Yeah, who'd think that something so small could actually hurt someone. But it'll get the job done."

I said taking it from his hands.

"What job?"

I got up, placing the gun on the desk. I began to pace.

"I didn't even know Mr. Leland had this type," Solly said. "I thought he just had hunting stuff."

"He's pretty well armed."

"Why?" Solly laughed and winced. He ain't in Alpha company anymore."

"I suppose, he's got to protect his wife and Lori."

Solly frowned, now holding his side. "He must have like twenty or thirty guns. That's real stupid."

"What's stupid about it?"

"He only has two hands."

I stopped pacing. "I guess it helps him to sleep nights."

"Is that what you got the gun for, Jonah," Solly asked, "Sleeping?"

That made me think. I mean really think and think and think and think. I thought until I was trembling all over and my head felt dizzy.

"Jonah? Jonah? Earth to Jonah? Come in Jonah?" Solly kept asking. He clapped his hands in front of me.

I snapped back into the present.

For a second or two, I took stock of his face noticing how clear and boyish it looked for a change. It wasn't acne that so often polluted his complexion since his father had been back. Usually after a beating, Solly was so bruised up that his face was distorted and outsized. This time he looked like himself, with his delicate features. How his father called him an Oink was beyond me. His nose especially was finely cut to even be mistaken for a snout. It looked like something a plastic surgeon would construct, a showpiece even.

"What's the job?" he asked me.

"Huh?" was my reply.

"You planning to stick-up a bank?"

I gave a nervous laugh then took a deep breath then spoke in a blue streak. "I've had it with your father, Solly. Ever since he came back he's been flying into his rages on us. I'm sick of being boot kicked and bitch slapped and thrown across the room. This shit has been going on for too long. Today, just capped it off," I told him. "Why can't we keep our own money? We earned it. That man wants everything. Everything. And I'm sick of it."

Solly's mouth was open. Then, he closed it. Then he gestured to the gun, "So what does the gun have to do with that?"

"I just told you, Solly, we're getting out."

"Out? Where out?" he asked.

"He'll cripple us if we don't."

"We can't leave. We can't leave Ma. What about her?"

I went back to pacing. I thought long before I spoke then considering heavily if I really wanted to say this next part. "What about her?" I asked finally.

Solly looked at me incredulously. "Well, we just can't leave her behind."

"She's the reason we're in this mess."

"How do you figure that?"

"She hasn't done one goddamn thing --"

"She's doing the best she can --"

"This is the best that she can do," I said lifting up his shirt.

He jerked my hands away. "That's not her fault."

"Yeah, right. She doesn't have to keep taking him back. She could stop this if she wanted to."

"What do you want her to do?" Solly asked.

"You're not listening to me," I shouted at him.

"I _am_ listening," he shouted back.

"Then why are you talking?!"

Solly gave me a piercing look and went quiet.

I began, "Last week, I promise myself the next time he puts his hands on us, he's dead --"

"Don't you have that kind of bass backwards? The next time –"

I spoke over him. "– What did I say about talking?"

He went quiet again.

"I got a gun, and I plan to use it."

This time he waited a good few seconds before he asked, "On my father?"

"Yes, Solly, yes," I said. "On your father."

At that instant, Solly's skin turned sweaty and clammy. "You decided this all last week, and you didn't clue me in before now?"

I nodded. "I know it is a lot to get down all at once."

"You only had a week to think of it... Jonah, you're really going to kill him? Like shoot him in the head or something?"

I shrugged (those were some blunt questions he was asking me). "I'll do what I need to do."

Solly didn't have much of a reaction after that. He just glanced away for a moment. He looked toward the window.

Outside, the dull yellow sun had set and pitch had settled in for the night.

Solly's eyes came back to mine. He said, "Good."

The Seventh Round
Bruce Harris

Twenty thousand saw the fights live. Another million watched in various theaters on large screens via pay-per-view. No one noticed anything underhanded before, during, or after the seventh round.

But the sonofabitch cheated. Not once. Twice.

"TNT" Tanner and I were on a collision course that came to a head like a plump cyst. Turned out, there was nothing square about that Las Vegas ring. The bout had been rumored for two years before promoter Reggie Watson inked the deal. That was no surprise. Many promoters slithered throughout the sport, but Reggie Watson was always front and center. Reggie reveled in the notoriety. He'd been in the news for tax evasion, accusations of domestic abuse, and a host of other unsavory activities associated with society's bottom feeders.

Nevada, two undefeated heavyweights. "TNT" Tanner. They called me "Coffin."

Cheap cigar smoke mingled with eight-hundred-dollar-a-bottle perfume, creating a 1940s-like Hollywood monster-movie mist. The hazy concoction blurred the lighting hanging over the ring like low storm clouds. The arena darkened. A spotlight illuminated my tunnel. As if on cue, the crowd's din stopped, heads turned in the same direction. Like a mole popping out of its hole, my manager emerged, leading the way. My head down, gloved hands outstretched, rested on his shoulders. On the ring's apron, he separated the ropes. I climbed in and raised my hands. To the delight of the crowd, I shadowboxed and danced around the ring, relishing in the attention and adulation. I was calm, confident. The referee had a few unintelligible words with me. I nodded. He rubbed my gloves against his starched white shirt, then walked toward one of the ringside judges.

An incredible transformation occurred: a make-believe on-off switch lowered the arena's volume. The crowd again became library-like silent. Heads turned in unison toward TNT Tanner's dressing area. Lighting shifted away from the ring. Aretha Franklin's "Respect" played at audiologist-unapproved decibel levels. Tanner's trainer was the first to emerge. TNT followed, arms raised, head nodding, smiling. His robe, white with gold trim, sported two lit crisscrossed dynamite sticks across the back. TNT beat on his chest in King Kong-like fashion. About half the sold-out crowd chanted, "TNT...TNT...TNT." The few pulling for me tried, without success, to drown out the TNT chant with their own COFFIN war cry.

You can look it up. The first five rounds were lopsided. I took charge early in the fight, pummeling my opponent while staying away from his power. The crowd sensed round six might be the end for Tanner, but the bell sounded and he lived to fight on. Round seven was next. I made reservations to send the sonofabitch to Queer Street.

Tanner's cut-man applied pressure to what was now an open gash above TNT's right eye. The ringside physician stood next to him, squinting closely at the wound.

"He's good, Doc," the cut-man lied.

"One more round, men," the doctor said. "If that thing opens up any further, I'm stopping it."

"It's a goddamned scratch is all," the cut-man said. "He's fine, Doc."

The doctor stepped away. TNT's corner got busy.

The call for seconds out. TNT Tanner and I headed for ring center. I wish I had known then—both his gloves were loaded with resin. Tanner's corner had done a nice job with the eye cut, but they didn't have sutures in the corner.

TNT's repaired cut begged for my left hand. I'd been in enough bouts to sense wounded prey. I moved closer. Tanner wasn't unbeaten for nothing. He feinted left, stepped inside, and landed a right to my kisser. An average punch at best, but things quickly turned surreal. Darkness! Blinking wildly, fighting a stinging burn, I froze. I backed up for the first time in the fight. I needed time to clear my head, my eyes. Tanner seized the moment. He rushed forward, overwhelming me, raining punches like an out of control windmill. I flailed wildly, badly missing the man in front of me. Tanner's adrenaline roared through engorged veins. He was careful not to let this opening pass. A one-two snapped my head back. I backpedaled against the ropes, screaming that I couldn't see. Rapid blinking continued. My eye sockets were on fire. TNT pressed his advantage. His left-hook opened a wide gash on my cheek, showering the first-row spectators with a sweat-blood cocktail. The bout's tide had turned on a single, mediocre punch.

"I'm blind!" I screamed, a second before Tanner's left-right combination separated me from my mouthpiece and a couple of teeth. I covered up, moved right. Tanner countered, planting body shots as easily as tulip bulbs. I had less defense than a hockey team with two players in the penalty box. I couldn't focus past the burning sensation ripping throughout both corneas and mucous membranes. My manager jumped into the ring, screamed foul to anyone and everyone. His words fell on deaf cauliflower ears. I momentarily lowered my hands to protect my midsection. Mistake. My jaw was no longer functional courtesy of a Tanner uppercut. I've seen photos of the punch. My elongated face resembled the image one sees when staring into a funhouse mirror. My resin-infused eyes rolled back into my head. Somehow I didn't go down, but I was out on my feet.

The ref stepped between us, waved off Tanner, ending the slaughter. Pandemonium ensued. It looked like half of Nevada's population was inside the ring. The first one in was Tanner's trainer. Before hoisting up his fighter, he stripped Tanner of his gloves and tossed them to one of the cornermen.

At the fight's conclusion, my handlers flushed my eyes with water. My eyes were clear by the time the ringside physician snaked his way toward me. Tanner was declared the winner, the undisputed heavyweight champion of the world.

My team and I continued protesting in the fight's aftermath and insisted that Tanner's corner had cheated. The charges were vehemently denied, but an investigation commenced. The results of Nevada's Boxing Commission tests on Tanner's gloves proved negative. Apparently, his cornermen got to his gloves first and cleaned them, No other foreign substance was detected other than minute traces of harmless particles typically found on a prizefighter's gloves.

Cries for a rematch began the day after the fight, but following a series of high-profile public appearances by Tanner and promoter Reggie Watson, a tidal wave-like force consumed the nation's psyche. Everyone in and out of the industry demanded TNT and I face off again to settle things once and for all.

Top Flight Promotions' Reggie Watson performed his magic. A rematch was set. "TNT – Can the Champ Put Another Nail in the Coffin?" he screamed into more than a dozen microphones.

Roughly one month away from the big event, my manager tossed a wrench into the mix. He said the only way I show up for the bout is if one of our handlers remained in Tanner's corner throughout the fight. My team wanted assurances that we could keep a close eye at all times on Tanner's gloves. It was normal procedure for a fighter's handler to visit the opponent's locker room prior to a fight for glove inspection. But, our request to have someone stay with the opponent in his corner throughout the fight was unprecedented. The two sides negotiated a compromise.

Reggie Watson announced, "Thanks to the dedicated, selfless hard work of so many individuals, we have come up with a solution satisfactory to both sides. Representatives from TNT and Coffin's teams will each inspect their opponents' boxing gloves during pre-fight activities. And," he added, "we will do something that's never been done before. These same representatives will also spend the entire length of the fight in their opponent's opposite corner." He paused for dramatic effect. Never known to be tongue-tied, Reggie Watson, born with diarrhea of the mouth, continued. "This will not only alleviate or assuage doubts, it will eliminate, terminate, annihilate, abolish, banish, obliterate, and quash once and for all, any notion or suspicion of nefarious or questionable behavior during this once-in-a-lifetime epic rematch." A nationwide sigh of relief was heard. Fight night was a month away. My training had gone well. I was well-prepared and confident.

Other than the venue change from Las Vegas to New York, Reggie Watson, working in conjunction with the boxing commission, was determined as much as possible to keep things the same for the second fight. The referee and the three judges assigned to score the fight remained unchanged, as did the ringside physician.

Like others at the time, I watched films of our first fight. Experts agreed I had the fight well under control. Something strange occurred in that seventh round in Las Vegas. There was no doubt in my mind as well the opinions of boxing experts that Tanner cheated to steal the fight. With the stringent controls in place for the rematch, I was confident the fight would be on the up and up. I was just as certain I'd have no trouble frustrating and defeating TNT Tanner. Oddsmakers made the champion a slight favorite. I disagreed. Sure, Tanner had the proverbial "puncher's chance," but against a motivated, skilled craftsman like myself, I didn't put much stock in it.

The bout took controversy to a new level. Round one of the highly anticipated rematch wasn't the only round that mirrored TNT – Coffin I. Reggie Watson should have named the rematch *Groundhog Day*. Boxers are who they are. No one expected Tanner to change his stripes. He figured to come forward, taking the fight to me, the same way he tried to do in our first meeting and throughout his career. Similarly, no one anticipated a quick knockout blow by yours truly. Despite the Coffin moniker, KOs weren't my style. My MO was smart, well-planned tactical fighting, using my jab, speed, and defense to win. And, that's what happened. At least for the first six rounds. To everyone's shock, TNT – Coffin II turned into a carbon copy of our first meeting. I took control early, pounding Tanner with rabbit-quick lefts, reddening his puss. With quickness, I stayed away from TNT's arsenal for six rounds while continuing to inflict damage on the pug. The cut-up and bloodied TNT hadn't won a single round on a single judge's scorecard.

Round seven. Tanner got in a shot to my face. I began blinking faster than a Pamplona bull runner. "I can't see!" Déjà vu. Burning tears dropped from my tightly squeezed eyes. I backed up, but Tanner stayed on me, throwing punches without a thought of defense. Half the blows landed. Blind and helpless, I backed against the ropes. The ref, concerned about Tanner's well-being seconds before, now shifted his gaze toward me. Screams came from my corner.

"He cheated! He cheated again! My man can't see!"

TNT's cornermen were elated, imploring Tanner to continue the onslaught. Next to them, a bewildered Hershel Morgan stood in disbelief. Morgan was the man assigned to keep an eye on TNT. It appeared as though Tanner had done it once more. The damned cheater hit me with tainted gloves. Nothing else could explain the burning and blindness. Yet, how was it possible? Morgan had watched Tanner's corner's every move.

I screamed. Tanner punched. The referee saw enough. He stopped the massacre late in the seventh round. Chaos erupted. TNT Tanner, who later that same evening required thirty-seventh stitches to close a labyrinth of lacerations across his face, retained the heavyweight championship of the world.

Tanner's gloves were tainted. But, how did he do it? Everyone focused on Hershel Morgan, longtime friend and my team's appointee to monitor Tanner and his corner. Hershel Morgan saw nothing! Boxing experts began questioning my heart. They concluded that once I took a shot to the face, I wanted no more combat. Total bullshit. Comments like that stung more than the crap TNT smeared in my eyes. I got over the words but never the mystery of how TNT did it. The 1970s-quality video replay of the seventh round between Tanner and me in Madison Square Garden became one of the most frequently watched two-minute, thirty-second segments in sports history.

*****

Reading the ringside doctor's obituary in the newspaper brought the two fights back into focus. The damned thing began to gnaw at me again. Before long, the two Tanner fights had again become an obsession. Maybe, after all these years, I'd find someone who knew something and was willing to talk about that damned seventh round.

The task wouldn't be easy. Most people intimately involved

in the two fights were dead. A little research revealed that in addition to the doctor, Tanner's cut-man, the referee, and my manager were all gone. TNT could tell his story to the worms. He got himself stabbed to death in a rundown Chicago bar a year after he retired.

Two important participants involved in both championship fights were still around. Hershel Morgan, the "eyes" on Tanner during the second fight, and promoter Reggie Watson. Neither of them ever publicly posited a theory or explanation as to how Tanner did it.

Reggie Watson's name was still associated with Top Flight Promotions, but he had little to nothing to do with day-to-day operations. I met him at a New York City nightclub, paradoxically named The Invisible Man. The years had been good to him. He still sported a shiny bald head, now reflecting the pulsating blue-and-red lighting aimed down from the warehouse-style ceiling. Wearing one of his signature exotic pocket handkerchiefs—a shocking pink with yellow polka dots—he gripped my hand with Jack Dempsey-like strength. Watson sipped a tall vodka on the rocks, three oversized olives resting on the glass bottom. A pair of gold pinky rings, rivaling the olives' girth, adorned both hands. The music's heavy bass pounded harder than a flyweight's jab. I couldn't hear myself think. Thankfully, Watson motioned me to a quieter back room. We sat, he ordered me a drink. I got right to the point. Guys like Watson don't like messing around. He didn't like the question.

His face became serious, concerned. "Any suggestion of foul play in any Top Flight Promotions bout is nothing but conspiracy theory stuff, you know, like UFOs, Bigfoot, the

Loch Ness Monster. Both fights have been analyzed and studied by others better than the two of us, and no one has been able to find a scintilla of evidence supporting nefarious actions. Each bout was properly sanctioned, signed for and sealed. No sir, I reject any suggestion that the fights were tainted in any way." A warm, ingratiating smile replaced the concerned look. "You still look good, Coffin. If I were you, I'd try to keep it that way. Finish your drink and take your white tuchus out of here."

Reggie Watson was the same piece of shit I remembered. I left but had a feeling I'd be seeing him again. I still needed to speak to Hershel Morgan, the man assigned to Tanner's corner. The more I thought about things, the more it stood to reason that Hershel Morgan was a traitor. He was either behind the deception or knew more about it than anyone else. I had only his word that he saw no one in Tanner's corner do anything to his gloves. He either lied or he was in on it. Hershel Morgan watched everyone, but no one watched Hershel Morgan! Sure, he was employed by my camp, but that doesn't preclude the possibility that he worked as a double agent for Tanner's people. Maybe Morgan had money riding on Tanner. He'd be in the perfect position to mess with Tanner's gloves, with or without the fighter's knowledge or permission. No other explanation made sense. It had been a long time. I needed to speak to him.

Morgan lived in a century-old house in a small coastal Maine town. He fished in summer, hibernated in winter. Unlike Reggie Watson, his bald head was not by choice. I explained my reason for the visit.

He spoke between sunken cheeks. "You mentioned you

spoke to Reggie Watson," he said. "How is Reggie? He still wearing those grotesque handkerchiefs?" I nodded. "He's always been a character, but make no mistake, he's a shrewd businessman. That son-of-a-gun knows how to fill arenas. I wouldn't trust him far as I could throw him…and I have a bad back," he added. "But you got to give him his due."

I told him about the ring physician's recent death. "That's rough. Not many of us still around from those days. Man, you had the fight won, same as the first fight. I gave up long ago trying to figure out how Tanner and his corner did it. I couldn't sleep for months after the rematch." He laughed.

"What's so funny?"

"The things you think of. I had a rabbit's foot in my pocket when I worked that second fight. A lot good it did me…or you," he added. "You may need one yourself if you keep asking questions. You know the old saying about what happens in Vegas."

I reminded him the second fight was in New York. Everyone knew better, but I figured I'd throw it out there. "Is it possible that the rematch was on the level? That Tanner didn't cheat?

Morgan grinned. "I guess it's possible. I guess it's also possible it will hit a hundred degrees in February in Maine."

I sucked in air. "Face it, we have only your word that you didn't see anyone tamper with Tanner's gloves. You had access. No one would suspect you. As they say, a perfect storm for you to pull it off. See what I'm getting at?"

Morgan grinned. "Go on."

"That's about it," I said.

71

"Coffin, I got what, three months at most," began Morgan. "That's what my doctor tells me. Cancer don't give a shit about defense. You can't stop it. Believe me when I say, if I knew, I'd tell you. What the hell is the difference at this point? But I don't know. Over the years, I've spoken to everyone except the fans in the cheap seats and the ring girls. Heck, I wasn't the only one looking closely at Tanner and his corner men. I just happened to be in his corner with the most access. He—"

"Wait!"

"What?" Morgan asked. He cocked his head to the side like a confused puppy.

"The ring girls!" I shouted.

Morgan's eyebrows rose. "What about them?"

"Has anyone spoken to them?"

He scratched his chin. "Hmm, not that I know of."

I'd forgotten about them. The fight videos I'd too often watched didn't include the one-minute rest periods between rounds. During the course of battle, I wasn't focused on them. Of course! "The ring girls were in the ring with us! Hershel, did you closely watch them while they strutted around the ring?" My heart pounded.

Morgan looked down. "I noticed them, sure, like everyone else noticed and appreciated them. But honestly, they were background stuff, more of a distraction than anything else."

"Who were they, Hershel? Do you have any idea?"

He shrugged. "None. You're going back too many years and I didn't know who they were back then. But, you might try Reggie Watson again. Seems like the sort of thing he'd know."

The trail quickly brought me back to the flashy promoter. After speaking to a receptionist at Top Flight Promotions and paying a small ransom, I was told the ring girls were hired by Madison Square Garden. A Howard Lazarus ran the department that hired the women.

Once inside the Garden's offices, to my amazement, I discovered Howard Lazarus was still employed there. Lazarus's office door was open. My jaw dropped at the sight of him.

"Something wrong?" he asked.

I stammered. "No…it's just that I expected to see a much older man. I'm sorry."

Smiling, he said, "Thirty-six is old enough." He paused. "I guess it's all relative."

"You're Howard Lazarus? I'm sorry, I thought I was seeing the Howard Lazarus who's worked here since the 1970's."

"Sit down, please. That was my father. I'm Howard Lazarus, Jr. "I'm afraid my father passed away years ago. This is the same office he used." He chuckled. "As you can see, not much has changed. What brings you here?"

I repeated my theory about how the ring girls might be the key to unraveling the mystery. "None of the existing films of the bouts show what happened between rounds," I stressed. "And to my knowledge, no one has spoken to any of the women at the time or since." I stared into the man's eyes. "Frankly, Mr. Lazarus, you are my last hope."

"Follow me." He led me to a crowded storage room down the hall. Within thirty minutes, he located the file. Back in his office, he produced the folder I'd been looking for. "Here they are."

I snapped photos, scribbled the names, addresses, modeling agency affiliation, and any other relevant information for the women. I made a mental note of Holly Strickland's face, the designated ring girl for the seventh round.

Holly Strickland was the key. If she was still alive, I needed to speak to her. I found her with the help of a private detective. She still lived on Long Island, less than thirty miles from Madison Square Garden, not too far from the address in her files.

The grandmother of six lived alone in a modest home. Her skin defied her age. Still statuesque, she had a far-away look when I told her the reason for my visit. I explained my decades-long fascination with the seventh-round mystery, and my hope that she might have seen something while she walked around the ring between rounds six and seven.

"I haven't thought about those days in a long time," Holly Strickland said. "It's too painful for me. I don't dwell on the past."

Not off to a good start. I felt horrible. Fearing she might become reluctant to talk about the fight for any number of reasons, I needed to be direct, to get her to focus. I asked her flat out about the seventh round of the second bout. "You had a unique vantage point. You were in the ring between rounds six and seven with us. Did anything unusual happen between rounds?"

She sighed. "You're wrong. I didn't work the night of the fight."

I raised an eyebrow. "Oh? I saw the records. It clearly stated you were the scheduled ring girl for round seven. Is that not accurate?"

"That's correct," Strickland said. "Would you like a cup of tea? Coffee?"

"Then I'm confused." I clarified, "Not about the tea or coffee. I'll take coffee if it isn't too much trouble." The two of us sat in her kitchen. She saw the WTF look on my face.

"You're right in saying I was scheduled to hold the round seven card. But..." She stared into her coffee. "...Amanda Freese worked the seventh round. She was originally scheduled to work round thirteen. At the last moment, the agency scheduled someone else for the thirteenth round. As you know all too well, the fight ended in the seventh round. I didn't strut around the ring that night or any other night. Other than sulk, I didn't do much of anything that evening."

"What happened? Why did this Amanda Freese take your spot?"

"Reggie Watson." She spat the words. "My agency was contacted by Madison Square Garden. They wanted me to be a ring girl for the big fight. I didn't then and don't now follow sports. I agreed, figuring it could help further along my career. I'd never been a ring girl before that. My job was to walk around the ring, holding a cardboard sign prior to round seven. We were trained how to walk, to smile, to nod, everything. Sure, it was about the sex appeal. Most boxing fans are male. I'm not naïve. My agency informs me a week before the fight that I'm to report to Reggie Watson's office. Reggie promoted the fight. He has a reputation."

"I know," I said.

"Well, I thought it irregular and questioned my boss at the agency. He was adamant that I report as this Reggie Watson person requested. I had a bad feeling the minute I stepped into his office." She paused. "His smile was…disingenuous. I can't describe it any other way. He had a proposition for me. He asked me if I wanted to make a lot of money walking around the ring for thirty seconds. I'm talking five-figure money. I didn't respond to him. He said all I had to do was to walk very close to one of the boxers."

"Why would he pay you that kind of money for that?"

"There's more. He said there would be some sort of powder, some harmless resin or something applied to my hip. The boxer was going to touch his gloves to my hip as I walked past him."

"Tanner."

She nodded. "Yes. That fighter, Tanner, he walked into the office during the conversation."

"What? Tanner was there?"

"Yes. Watson wanted to be certain that I knew which fighter he was referring to."

Holly Strickland closed her eyes, her body jerked, the result of an uncontrolled chill. She continued.

"It was awful. That Tanner. He grabbed my arm. Hard. He hurt me. He lowered his head so that it was inches from mine…told me to remember his face…the face of a champion, he said. He had gold teeth. His breath was hot…horrible. I thought he was going to kiss me, but Reggie Watson came out from behind his desk and pulled this Tanner away. Tanner just grinned, showing those hideous teeth. He winked at me, shook Watson's hand, and walked out."

"I'm sorry," I said, feeling nauseous. Jesus, why was I asking this woman to relive this pain? Ironic. I finally knew how TNT Tanner cheated me not once but twice out of the championship, yet at the moment, it seemed small.

"I take it you didn't agree to Reggie's proposition. What happened after that?"

"No. I didn't trust him from the start. I felt threatened by him and that boxer. I refused right then and there. Watson became upset, belligerent. I made a move to leave. He blocked my path, intimidating me." Holly Strickland again shook recalling the details. "Reggie Watson called me an ignorant fool. He said no one says no to him, that he'd personally see to it that I never got another modeling job in this or any other city ever again. He was inches from my face, like Tanner had been. He repulsed me. As he spoke, his spittle rained on my face. It was the worst day of my life. He was right about one thing. I never got another modeling job after that meeting." She glanced at a cross hanging on the kitchen wall.

"And you never said anything to anybody about this?" She looked at me, said nothing. I heard her silence. "He threatened you if you spoke out, didn't he?" More communicative silence.

Strickland noticed my empty mug. "More coffee?" she asked, returning to the present.

"Sure, thank you." I pressed on.

"So, this Amanda Freese, the woman who took your spot, she took Watson's deal?"

Strickland lowered her eyes. "Poor Amanda. Yes. A day or

two later, my boss at the modeling agency wanted to see me. He was furious. He informed me that I wouldn't be working the fight. He didn't give me a reason. He didn't have to. Amanda modeled for the same agency as I did. I knew she had some trouble in her life. I never pried, but heard stories… drugs, that sort of thing. Such a shame. She was a pretty woman. Smart too. But somewhere she went off the rails. She died a long time ago. A wasted life."

I knew how Tanner cheated. That should have been the end of it.

*****

Reggie Watson's receptionist looked like she'd seen a *Wizard of Oz* flying monkey when I burst in, gun in hand. Watson looked up. He heard the commotion. He ordered me out. "I'm firing at the count of five," he yelled through the open door. The first bullet came at "two." Luckily, before the lowlife said "one," I grabbed the receptionist and we both ducked behind her desk. She screamed with each shot. After the sixth round, I waited. Nothing. I didn't give him time to reload. I got up, walked into Watson's office, and approached. I decided right then and there this assault would be aggravated, but sans deadly weapon. I was going to squeeze his neck.

He sat there, watching me come closer.

"Out of rounds?" I asked.

The smile. The same one Holly Strickland had seen. Watson said nothing. The pocket pistol he pulled from his vermilion handkerchief spoke.

No Way Out
Robert J. Mendenhall

Had I known when I started tailing this guy three days ago I'd wind up as a hostage in a diner with one dead cop and another bleeding out at my feet, I might have not taken the case. But there I was.

I don't normally take PI work. The private security piece of my company, Nighthawk Security, kept me plenty busy and well fed. Not that I didn't enjoy private investigations; I spent a dozen years on the Saint Thomas, Illinois Police Department, more than half of them as a homicide detective. There just wasn't enough time for me to devote to the investigatory piece. But this was a favor for an old friend of an old friend, so I shuffled schedules and juggled jobs. It was a no-brainer any first-year PI apprentice could have handled— follow the sleazy husband of the client's daughter and get some pictures of him cheating on his wife. Slam dunk.

The husband's name was Gerald "Gerry" Roth. He was a nervous young guy looking like a gang-banger trying to go legit. He wore brown Dockers faded at the knees and a tan, short-sleeve golf shirt sporting a *So-Quick Gas and Mini-Mart* logo and the shadows of old coffee stains. The tattoos on his neck and arms advertised his past gang affiliation. He tried combing his unruly hair into a semblance of grooming, but it remained a greasy mop.

For three days the guy did nothing but go to work at the

So-Quick. Each night he would go home to his wife, then slip out after she went to bed. I tagged Roth's old Jetta with a GPS tracker on day one, so I had a real-time log of the car's movements. Dad was not going to like it. The kid was delivering pizzas. That's it. He wasn't stepping out on his wife, he was working two jobs. I felt kind of sorry for him. I figured I'd finish out today, then invoice my client and close the case.

But this morning, it all turned to shit.

Roth stopped at Marcie's Diner on his way to the So-Quick. Marcie's was a quaint little dive on Saint Thomas's lower west side, the kind of place where the scent of bacon adhered to the walls like a coat of paint. Roth took a seat at the counter and ordered a light breakfast. I took a booth by the window, close enough to watch him, but far enough away to be inconspicuous. There were three other customers in the place, a young man and woman with a toddler at a booth by the door. I noted a narrow hall near the counter that probably led to the kitchen and public restrooms. I heard hot grease sizzling and a Rod Stewart song from the seventies playing low in the kitchen.

There was only one server working and it took a few minutes for her to get from the counter to my table.

"What would you like?" she asked. Her voice sounded a bit husky, like someone who smoked too much. I glanced at her briefly. She was slim and appeared in her early forties or, generously, in her late thirties. Tinted hair straddled hunched shoulders. She looked tired. Veins of red took attention from the blue in her eyes and no amount of makeup could conceal the dark patches beneath them. Even her skin appeared fatigued. I expected her to be chewing gum, and was a bit disappointed she wasn't.

The aroma of bacon and coffee made me hungry. "Coffee," I said. "And a breakfast menu."

She pointed her pen toward the napkin rack at the window end of the table, then ambled off. I pulled the menu and flipped it open. I glanced at Roth. I glanced at the specials. Another glance at Roth. Another glance at the specials. This went on for another minute before my weary server brought an empty mug and pot of coffee.

She poured the coffee expertly. "Decided?"

I ordered one of the specials. She wrote it down on her pad and I noticed she was left-handed. A quick glance at her name badge. Jessica. There was no ring on her left hand.

She ripped the sheet from her pad and swayed toward the open kitchen window behind the counter. She stuck the order on a tin carousel, gave it a little spin, and double-tapped a silver service bell. A hairy hand in the kitchen snapped it up as an oldies radio station jingle segued from Rod Stewart to Elton John. Jessica made her way back to Roth, coffee pot in hand.

The door jangled open and two uniformed police officers strode in. They were young, twenties maybe, and went right for the counter. I could tell they were rookies by how little attention they paid to their surroundings. They didn't look to see who was already in the diner. Failed to check to see where the other exits were. Laughed distractingly at each other. And took stools at the counter with their backs to the front door. If I was their shift sergeant, they'd have been back with their field training officers.

What really pissed me off was they blocked my view of Roth. I shifted in my seat a bit, but only succeeded in jabbing the butt of my concealed Beretta .40 into the small of my back.

Jessica brought my breakfast. Steam wafted from evenly

scrambled eggs and sizzled bacon. A patch of crispy hash browns accented the plate. The freshly squeezed orange juice was chilled enough for condensation to bead up on the outside of the glass.

"Looks great," I said.

"You know that I didn't cook it, right?" She managed a lazy 'whatever' look and headed back to the counter.

I dug into my breakfast, still unable to see through the two cops at the counter. I did, however, have a partial view of Roth in the convex mirror mounted in a ceiling corner near the cash register. He was no longer eating. He sat still, rigid. Uneasy.

I don't recall cops being so young when I was on the job. Nowadays, they looked like college sophomores, fresh-faced with trendy haircuts and white-framed sunglasses. And a swagger that said *Don't mess with me, man. See my badge? I'm the police.* That kind of attitude was a disaster waiting to happen.

The cop closest to Roth leaned into his partner's space and whispered something in his ear. My guess is it wasn't sweet nothings. The partner tensed and they both glanced at Roth. I put my fork down and ran a paper napkin over my mouth. I wasn't liking this.

The cop closest to Roth stood and approached him. In the mirror, I watched Roth stiffen.

"Hey, buddy," the cop said to Roth, standing over him in an intimidating stance. "Don't I know you from somewhere?"

Roth did not look up at him. "Don't think so," he said.

"I'm pretty sure I know you," the cop said. "You with the Kings? Naw, the Saints. Those tattoos on your neck look like you're with the Saints."

Roth covered his neck with a trembling hand. "I'm not in a

gang. Not anymore. I got a job. I got a wife."

"Hey, Malenke," the other cop said. "Leave him be. Let's finish our breakfast."

Malenke didn't listen to his partner. I took a sip of my coffee.

"Let me see some ID," Malenke told Roth.

At this point, Officer whatever-his-first-name-was Malenke had no legal justification to ask Roth for his identification. I knew this was not going to go well for Roth. And Officer Malenke was setting himself up for a civil rights law suit.

Roth slapped the counter with both hands. His fork clinked on his plate. "I-I ain't done nothin'," he stammered.

Malenke's partner stood and angled himself next to Malenke in an aggressive manner, his right hand finding the butt of his holstered side arm. I watched his thumb slip the security snap free. What the hell were they teaching these guys at the academy?

I glanced at the family in the booth by the door. They were no longer laughing; the woman pulled the boy closer to her.

"That's what you say," Malenke said. He leaned down, close to Roth's face. "I say once a banger always a banger. Now, let me see some ID." Malenke's hand went to his own holster and snapped the thumb break open.

I got out of my seat quietly. Jessica came out of the kitchen, but stopped short when she saw the situation at the far end of the counter. She glanced at me. I motioned for her to stay put.

"I don't have to," Roth persisted.

"I'm not going to ask you again," Malenke said. "ID."

Roth's eyes were wide, panicked. "Why won't you just leave me alone? I don't do that anymore. I'm straight. I gotta wife, now. A baby comin'…"

I inched my way toward the confrontation, wary not to spook either Roth or the gung-ho uniforms.

Jessica inched backward. Her hip made unexpected contact with the rear counter. She reached back blindly and her hand swept a juice glass from the counter. The glass hit the floor and shattered.

Malenke jumped at the sudden crash. He partially turned toward the sound and as he did, his hand came off his gun.

Roth flew off his stool. He ripped the gun from Malenke's holster and back-stepped, thrusting the gun in the direction of Malenke's partner. I recognized the gun immediately. Glock Model 22, .40 caliber—*no external safety.* Roth gripped the gun clumsily in both hands, stiff-armed, as if he were unaccustomed to handling firearms. His finger tensed on the trigger.

He backed into the stool.

The gun went off.

The shot was like a pipe-bomb had exploded in the cramped diner. The woman by the door screamed.

Malenke's partner fell, his own gun still partially holstered. The bullet drilled a fine hole into the boney brow above his right eye and exploded out the back of his head in a coarse spray. He was dead before he struck the black and white tiled floor.

I leapt from my seat and dove for Malenke as Roth turned the gun in his direction. Roth shot twice.

I tackled Malenke even as the first shot tore through his shoulder. The second round whizzed past my ear so close I heard the rush of air along the bullet's path.

The boy in the booth screamed. The man came out of his

seat and gathered the woman and child into a protective huddle.

The cook barreled out of the kitchen.

"N-nobody move!" Roth screeched. He stood awkwardly, both hands gripping the Glock in a shaky stance. He pointed it here, then there, then back again in a panic.

I rolled off Malenke. Blood soaked the front of my shirt. The brassy tang of so much of it flared my nostrils.

The gun pointed at me.

The cook backed up.

The gun pointed at him.

"I said nobody move!" A wispy haze hung above Roth's head, residual smoke from the three shots.

"Easy, now," I said. The gun pointed back at me. "No one else has to get hurt."

Roth pointed the gun at the family. The child whimpered, the woman sobbed. My ears rang.

The gun whipped toward Jessica. She brought her hands to her face and flinched.

"You. The cook," Roth said, still pointing the gun at Jessica. "Is there a back door?"

"Yeah," the cook said. He rubbed sweat from his balding pate and puffy, stubbled cheeks with a hand-towel. Grease stains and perspiration marks muddied his once-white t-shirt. His belly bulged behind a discolored apron.

"Go and lock it. And get right back here. If you don't get right back here, I'm going shoot her. You g-got that?"

"Yeah. Yeah." The cook stuffed the towel in his back pocket and wiped his hands on his apron.

"Ten seconds and you ain't back here, she's dead."

"Okay, Mac. Okay."

He was back in five.

"It's locked."

"Now go lock the front door. Flip that Closed sign. Pull down the shades."

"Okay," the cook said.

Roth bent at the knees and pulled the dead partner's gun from its holster. He slipped it into his waist band and straightened. His eyes, frightened before, were now crazed.

"Why why why…" he muttered. "Why couldn't they just leave me alone?" He swung the gun toward Malenke. "Why couldn't you just leave me alone?"

Malenke flinched, first at the gun, then at the fire in his shoulder.

The diner's phone rang. We all looked at it.

"Don't answer that," Roth ordered. "Shit. Cell phones. Everybody gimme your cell phones. Hurry up."

I slid my smart phone toward him. Roth kicked it behind him. The two adults in the booth put theirs on the table. Jessica and the cook set theirs on the counter. Roth pointed the gun at Jessica.

"Okay. Okay. Waitress. Go gather up all those phones. That one and the ones on the table over there. Go."

Jessica did as she was instructed. The diner phone stopped ringing. In the kitchen, Elton John segued into Billy Joel.

"Just drop them on the floor behind me," he said moving out of her reach.

"Now get back over there," he motioned to the counter.

"This cop is bleeding to death," I said.

Roth waved his gun at me. "He should have just left me alone. Why didn't he just leave me alone?"

"I don't know. Maybe he was just being overzealous."

"I dunno what that means. He was being an asshole. I wasn't doing nothing." He scanned the diner frantically, the gun always in motion. His finger remained white-knuckled on the trigger.

The hard angles of my Beretta dug into the small of my back, but I knew while he was aiming at me I wouldn't be able to get it out of my holster and trained on him before he riddled me with bullets. And I wasn't wearing an ankle holster. That thought triggered another and I looked down at Malenke's ankle. No back-up gun there, either. A side glance at his partner's askew legs... nothing. I needed to win Roth's confidence.

"My name's Adam," I said. "What's yours?" It was a weak effort and I knew it.

The gun swung back in my direction. That was good. Not for me, of course; Roth had already killed an armed police officer. But, if I kept him focused on me, his attention wouldn't be on the civilians.

"Shut the fuck up. I'm not your buddy."

"Okay. Okay. But, how about you let me help the cop."

"Fuck him."

"You said you have a wife, right?" I pointed to Malenke's left hand. "He does too. She'll be a widow unless you let me stop his bleeding."

A grimace of anguish washed over the fear in his face. He looked at the dead cop then down at Malenke.

"Okay," Roth said. "Fix him up." He swung the gun back toward Jessica. "But if you try any shit, I'll shoot the waitress right in the face. You got that? You got that?!"

"I got it," I said with a glance at Jessica. She didn't meet my eyes. I knelt, careful to keep my back away from Roth. I certainly didn't want my jacket to ride up and expose my gun. I'd be lying next to Malenke's partner, just as dead.

Malenke groaned. I unsnapped the belt keepers holding his duty belt to his pants belt and pulled the rig off. I slid it to my side, one eye on the can of pepper spray secured in its own little holder on the rig. I also eyed the small, Asp baton in a similar holder. And his portable radio. Which wasn't even turned on. *Shit.*

"Uh-uh," Roth said. "Slide his Batman belt over here." I did.

I unbuttoned Malenke's uniform shirt and peeled it back to expose a t-shirt that was probably white once. It was scarlet now, damp with blood that flowed from the bullet wound. From what I saw, the round tore into his shoulder below the clavicle. I guided my hand between the shirts and gingerly felt for an exit wound. Malenke stifled a cry. His wet shoulder blade felt splintered. If Malenke was wearing his body armor properly, higher and tighter on his torso, the bullet would have knocked him on his ass. He'd have been sore and bruised but otherwise undamaged. I eased him back over and applied pressure to the entry wound. This time, Malenke didn't stifle.

I looked up at the cook. "Do you have a first aid kit?

The cook shook his head. "Only some bandages and peroxide."

I looked at him like, *Really?* "Okay. Do you get your aprons from a service?"

"Yeah. So?"

"Bring me some clean, white aprons. A lot of them." The cook shot a nervous glance at Roth. "And the peroxide," I added. "Now."

Roth swung the gun back at me. "What…what do you need

that for?"

"He has two holes in him," I said slowly. "One in front and one in back. I need to plug them both with whatever sterile packing material I can get. The aprons will be the cleanest things here."

Roth eyed Malenke. Then the cook. The gun was all over the place.

"No tricks," I assured him. "I just need to staunch the bleeding."

"I'm not a fuckin' doctor. I dunno what that means."

"Slow the bleeding down. Stop it, if I can."

Roth swung the gun back toward Jessica. "Go get the aprons," Roth told the cook. But just like the back door, if you ain't back here in like fifteen seconds, she's dead."

"And the peroxide," I added as the cook darted into the backroom.

Fifteen seconds passed quickly. After twenty seconds the cook still hadn't come back. Thirty. Billy Joel played on.

"Where the fuck is he?" Roth stammered.

"Give him some more time," I said evenly. "He probably had trouble finding—"

"No! No more time!" Roth thrust the gun forward, extending both arms toward Jessica. "Wait," I shouted, ready to launch myself at Roth.

"I got 'em," the cook called out. "I got the stuff you need." He stomped out of the backroom, a bundle of aprons wrapped in tight, clear plastic in his arms.

Roth eased his stance and jerked the gun back in my direction. The cook angled toward me and dropped the aprons on the floor next to me. He held a brown, plastic bottle of hydrogen peroxide.

"Okay, I'll need your help, here," I said to the cook. "What's your name?"

"Eddie."

"Okay, Eddie. First open the bottle." He did. "Now, open the bundle. Pull out an apron."

Keeping one hand firmly on Malenke's wound, I took the peroxide bottle and poured half the bottle onto the apron. I handed the bottle back to Ed and eased Malenke back onto his side. I took the apron, maneuvered it around his back.

"This is going to hurt," I said as I pressed the apron into the wound. Malenke concurred loudly. I rolled him back over. The pressure of his body weight kept the apron tight in the wound.

"Another apron," I said to Ed. Then to Malenke, "This is going to hurt more." I poured the rest of the hydrogen peroxide directly into the entry wood. As Malenke shrieked, I snatched the apron and pressed it hard onto the wound.

Malenke passed out.

"Eddie, I need you to apply pressure to the apron. Both hands. Lean into it."

"Okay." Eddie did as I instructed and I stood.

"Whoa," Roth jutted the gun toward me. "Where do you think you're goin'?"

I raised my dripping hands. "Just want to clean my hands. I can use the sink behind the counter so you can keep an eye on me. May I do that?"

Roth's eyes shifted left and right as he thought. "Sure. Okay. But no funny shit." The gun shifted back to Jessica.

I kept my hands raised and angled my way toward the counter. I stopped at the sink, ran water, and rinsed my hands, one eye on Roth.

I grabbed a towel from counter, wiped my hands dry, dropped the towel on the counter, and made my way around it. The charcoal and sulfur odor of gunpowder still hung in the air. I could taste it.

Roth muttered to himself. I couldn't make out much of what he was saying, but I recognized what was happening. He was coming to terms with what happened here. Of what he had done. Of his situation. Tears welled in his eyes.

This was not going to end well.

My mind raced through scenarios. Contingencies. If he did this, I could do that. If he did that, I could do this.

The boy in the booth started crying again.

"Shut that kid up," Roth whined. He turned the gun toward the family.

"Whoa," I said moving a step toward him. "He's just a kid."

"Stop!"

I stopped, but Roth did what I wanted. He pointed the gun back at me. I kept my hands at shoulder height where he could see them. I had to try talking him down.

"Look," I said trying to keep my voice even and reassuring. I may not have pulled it off. "This was an accident. I saw what happened. You didn't mean to kill the cop. The gun went just went off."

"I-I know that! But do you think anyone else is gonna believe that?"

"I'll tell them. I saw it go down. The cops were harassing you. You were minding your own business."

The toddler's cries grew louder. Her mother tugged the boy close. The father drew them both in, but the cries continued.

Roth started to swing the gun around again.

"It wasn't your fault!" He brought the gun back in my

direction. "It wasn't your fault." I repeated more softly.

"It don't fuckin' matter. They'll always think I'm a banger. It don't matter I'm not any more. I can't ever get away from it. No one trusts me. Not even my wife's old man. To him, I'll always be no good. I was… I was gonna get my GED, man. Get a real job…." Tears streamed from his reddened eyes. He visibly shook.

I got to know something about Roth in the last few days. He'd tried to put his mistakes behind. Tried to make a fresh start. Earn trust. He fell in love. Started a family. Became responsible. How many others in his shoes had not even tried to straighten out their lives? I genuinely felt for him.

"Look," I said. "I know some cops. I'll talk to them. I'll make them see this was an accident. You just need to put the gun down." I lowered my hands slowly, hoping the motion would subliminally suggest he do the same. It didn't.

"You know cops?"

"Yes. Some pretty important ones, too. They can help." My arms were at my sides. I eased my right hand behind my leg.

"You're fuckin' lying. I just killed a cop. Shot another one." The tears stopped. His eyes were round and distraught. Tension lines ridged his neck. "They're gonna kill me. First chance they get. I got no way out, man. No fuckin' way out!"

My gut churned. I knew he was right. Even if I talked him into giving up, his life was essentially over. His dreams of a better life. Of a family. Kids. He had nothing going for him, now. And nothing more to lose. In the kitchen, Carole King played on the radio. *It's too late, baby, now, It's too late…*

The child wailed. My fingers slipped under my jacket, reached for the small of my back. I didn't want to do this. I silently pleaded with him. *Gerry, don't make me do this.*

"I said shut him up!" Roth howled and turned the gun toward the family. I saw his finger start to compress the trigger.

I pulled my Beretta free, thumbing the safety off as I swung the gun around.

And shot Gerry Roth through the side of his head.

*****

Saint Thomas PD Patrol units set a perimeter around the diner and secured the front and back doors. Paramedics loaded Malenke onto a gurney and wheeled him out the front door to the waiting ambulance. Detectives interviewed, Eddie, Jessica, and the family. Crime scene technicians placed little yellow cones around the floor and photographed points of evidence. Medical Examiner personnel huddled around the body of Malenke's partner.

I had already surrendered my Beretta to the lead detective and given her a preliminary statement. I would have to go downtown later for a more in-depth interview with the State's Attorney to determine if charges would be filed against me, but it was a clean shoot, so I wasn't worried. I expected to be questioned by STPD upper brass long before then.

The detective interviewing Jessica moved off. Jessica wiped her cheeks with both hands. She sat on a stool in front of the counter. I eased my way over to her. Someone had turned off the radio.

"How are you holding up?" I asked, slipping onto the stool next to her. I offered her my handkerchief.

She took it without thanks and dabbed her eyes. "Super," she said, her voice husky.

"Not an easy day," I said.

She scowled at me. "You seem to be doing okay. Doesn't it

bother you? Killing that boy?"

"I've learned how to mask it, but, yes. It bothers me. A lot. I didn't want to shoot him, Jessica. He was a troubled kid trying to climb out of the mess he'd made with his life and wound up in a situation he didn't choose and couldn't handle. But, I couldn't let him kill anyone else."

"So, why didn't you just shoot the gun out of his hand, or shoot him in the leg, or something? Why did you have to kill him?"

I didn't answer. It was pointless to try and convince her that shooting the gun out of the bad guy's hand only happened in the movies, and shooting him in the leg wouldn't have stopped him from pulling the trigger.

"You're just as bad as them," she said and walked away from me. I didn't know if she meant the gangs or the police.

Two deputy chiefs in full dress uniforms walked in, spotted me at the counter, and angled my way. I stood, the remorse in my gut festering into anger. I had a lot to say about how this went down. About their lackluster training methodology and how the responsibility for these two, meaningless deaths was solely on the department.

"Adam Pike?" one of the deputy chief's asked.

"That's me," I said. But before they could ask me any questions, I launched right into my tirade. While I watched their faces solidify into stone, I wondered, in the back of my mind, if Jessica had been right. I've had to do a lot of things that troubled me in my career, and learned to live with them. Even so, I would never forget the moment I pulled the trigger and blew Gerry Roth's brains out.

Never.

We'll Take a Cup of Kindness Yet
Shawn Kobb

I set two drinks down onto the weathered wooden table. I drank beer. I couldn't say what kind. Whatever Dez poured when I said "beer." True to tradition, my friend had requested a random cocktail, the more obscure the better.

"Your *sidecar*." I slid into the booth across from Billy.

He raised his murky orange drink and I reciprocated.

"To another year of friendship."

The toast never changed, even if the relationship over the years had. It'd morphed and mutated into something more complex, less manageable. Gone were the easy days of high school, cutting classes and chasing girls. Was life tough back then? Maybe. I remembered complaining about the unfairness of it all, every little slight a mountain of injustice.

"Another year." I clinked the pint glass and took a drink. "Next year you buy the first round." Another part of the tradition. Billy never did. He never would.

"Next year."

He was quiet. Distracted.

I didn't ask. We'd been friends too long to need to. He'd

talk when he was ready. As much as we both played up the friendship in our annual New Year's Eve toast, we held our secrets close. More and more secrets accumulated over the course of the year, and they fed on each other like piranhas and grew like the interest on one of Billy's loans. Eventually it was impossible to pick out the little nugget of truth buried under the calcified layers of deception.

We drank in silence, muted conversation of other patrons in the background, occasionally punctuated by a sharp laugh or shouted punchline. Frills of green and silver Christmas garland hung over the bar, woven in and around dusty cocktail glasses that saw little use in Maxie's Bar, apart from when smartasses like Billy showed up and ordered a Gibson or a Brooklyn or a fucking Sazerac.

These days it would be trendy to call Maxie's a dive, but it wasn't that. Dez kept it clean—Maxie retired six or seven years back and checked out permanently not soon after—and the food wasn't half bad in the place. It was a place without pretense. It didn't show up in any "best kept secrets of DC" lists or do two-for-one specials to lure in tourists from Des Moines in town to see the Lincoln Memorial or gawk at the Spirit of St. Louis down at Air and Space. If you didn't know about Maxie's, you didn't go to Maxie's. And if you didn't grow up in this neighborhood, like Billy and me, you weren't in the know. It suited us just fine.

"You know we been doing this ten years now?"

I thought on it. Somehow that first reunion felt like both ancient history and yesterday. "Yeah?"

Billy pointed to a booth closer to the bar. "We sat over there. It wasn't New Year's Eve that first time. A few days before, but close enough."

"Sounds about right. I wasn't sure it was a good idea. That call came out of nowhere and—"

"Probably wasn't a good idea, but here we are."

I looked at my old friend. His face had a blue tint from the buzzing glow of the Pabst neon hanging on the wall. Same smile as always. That "fuck it, we're all going to die in the end anyway" grin that got me, got us both into so much trouble back in the day. That smile was there, but something else too. Something in his eyes, the set of his jaw.

"Here we are."

"Here we are," Billy repeated.

A television hung in the corner, a big, old picture-tube set with a VCR built into it. I wondered if Dez, or Maxie before him, had ever once slid a videotape through that little gray flap. A man and a woman were on the screen, bundled in stylish black overcoats, smiling into microphones. The psychedelic rainbow of Times Square and a few hundred thousand drunks served as backdrop. A countdown in the corner told me we had twenty-three minutes until the ball drop.

"Big things coming down the pike?" Billy asked.

I kept my attention fixed on the D-grade celebrities. I didn't trust my face to not give anything away if I looked at my old friend too quickly. Billy didn't ask about my work. I didn't ask about his. Not on this night. We were two lanes of a highway headed in different directions, and there was supposed to be a solid barrier of concrete and steel rebar running down the middle to keep those routes from crashing into each other. Billy had just gone and hopped right into oncoming traffic.

"Little of this, little of that." I took another drink of my beer. "Why you asking?"

Billy shrugged as though it was nothing. As though he hadn't just snatched the last remaining remnant of the friendship we'd forged in childhood and ripped it to shreds in front of my face. I won't claim what we'd had was anything special, anything different than what a million other kids around the country had. We bonded over a shared love of Zeppelin and AC/DC, bitching about our parents and our teachers, arguing over who was the hottest girl in school, and being too chickenshit to talk to her.

After high school—we both graduated, but I'd had serious doubts about Billy for a while—life took us different directions. I "got my shit together" as parents like to say. Army then police. Billy didn't. Or, at least not in the way you're supposed to. Billy could afford to pay for drinks. Billy could buy the whole damn bar if he wanted to. Billy could get you all the money you needed, but mind those strings. They were long and tight and would choke you dead if you weren't careful.

My friend stood up so suddenly I felt the involuntary twitch of my right hand toward the holster I wore. Even then, with my friend. If Billy noticed, he didn't say anything.

"Grabbing the next round. Be right back."

I nodded, polished off my beer, and pushed it away from me. I surveyed the room, but if anyone was paying me any extra attention, I didn't spot it. Billy was chatting up Dez at the bar and had pulled out a sizeable roll of cash. The usuals at Maxie's knew who Billy was and they knew who I was and were smart enough to leave the both of us alone. All the same, I felt eyes on me. A few years of being a cop makes you paranoid. A few more teaches you that paranoia doesn't mean they aren't also out to get you.

Billy sat and we clinked glasses once more. He'd switched from a cocktail to a beer, same as me. A second round wasn't something we normally did. The point of this annual reunion wasn't to get shitfaced. I wasn't sure what the point even was anymore. Guess we just wanted a tangible reminder of what we'd once had. Wanted to pretend that although life dumped us in boats and pushed us down branching forks in the river of destiny, we still weren't all that different. When I was feeling petty on these nights, I'd think this was me doing Billy a favor. I might be police now, but I was still that kid he'd cut class with. He wasn't just a crook to me. Wasn't a loser. I knew he was more than his rap sheet.

Truth was, this was Billy doing me a solid. He didn't need my friendship to feel like he was worth a damn. He sure as hell didn't need my protection. If anything, I needed his. I'd hit him up a few times over the years for tips, street chatter from people I couldn't be frequenting. My friend had never approached me for a favor in turn.

Billy was nursing his beer and watching the television. Far as I knew, he didn't even like beer. Nothing was right this New Year's Eve. I'd expected some of it, but not all of it.

The timer told us we had just over eight minutes left in the year.

"I always liked *Auld Lang Syne*. We usually sing it at happy occasions, but it's sad, too."

Billy was quiet when he spoke, the words for him as much as for me.

"The song?" I asked. "Never thought much about it. Guess so."

"And surely you'll buy your pint cup, and surely I'll buy mine." Billy sang softly, his voice just barely carrying over the human hum of Maxie's Bar. I didn't know I'd ever heard him sing before. Wasn't like we went to karaoke. The line was unfamiliar, but I knew the tune.

"Sounds like us," I said. "I buy for you. You buy for me."

Billy nodded, still not looking at me. "The song's supposed to be optimistic. There's a bit of melancholy to it as well though. Two friends sharing drinks in the spirit of good times. Two friends who paddled in the same stream, but now a roaring ocean separates them."

It was just over twenty-five degrees outside, and people came and went from Maxie's, stepping out for a cigarette or bit of fresh air. We weren't sitting far from the door, but even that cold air blowing in wasn't helping now. It was hot in the bar, wet and sticky like a steam bath at the gym. If Billy felt it, he didn't show it. He had the same distracted look about him, could have been sitting in his own living room, watching a documentary about the origin of holiday music for all I could tell. I reached with my left hand to take another drink of beer, at the same time casually dropped my right to the comfortable plastic and leather bulge of my service Glock.

"Can't say I know the lyrics as well as you, Billy. You always were better at that. Best I can manage is to hum the melody."

He did look at me.

I was fried. I couldn't say how he knew, but he did. Clear as crystal it showed in his eyes. This would be our final New Year's Eve toast together. I'd known that walking into the bar that night. I didn't realize Billy knew it too. He wasn't supposed to. But he did. He definitely did.

"Nothing lasts forever, Malone. I don't think it's meant to. Traditions, friendships, none of it. Sometimes we think it will, but that's because we're all short timers here. In the big picture? We're just a blip. The pop of one of Dez's knock-off Champagne corks."

"It doesn't have to go down like this, Billy."

"What'd you think? You thought you could sniff around in my life? Share my business with your cop friends? Business I told you about because you asked? Because you were my friend? You thought you could do that, and I wouldn't find out?"

My buddy didn't sound angry. Didn't raise his voice or slam his fist on the table or jab a finger in my face. If anything, Billy sounded sad. I'd like to think we both were, but if I'm being truthful with myself, I hadn't felt that bad about the idea of finally bringing him in. What was this yearly drink other than a chance for me to feel good about myself? Look at Malone, still hanging on to a friend who'd gone bad. Look at that loyalty.

It was all a load of bullshit.

Turned out it wasn't bullshit to Billy. This wasn't two high school friends going through the motions. It was something real, an honest to God connection to the old days. I hadn't fully realized that until that moment.

"We couldn't keep this going forever. I'm police. And you're a criminal."

Billy laughed, the single short bark of a kicked dog. "You just catching on to that? News flash, Malone. I've been a crook for a long time. You've been a cop almost as long."

"Shades of gray. I can look the other way on some things. No one's getting hurt. No one that didn't bring it on themselves, at any rate. But what I'm hearing now? What you're into?"

I shook my head. One informant I could ignore, even if it had the ring of truth. A second with same story? I'd had no choice, but to run with it. I gave my old friend every benefit of the doubt I could swing, but trail after trail I ran down lead to the same black hole. Coming into Maxie's this night I had thought I'd explain it to Billy this way, but I didn't need to. He knew. I hadn't been as quiet as I'd thought. No amount of justification would make him see what had to happen.

Dez turned the sound up on the television and the announcers nattered on about the "big moment." Less than a minute to the New Year. Dez pulled the big bottle of bubbly out from under the counter. Every year he'd pop it right at midnight.

I scanned the crowd again. Most were turned to the set, not wanting to miss the moment the clock hit midnight, as though the New Year wouldn't be born without a witness. A big guy in the back of the bar hooked my eye for a brief moment, but then turned away. Did I know him? Hadn't I seen him here before? Or was he one of Billy's men? My right hand rested on my sidearm.

"You know the last stanza?" Billy asked.

It was hard to hear him over the increasing volume of the crowd and the television blasting in the background.

"Last what?"

"Stanza. Last bit of the song?"

"Can't say I do."

"And there's a hand, my trusty friend," Billy sang again, his delicate tenor louder now to compensate for the noise. He reached his right hand out across the table toward me. "And give me a hand o' thine."

He waited, eyes locked on my own, to see if I would offer my hand. The hand curled around the molded grip of my gun, ready to draw, ready to shoot down my friend should any of his henchmen come out of hiding.

Around us the crowd counted down the remaining seconds of the dying year. Billy's face relaxed, eyes turning sad when my right hand failed to make an appearance above the table. He gave the slightest shake of his head. It was the look of disapproval the two of us had shared from teachers so many times after being caught skipping school or smoking behind the utility shed or slamming our locker doors.

I saw what I was losing. The friendship I was giving up. It had been real once, so many years ago. It was a bond we thought could hold, but it had been broken by time and fate and simple shitty luck. Ten years ago we thought we could re-forge that bond, we could pretend I wasn't what I was and he wasn't what he was, but over time the glue we'd used to patch that friendship back together grew weaker and more brittle until one day, this last day of the year, it finally shattered.

I began to relax my grip from my gun, hoping we could walk out of here, the two of us free of bullet holes. The friendship was over, but it didn't have to end in violence.

Three!

Two!

One!

Billy's eyes darted to something over my left shoulder. It was quick, maybe an involuntary tic. Might have meant nothing at all.

At the same time, the second hand hit the twelve and Dez popped that bottle of cheap sparkling wine.

The sound of the cork reverberated in Maxie's Bar.

I pulled the trigger and echoed it.

Oliver, Marty and Me
Dan Meyers

"So you think my sister's a whore?"

"Not your sister. Your sister's an angel. I said your mother is a whore."

At the other end of the empty bar, Oliver asks, "Is that conjecture or opinion?"

I swallow the contents of my glass, put it back on the bar top, and look Oliver in the eye. "Neither. Just stating a fact."

Oliver smiles – showing teeth like a long abandoned graveyard. "Well, that makes it indisputable." He slides his empty glass down the bar to me. I line it up with the other two empty glasses and then pour triple shots of vodka into all three.

"Here, see if you can manage to catch the glass this time." I slide his drink along the bar, watching as he barely manages to stop the glass from sliding off the end. He grins like a mule eating garlic. I say, "I've told you, I'm not going behind the bar again to get more glasses just because you want to fuck around." We'd started off with half a dozen highball glasses, then moved on to whiskey tumblers when the highballs became victims of gravity.

I look at my watch. 2:27 a.m. No sirens or flashing lights outside. I'm not too sure if the pool of blood around Oliver's bar stool is getting wider. The tourniquet encircling his left thigh should've been slackened and reapplied over an hour ago. But then, why bother? He's going to lose it anyway. Serves him right for being such a shit getaway driver and wrecking the car. Hell, in thirty years' time that car would've been a classic, had it survived.

I raise my glass and say, "Here's to survival," and take a swig of the clear liquid. Oliver takes some vodka, then says, "Has Marty stopped drinking?"

"Ooops! My bad." I lean over the bar, pick up the third glass, and pour the alcohol as close as I can into Marty's open mouth. He's flat on his back. Hardly surprising considering Oliver put several .38s into him – one I'm sure went through Marty's heart. Some of the vodka goes up his nose, and droplets splash into his still open eyes, but most of it dribbles out the corners of his mouth. Maybe it's time to cut him off if he can't hold his liqueur?

I sit back down on the bar stool, just in time to go through a coughing fit. I wipe my mouth with a napkin. More blood than spittle. What the fuck is it with little old ladies and .22 caliber guns? Oliver's looking at me – his glass paused half way to his lips.

I say, "You shouldn't have killed her. She was probably someone's grandmother."

"Fuck you, asshole. You're lucky she only pulled a .22 out of that bag, and not some old .45 long barrel. That would've gone straight through you. Ripped your spine out and pinned it to the far wall."

106

It was supposed to have been a simple backwater bank job. Marty had talked us into it one evening two months ago, here in the bar.

*****

"I was passing through there 6 years back, driving on down to the Keys with Michelle. She's the blonde." He points to the row of three framed photographs – his ex-wives club. Each photograph had been pinned to the wall using a nail gun – a nail through each of their foreheads. "Anyway, we're way out in the boondocks, staying in the local hotel for several days, and I got to thinking…."

That's when we should've known it was all destined to fail – using the words 'Marty' and 'thinking' without putting 'you're not' in between the two was a total oxymoron. But we still let him carry on talking.

"There's a big processing plant about 10, maybe 15 miles away, pays its workers monthly by bank transfers. Sort of like electronic cheques."

He pauses, and Oliver calls it first. "You're not thinking of hacking the bank transfers are you, you dumb prick? That's just pure Hollywood. Jesus H. Christ!"

Marty gets bitchy. "If you'll just shut the fuck up for a minute? We're not looking at the transfers, or any account details either. We're looking at cash from the local retailers. The bank is the only place in the town that has a satellite link to the internet. Hell, there's not even any cell phone reception out there. It's all old fashioned overhead cables and landlines. No cell provider's prepared to run a service to out-of-the-way Hicksville, so most of the businesses rely on cash that people draw out from the bank – either over the counter, or via the ATM. That means the town has a fair amount of good old re-circulating non-traceable greenbacks sloshing around in the vault."

Oliver's about to say something snarky, so I cut him off at the pass. "I know you're not going to suggest mugging every person we see coming out of the bank, so what's the deal?"

Oliver turns to me. "Are you seriously listening to this guy, Bobby Gee?"

I make the second fuck up of the night. "Can't hurt to hear the man out, can it. Go on Marty, having set the scene, what's the play?"

"With all the usual big city facilities non-existent, when the pay gets transferred to their accounts on the last Friday of the month, most of the citizens withdraw a big wad of it in cash. So we go in on the last Thursday of the month, when the bank's still full of ready money."

I say, "Any bank job needs research, surveillance, scoping out – so it's going to take some time just to put everything like that together."

Marty smiles, all toothpaste and strawberry mouthwash. "Done all that already. Hang around after I close and I'll walk you all through it."

*****

Of course, what could go wrong did go wrong. The latex zombie masks were a size too small and damn uncomfortable even before the three of us piled out of the car. Marty had the lead with some cheap shit Russian pump action shotgun. In through the doors, two in the ceiling, "Everybody down on the floor now!" Oliver and me we're following behind, waving big black 9mm automatics and sweating like a pair of pedophiles in Santa suits.

Only, after the first skyward shot of double-ought, the second one got jammed up with a crunching noise you could've heard all the way back to the State line.

Some people had already dropped to the floor on the first shot, but others had gone to the sides, or dived under nearby desks. Several tellers were looking on behind bullet proof glass while the manager in a lightweight grey 2-piece was desperately trying to punch in the security door combination so he could get through into the back offices.

Next thing I know, Marty's thrown the shotgun to one side, turned and barged between Oliver and me – shouting, "Out-out-out!"

I'm almost through the door when I feel a poke in my back. I turn round, and see a 60-something mom – hair up high and more make-up than a rodeo clown in a dress – standing behind a desk and pointing a chrome .22 revolver. Oliver turns, not even slowing down, and lets one lose. All that training in Helmand finally paid off. She goes down, and I know she's not going to get up again.

We all pile into the SUV Marty had kitted out with fake plates – Oliver driving, me up front, and Marty in the back – and we manage to get the fuck out of town. Didn't even stop when we dumped the zombie masks as we passed the *Welcome To…. Home of the pickled pig's foot* city limit sign – or some shit like that.

Then it was a long, hard, 12 hour straight drive to get back home. All the way up, Oliver and Marty kept needling each other like a couple of teenagers. I try to sleep, then drive, then try to sleep again – forever feeling a tacky wetness on my back, and a stabbing pain every time I breathe in deep.

Finally, around 1 a.m. this morning, we see the sign *Heggety's Country Bar* up ahead. But the two of them are still verbally tearing chunks out of each other – so much so that Oliver almost misses the turn into the parking lot. He yanks the steering wheel sharply to the left, only he doesn't stop to open the gates first, so we grind to a halt with the gates ripped off their posts and wrapped around the front of the car.

By that time I'm stoically philosophical. Whatever else can get fucked up will get royally fucked up, regardless of what we do.

I climb out, only to find Oliver and Marty are still facing each other in the middle of the car park, both ranting and raving. Then, from nowhere, Marty pulls out a knife, and next thing I know, it's sticking out of Oliver's thigh. In retaliation, he pulls out a little snub nosed .38 and gives Marty two, up close and personal.

Marty does the decent thing for once and drops like a sack of shit, while Oliver finally realizes he still has the knife stuck in him.

I'm now starting to wonder if any of the neighbors heard the crash, or the gunshots. As Oliver puts the revolver away, he says, "Gimme your belt."

"What?"

"Your pants belt. I need it."

So I pull the length of leather with a brass pin buckle out

from around the waistband of my jeans and pass it to him.

Guy doesn't even say 'Thank you.' He just wraps it around his upper thigh, pulls it tight and locks the buckle so it doesn't come loose.

He looks off into the distance and says, "Now for the hard part." And before I can stop him he's yanked the knife out, and for a moment I think the bleeding gets worse.

We both look down at Marty. I say, "Best get him inside."

So we get his keys out of his pocket and drag him into the bar, turn on a couple of lights and drop him behind the counter.

When we're done, Oliver says, "Well, Bobby Gee, this really is one mighty bad SNAFU. Still, I guess Marty's in no position to complain if we help ourselves to some liqueur, now is he."

*****

I take another look at my watch. 2:41 a.m. Still no sirens or flashing lights. I look across at Oliver again. The red around his bar stool has spread. I know because I can see my leather belt hanging loose where he's slackened it off. Oliver carefully drains his glass, then puts it on the bar top, upside down.

"Sorry, Kimosabe," He looks down the bar at me, his eyes heavy lidded and half closed. "I think it's time I finally caught up with my sleep. See you wherever, whenever that might be." He folds his arms on the bar top and rests his head on them.

I go into another coughing fit – the worst so far – screaming pain in my chest, hard to breath in, and the back of my hand is coated in dark red. It'd be nice to just go to sleep, but I've still got one more thing to do.

I rip the pocket off my shirt, soak one end in vodka, and with a book of matches from a bowl on the bar, I set alight to the other end. Vodka doesn't burn unless you heat it first, and I figure Marty's soaked shirt would've warmed up enough from his remaining body heat.

I lean over the bar again, watching the burning cloth and seeing the alcohol start to burn blue. Then watch it drop onto the middle of Marty's shirt. When the flames take hold I sit back down on the bar stool again, involuntarily hawking up a chunk of blood and phlegm, and spitting it into the remaining empty glass.

Every account I've read has always stated that people die of smoke and fumes long before the flames reach them.

I pick up the vodka bottle and pour some over the blood clotting in the glass, turning the whole thing pinkish red. I take a sip, and hope for once that Lady Luck is on our side, and that the Fire Department won't get here in time.

Black Market MPs
James Roth

"Ain't this country the fucking best thing that ever happened to you?" Vaughn said. That's when it all started off for me, and not for the better.

He'd said this more like he was talking to himself than to me. Except for maybe the girls, I wasn't sure what he'd meant. My girl, I thought then, was just fine, because except for the girls most of what I'd seen of Japan was burned-out buildings that smelled like pissed on ash heaps and people as scrawny as mongrel dogs.

I said, "Never thought I'd be fucking a tattooed dame."

Vaughn turned to me and said, "You ever think about how many GI cocks she saw before you fell in love?"

That's how Vaughn was, not easy to be around. No one liked going on patrol with him.

"You're in Japan," he then said, "not fucking Kansas," to piss me off even more.

"Idaho," I said, "Twin Falls, near Yosemite."

"Big fucking difference, farm boy. South Boston born and bred." Then he bellowed like a minister from a pulpit, "Praise the Lord, this country is para-fucking-dise!"

I said, "My family owns a ranch."

Vaughn said nothing. What an asshole, calling me a farmer. He didn't know the difference between a steer and heifer, the South Boston thug. But in the end, things didn't turn out well for either of us. But better for me than him.

At about this time the deuce and a half we'd been tailing went down a side street and stopped behind a warehouse. It had been raining earlier, and the city's streets had a sheen to them in the moonlight. What I would've thought of as something that had beauty back home in the mountains was sinister and threatening in the city, the way the streets rolled out, black as tar, and the buildings, dark and empty, looked like creatures ready to collapse on top of us.

Vaughn slowed the Jeep down to a crawl. He'd already switched off the headlights. The driver of the deuce backed it up to the loading bay.

"I'll call it in," I said.

"Are you fucking dumb or what, country boy?" Vaughn said.

"It's procedure," I said, reaching for the mic, but thinking that all the talk I'd heard about him from other MPs about his South Boston ways was probably true.

He grabbed my wrist. "We're sitting on a gold mine. You understand?"

I let go of the mic.

He grinned so widely I could see down his throat, toward a dark pit, then he looked back at the deuce and eased the Jeep over to the curb and shut it down. Not long after that two GIs and a couple of Japs unloaded the deuce, taking rations and crates inside on dollies along the wet, dark loading dock. It was a helluava haul, mostly rations, which are more valuable than gold when you're starving, but cigarettes and booze, too, all worth a fortune on the black market, and medical supplies, too, including vials of morphine. Both Jap soldiers and our boys were hooked on it.

"Para-fucking-dise," Vaughn said again, drawing out his .45.

"They're GIs," I said, "like us." I was thinking of those dead GIs and marines who'd washed up on faraway beaches.

"They're thieves," he said. He grinned again, showing his tobacco-stained teeth and issued a stench of tobacco; he had a wad of it packed up against a cheek. Looking at him, with his eyes bulging out, was like looking at one of those devils with horns that my girl Shoko had showed me at a temple in Asakusa, a district that had mostly been laid waste by LeMay's B-29 firebombing of eastern Tokyo.

Vaughn took a roll of duct tape and ripped off a piece and gave it to me and said, "Cover your name."

I did and knew then that I was fucked.

"Guard the door on the loading dock," he said.

"Where're you going?" I asked.

"You ask too many fucking questions, farm boy. Don't let anyone get past you," he said. "If they try to." He tapped his .45.

We got out of the Jeep, and he went around to the front door. I covered the back. I'd only been there thirty seconds or so, looking at a puddle of rain water at my feet, a full moon reflected in it, when a little Jap came running out and bounced off me, landing onto the concrete of the loading dock. I pointed my .45 at his forehead, and he started jabbering away, holding up both of his hands, as if his hands could stop the slug of a .45. Not hardly the samurai warrior I'd heard about from GIs who'd seen action. He pissed in his pants even, farted, and farted some more until the farts were no longer gas. The stench!

"Get up!" I said. I grabbed him by the arm.

He pushed himself up. He stepped in the puddle of water, leading me back across the dark loading dock into the warehouse, where there was another Jap, a little one like the one I had, but wearing a white shirt and tie, a boss, I guess, and a couple of GIs, one, a sergeant, sitting behind a table that had stacks of dollars on it.

The sergeant's nose and ears were cauliflowered, like he'd spent some time in the ring. His head looked like a potato it was so beat up. The other GI was a private, just a kid with pimples, a few years younger than me, maybe nineteen.

Vaughn helped himself to the money. "Thank you very much," he said.

"Put it back," the sergeant said, staring up at him. He'd spoken as if he was issuing an order.

"Or what?" Vaughn grinned.

"You don't want to know," he said.

Vaughn went over to him, drew out his .45, and pistol-whipped him across the forehead, opening up a deep gash, but it was like his .45 had hit the barrel of a Sherman. He didn't flinch. He just let the blood flow down over his eyes, into his mouth, down onto his chin, and drip from it onto the concrete floor, splat, splat, splat. Damn, he was tough. Terrifying. And, to my misfortune, I'd see him again, under circumstances I couldn't have imagined.

His name was O'Shaughnessy, from South Boston, too. Hell, Vaughn and he might have known each other, or heard of the other, long before the war, maybe run in different gangs, which would've explained a lot. But I didn't know. I'm a cowboy. Or was until that night. Being on a saddle in the high country, bringing down the cattle during the first snow, my beard iced up, that seemed better than being in that warehouse.

Vaughn went over to the private, holding the .45. He pissed in his pants. "Please! Please!" he begged.

"I knew you were a pussy," Sergeant O'Shaughnessy said.

"Please! I just wanted to earn a few extra bucks for my girl."

Vaughn holstered his .45. He held out a twenty for the kid to take.

"I can' take that," he said.

"Afraid to?"

The kid looked at O'Shaughnessy.

Vaughn went over to the kid and stuffed the twenty into a pocket of his field jacket. The kid took it out and tossed it on the floor. "Hell, no! I'm not stupid."

"You saying I am?" Vaughn asked.

"No! Please!"

"You and your friend are making a big mistake," O'Shaughnessy said, "a real big mistake."

"Are we?" Vaughn said. He then saw the crates of medical supplies and had the little Jap pop the top off of one and reached in and pulled out several vials of morphine. "You haven't changed your ways," he said to O'Shaughnessy. He took several of the vials and put them away in his field jacket. He tossed one to me. I almost dropped the damn thing, I was so nervous.

"You did good, farm boy," Vaughn said, "you deserve one." Unlike the kid, I was stupid. I didn't toss the vial back.

Vaughn then drew his .45 out and let go with a round right over O'Shaughnessy's head. O'Shaughnessy just laughed. "You should've put it through my forehead," he said.

"A dead man ain"t worth nothin' to me," Vaughn said.

As soon as we'd made it outside, I heard O'Shaughnessy laugh so hard that the loading dock doors of the warehouse rattled. Hearing that laugh, I thought I might piss in my pants. It wasn't like he was laughing at someone's joke.

I followed Vaughn back to the Jeep across the damp street, my legs wobbly, and got in and Vaughn started the Jeep up and he drove off. He didn't say anything, was just grinning. Then he started to sing, "On the first day of Christmas, my true love gave to me. . ." He turned to me. "What the fuck did she give?"

I couldn't speak.

"You're not in a festive mood." Vaughn stopped the Jeep up against the curb. A couple of drunk Japanese businessmen stumbled by. One stopped to piss against a building, while the other puked in the gutter. This was MacArthur's idea of democratization? I thought, a country of drunks, kids with hair lice, and people who were starving. Vaughn stuffed a stack of dollars inside a pocket of my field jacket. Those damn jackets, they had pockets all over, deep ones.

"I don't want it," I said.

"You're taking it," he said, "farm boy, whether you want it or not. Merry fucking Christmas. Now how does that song go? On the first day of Christmas, my true love gave to me . . . Fuck, taking is more my way of celebrating Christmas. Giving is for suckers."

"Then take this money back," I said.

"You calling me a sucker?"

I didn't say anything. I was in deep and words would just get me in deeper.

He started up the Jeep and drove off. The headlights shone on the wet street and glass of shop windows. Vaughn started to laugh to himself, shouting now and then, "Para-fucking-dise, this country. All those GIs dying for what? Poor bastards. Some foolish idea. Only fools die for ideas." He tapped his field jacket, where the money and vials of morphine were. "Money. That's what they should've died for," he said. "What can an idea buy me?"

I later thought about him saying that, and it made things a lot easier for me. But at that time I was thinking about how to get out of this mess I was in, if I should tell the lieutenant. Shoko, my girl, would help me with that decision, I thought; I always ran things past her, her knowing how things were in Japan, even how the U.S. Army worked. She really knew, all right.

When Vaughn and I finished for the night, I went back to my barracks and threw some civilian clothes in a duffel, along with a razor, toothbrush, that sort of stuff, and it was only then that I remembered the vial of morphine. I found it in the pocket of the field jacket and put it in the duffel too.

Shoko had a room above a noodle shop, not too far from Ueno station, a major train station that hadn't been turned to ash by the incendiaries. I went to stay with her during my off-duty days.

Right off she served me tea on a round cherry wood tray, the way she always did, along with some *sembe*, rice crackers that have absolutely no taste. I opened a tin of Uncle Sam's strawberry jam I'd given her and smeared some of it on one, and she said something in Japanese, to express her disgust, no translation necessary.

We were sitting on the floor, she with her legs tucked under her, very elegantly. Me cross-legged, slouched over, the way, yes, a cowboy would sit on a log near a campfire. There was no furniture in her room, only six tatami mats, the way the Japanese measure rooms, and a sink and a squat Jap toilet. The only heat was from a charcoal-burning hibachi. There was no bath. We used a public bath down the street. Most Japanese did. That took some getting used to, being naked, shoulder to shoulder with another man, but I warmed up to it after a while, started to enjoy it even. Damn, the water was hot, just like coming out of a geyser almost.

Shoko was wearing a yellow robe, with patterns of green bamboo on it, nothing underneath. The nipples of her little tits poked against the cloth, hard and eager, but even the sight of them didn't give me a hard-on. She, after sipping her tea, put a hand on my crotch.

"What matter, Spencer?" she asked.

A boner started to take shape, and she knew then that I'd

talk. There's a saying in Japan that women have of men: When the little head is hard, the big one is soft.

Shoko had a shiny black snatch of hair that drove me nuts, just a glimpse of it, and she knew it, and so when she opened the robe a bit and I saw some of it, and her tattooed shoulder, tea time was over. The tattoo is of a koi, like a damn painting, it is. Never thought I'd say that about a trash fish.

We fucked raw on the tatami, under a quilt, it was so cold in the room, and after the fucking my elbows and knees burned the way they would if we'd been doing it on sandpaper, because they'd been scrapping on the tatami, but while we were fucking I didn't feel any pain, none at all. Not one bit. That's a perfect fuck, when a man's thinking is focused only on the fucking. When the little head is hard, the big one is soft.

As I lay on my back afterward, both my big and little heads soft, I said, "It's Vaughn. I'm in some deep shit because of him."

"You tell," she said.

And I did.

When I'd finished, she said, "You tell lieutenant. He officer."

I just lay on my back, smoking a Chesterfield. She plucked it from my fingers, crushed it out in a porcelain white ashtray, and said, "You listen me, Spencer? You listen?"

"I'm listening."

"You tell lieutenant."

With her, it was sometimes difficult to know if she was issuing an order or asking a question. A lot of Japanese spoke English that way. I said to her, "I have to get by Sergeant

Nowak, the thick-necked Pollock. I can't just walk into the lieutenant's office."

"You know to do so."

I wasn't sure what the hell that meant.

She knocked out another Chesterfield from a box of them lying nearby and stuck it in my mouth and lit it, and I drew on it, blowing the smoke up toward the ceiling in one long stream. Then Shoko took a drag herself and handed the Chesterfield back to me, all red, the tip, from lipstick I'd scrounged up for her on the Ginza.

Lying there on my back after a good fuck, smoking a Chesterfield, my mind started to wander, and I thought of myself back home on the ranch, sticking a hot branding iron to a calf. That's what I wanted to do to Vaughn, right on his ass, the brand of the Broken Y.

Then I remembered the vial of morphine and got it out of my duffel. Holding it in my hand, I didn't know what to do with it.

"Morphine," Shoko said. She was a quick study. "I have friends. Give me."

She had friends, all right. I handed the vial to her.

"Fine," I said. "I don't want that stuff near me. I'll be doing KP in Leavenworth for the rest of my life."

"What?"

I didn't want to explain.

"You not worry, Spencer," she said. She opened my fly and put a hand inside and, well, that was how she operated, by getting the small head hard.

On my next duty day, I went to see the lieutenant. Nowak asked me, "What is it, Robertson?" He was pushing around some papers. He was always pushing around papers, to make it seem that he was more important than he was.

"I want to see the lieutenant," I said.

He stuck the pen he was holding above his ear. "What about?" he said.

"It's a private matter," I said.

He pushed himself back in his chair. The springs squeaked. "I run this outfit," he said. "You know that?"

"Yes, I know, sergeant, and you do a helluava job."

We just stared at each other. He knew I wasn't going to tell him anything.

"A private matter, is it?"

He got up from his desk and knocked on the lieutenant's door, and the lieutenant said, "Yes?"

Sergeant Nowak said, "Robertson here wants to have a word with you, sir."

"Send him in."

"I'll find out about your 'private matter,'" he said.

I went into the lieutenant's office. He was smoking a cigarette, had a cup of steaming coffee on his desk, not a scrap of paper, no Army forms in sight. Just a baseball in an ashtray. He'd been a pitcher at his university, some private school back east. He was tall and lanky with a good curveball, I'd heard, and had been scouted by the pros. Then Pearl Harbor came along. He ran his outfit the way most officers I'd seen did, by sitting on their ass smoking and drinking coffee and probably thinking about the life that had passed them by.

I stood in front of his desk and said, "Good morning, sir."

"Good morning, Robertson. Something on your mind?"

"There's something you should know about Vaughn, sir, that happened when we were last on patrol," I said.

He leaned forward, both of his elbows on his desk, picked up the baseball, tossed it back and forth between his hands, and then caught it in his left one and said, "What?"

I told him.

He leaned forward, staring at me. "You waited three damn days to report this?" he said.

Well, I couldn't really tell him why I'd waited, that I'd been shacked up with Shoko, fucking my kneecaps off, even if he had a shack job, too. We all knew he did. And he was married, the cheat. But him being my CO, I had to let all that pass.

"I didn't know what to do, sir," I said.

"How do you expect me to protect you when you're with your girl? That's where you were. Right?"

"Yes, sir."

"I'm not stupid, cowboy."

"No, sir. I didn't mean for you to take it that way."

He leaned back in his chair, smoked on his cigarette, pitched the baseball back and forth, from one hand to the other, then put the ball down and reached for his coffee mug. He sipped some coffee. "You cowboys must drink a lot of coffee," he said.

"Yes, sir." That's where I wanted to be, sitting on a fence

railing drinking coffee.

"You should've come to me with this right after it happened. Get out of here and tell Sergeant Nowak on your way out."

I just stood there. He knew what I was thinking, too. He said, "Okay. You've made your point. Fuck. Everyone has got their hands into something over here. You said O'Shaughnessy, right? He's not the only one. Fucking half of Uncle Sam's rations are on the streets. Now get out of here."

"Yes, sir."

"And be careful," he said. "That's all I need is a corpse to explain. The paperwork!"

I saluted and left and walked right past Sergeant Nowak's desk. He grumbled, "I'll find out, cowboy."

I went back on duty that night with Laroach. We called him Roach. He was from Louisiana. He sure as hell knew how to talk food, what we could understand of what he was saying. He had a shack job, too, and he was taking rations to her family and cooking them up for her. He could mix vegetable slices with this god-awful salt pork and turn it all into something that looked like what a waiter at a fancy French restaurant would serve on a silver tray. He was learning the lingo, too. I heard he ended up living in Japan, started a family, unlike me, who stayed on, too, but not quite under such pleasurable circumstances.

Laroach and I talked shit all night, baseball and girls and the war, the bombings of Hiroshima and Nagasaki, and about the defeated Japanese who never showed any hostility toward us, but seemed thankful that we'd put an end to the war with those two bombs. Even the firebombing of Tokyo in March, that killed more people than the atomic bombing of Hiroshima; they just wanted to put the war behind them and build back their country. I'm not sure an American could've done that. The GIs from down South were still fighting the Civil War. "The War Between the States," I'd heard more than one of them call it. Not really.

We finished our patrol and returned to the office and were doing our paperwork when Gomez came in and shouted, "You are hearing about Vaughn?"

"Are you going to tell us?" I said.

"His body was found floating in that canal in Nihonbashi, his throat slit. You know that canal?"

As if I cared about that canal, its location. That little Jap came to mind and this time it was me who had to hold back pissing in my pants.

I changed into my civies and went straight to Shoko's. We walked up the street to a sukiyaki place--supplied with American beef, of course--and as we were eating and drinking Kirin beer I told her what had happened to Vaughn.

"What we do?" she said, as if she wasn't making plans.

The bowl of sukiyaki was there in front of us, steaming. We just stared at each other through the steam. Shoko was wearing a real fine blue silk dress. Her long hair was tied back into one long ponytail, braided. I was thinking, I'd never seen anything like her in Twin Falls and never would. She was beautiful. I said, "I don't know."

She set her chopsticks down and looked at me real serious like, the way only a small dame can and get away with, and said, "I from Kanezawa."

I didn't catch on to what she meant right away; a lot of Japanese speak that way, hinting rather than saying, with you having to fill in what they haven't said.

I said, "So?"

"We safe there."

"And where are we going to stay?" I said.

"I have friend. Room. It's good. Kanazawa have beautiful park. I show you. Very famous. Kenrokuen."

I wasn't really too interested in sightseeing, but, well, I couldn't tell her that. Yeah, she had it all planned out, even the walks through Kenrokuen.

We continued on eating, and as we did she told me about her hometown, Kanazawa, and how we could take a train there.

"Kanazwa have good crab," she then said. "Delicious! Winter crab ichi-ban."

Hell, the way she talked about me going AWOL made it sound more like a honeymoon. We even started to joke about it, how much fun it would be to go to Kanazawa and walk in the park and then go back to our room and fuck.

We left the tavern, *izakaiya*, as they're called, and headed back to her place, along a narrow street lined with shops-- liquor stores, tailors, and places that sold ancient woodblock prints of Japanese men and women fucking, stuff that would never be shown on a street in the U.S. Never. Those woodblock prints made me think, maybe it's American culture that's got sex all wrong, the way people think of it as something indecent.

Along the street GIs were walking along with their arms around their shack jobs, all smiles, having just gotten laid, or about to get laid, the GIs casting a knowing wink to each other, not caring if they stepped into a puddle of water. Then Shoko stopped suddenly, just up the street from her room, and through the crowd--and I don't know how such a small girl could manage it, but she did--she saw what I couldn't.

She said, "We can not go my room."

"Why?" I asked.

"Them," she said.

I looked over the tops of the heads of the people and saw two Japanese men wearing suits, sort of odd, and both had crew cuts and sunglasses; not a common sight, those two, the way they were dressed or their hairstyle.

"Yakuza," Shoko said.

"What?"

We tucked into the entrance of a shoe shop and watched them for a few minutes, as customers from the noodle shop under her room came and went, hoping they would leave, but they didn't. And then what had been rain turned to snow, not the dry snow I as familiar with, but sloppy wet stuff, like mud. "We go to Ueno Station," she said. "You have money?" She popped open an umbrella she had brought along, and I took it from her and held it over us. I counted my money, U.S. dollars. I had twenty-seven dollars and thirty-seven cents, and yen, just over two thousand. "Enough," she said.

We went back up the street toward the sukiyaki shop, then she took me down some back alleys, one coming out onto a main street, which only had a few cars, and some Jeeps, MPs in them, same as me, patrolling, and crossed it and went down some more alleys until I was lost, and remained so until I saw the entrance to Ueno Station, passing by a "Prophylactic Station." No shit, the U.S. Army was passing out rubbers to GIs all over the country. Even I had a few in my pocket. An Army of drippy dick soldiers isn't an Army and MacArthur knew it.

We went in the station, and I bought two tickets, third class, for Kanazawa, the only tickets left, on the last train, and you can't imagine what that was like, really you can't, riding third class--discharged Japanese soldiers wearing the only uniform they had, smelling of urine, pregnant women, or women with a kid on their back, another holding onto their hand, and old men smoking a cheroot. It was hell. And it was hell for more than twenty-four hours, as the train went along, chugging up snowy mountains, going through tunnels. The windows fogged up, even became icy inside the damn train, but, well, the two of us, we did have a seat, unlike so many pitiful Japanese.

We did manage to sleep a little, our heads leaning together, and when dawn came there were fallow rice paddies covered in snow and mountains and more tunnels and soot from the engine coming in the car and more tunnels and more soot, until the tracks came out onto a wide plain, rice paddies covered in snow as far as I could see, like hay fields, mind you, on the Broken Y, and it was at about this time that Shoko said, "Now not far."

"Thank god," I said.

Another couple of hours later the train pulled into Kanazawa station, and Shoko and I got a taxi to her friend's place, thirty minutes away, in the direction of the park, Kenrokuen. Her friend's place was a traditional Japanese inn above an *izakaiya*, one that grilled fish over charcoal, so that the fish smell smoke rose right up into the rooms. We'd exchanged a room over a noodle shop for this one that smelled of grilled fish.

The room was six-mats, the same size as Shoko's back in Tokyo, and was in the back of the building, facing Kenrokuen, which was a few blocks away; we could see the pines from it over the roofs of other buildings and flimsy Japanese homes of wood and paper that had a charm about them, I have to admit, real charm, like a scene from a fairy tale.

Kanazawa was only bombed here and there, as if a pilot had only dropped the bombs to get rid of them, so as not to come back to Iwo or Saipan with them and risk getting his ass chewed off from not unloading them. There was a harbor not far off where most of the bombs seemed to have fallen on some fishing boats or freighters that had been hit and had rolled over and sunk, the hulls painted now with seagull shit.

Kenrokuen was like no other park I'd been to. I'd imagined a park like back in the U.S., with picnic tables and places where kids could play--monkey bars, a swing, and a carousel--so I learned something about Japan, seeing Kenrokuen, I did, and Shoko was proud to tell me about it, too. The Maeda clan--the *daimyos*--started construction on it in the sixteenth century, and it wasn't finished until the middle of the nineteenth century. The Maedas controlled that part of the country, and the warlord there, if that's the word for him, and his entourage--lieutenants and concubines--would take walks through the park from time to time. The Maeda clan's castle was nearby.

The park was designed to look like a scene from nature, like a valley I'd come into on my horse that no one had seen before. There were pines and cherry trees and a small stream that flowed through it. The only tip-off that none of it was natural were the gravel paths leading through the park and a teahouse, part of which was on pilings over one of the lakes.

Shoko and I would go to the teahouse from time to time and have tea and look out over the lake, where koi swam peacefully by. Watching those koi, I never thought in my life that I would be sitting on my ass on a mat drinking tea admiring carp, but thinking about Vaughn with a smile cut into his throat and what had happened to him changed the way I saw things.

Shoko and I got our food from the *izakaiya* on the first floor, and even from a few GIs I hit up for some rations, telling them I was with my girl after going AWOL because of an asshole sergeant, which they all understood and sympathized with. They, many, had been under the thumb of an asshole sergeant and usually said something like, "Fuck it. I wish I had the balls to do what you did. Either that or shoot the son of a bitch in the back of the head. What'ya need?"

Shoko and I slept on a futon on the tatami. She always put it away in the morning and swept the tatami clean and had a girl bring us tea and eggs for breakfast.

We had our dinners in the *izakaiya*. One night Shoko and I were having saury grilled over charcoal. Saury, the first time I saw it, made me think I was eating a baitfish, something trolled off the stern, but I got used to it and even enjoyed the oiliness of it and the *daikon*, the grated radish that was always served with it.

The *izakaiya* was small, the way most *izakaiyas* are. A counter ran along the length of one side of it, and between the counter and some Japanese tables on tatami there was a passageway that led back to the kitchen. Shoko and I always ate at one of the tables, even though I could hardly get my knees under it and doing so made the small of my back ache. A log, that's what I wanted to sit on. Shoko was all dainty, sitting on her legs, making me feel as delicate as a rodeo bull.

We had just about finished our fish and miso soup and rice and were working our way through another bottle of Kirin when Shoko said, "Excuse me."

She couldn't hold her beer. She always had to take a few trips to the lady's room. So I didn't think anything of it. And then, not long after she'd left, this Japanese man sat down where she'd been. His hair was greased back. A real fashion plate, he was, in his forties, I guessed, wearing a double-breasted dark jacket, white shirt, and scarlet tie.

"Mr. Robertson?" he asked.

"Who are you?" I said.

"In due time," he said. "You've become accustomed to Japanese food? It's very healthy."

"Who's asking?" I asked again.

Standing behind him was a Jap with shoulders as wide as a grizzly's and with a grizzly's snarl on his face. Two fingers were missing from his left hand, and he hadn't lost them from being thrown from a rodeo bronco. Hardly.

Fashion plate unbuttoned the middle buttons of his white shirt and pulled it open, showing me a tattoo of a sword among some blossoming chrysanthemums. I knew about Japanese tattoos. Shoko had gotten her tattoo because she'd had a yakuza lover and wanted to prove her loyalty to him. And then he got mortared on Peleilu. His remains, some sand and ash in a pine box, was sent to his family

"Shoko is a beautiful girl," he said.

If I could've gotten out of there I would've; I'd have gone straight to the first MP I saw and turned myself in. A few years in Leavenworth was better than where this conversation was heading, and I knew it. But I was trapped; making my way past that grizzly who wanted to bite my head off wasn't a very smart thing to try. I knew grizzlies all too well. What could I do but try to talk my way out? A losing proposition, I knew. I'm not a talker. But I tried. I tried. His name was Yamaguchi, a member of one of Japan's largest yakuza clans.

"Your English is pretty good, for a Jap," I said.

"I lived in L.A. when I was younger. USC, class of twenty-nine, the year of the crash. Ever seen a Rose Bowl parade?"

"No."

"Americans have a way of turning simple events into obscene spectacles. We Japanese, we prefer restraint, austerity--the petal of a cherry blossom settling onto the surface of a brook, flowing away as a representation of lost beauty."

"I've been to Kenrokuen," I said.

"So you feel at home in Kanazawa?"

"What kind of bullshit question is that?"

"You're AWOL, aren't you?"

"What do you want? You've interrupted our dinner."

"Forgive me for being Japanese. It's our nature to be polite. We Japanese want you to feel at home here in our country, and it is *our country*. We want you to feel that you're part of *our* family," he said. He smiled. One of his molars had a gold crown. I think he took some delight in showing it, that he had money. Plenty.

I had nothing to say.

"I'm a businessman," he said. "And businessmen are always looking for opportunities to expand their business. It's a consequential result of the invisible hand theory. Of course, you're familiar with Adam Smith?"

I don't like a Jap talking down to me. It isn't right. I wished then that I'd seen some action and put a slug between the eyes of a few Japs. They deserved as much, being so proud. That thought became a knot in my stomach and a tightness in my neck when he reached into a pocket of his jacket and took something from it and set it on the table, a vial of morphine.

Looking at the vial, I said, "I'm a cowboy. We ride horses. Brand cattle. Sit around campfires to keep warm, things you and Adam Fucking Smith wouldn't know anything about. I don't know nothin' about that," I said, looking at the vial.

He buttoned up his shirt back up. Then he slipped his hand inside his coat and pulled out a U.S. Army .45 from a black leather shoulder holster and laid it on the table. "I believe Sergeant O'Shaughnessy is an acquaintance of yours?" he said.

I remembered him as I'd last seen him, with blood dripping off his chin. "Another one of your polite questions?" I said. "We've met."

"I can't help myself," he said. "I'm Japanese." He looked down at the .45, then at me. He grinned. The gold molar flashed.

I looked at the .45 and grunted.

"That's rude," he said.

"Pardon fucking me," I said. I grunted again.

He flashed his gold molar. "You have humor," he said. "Americans are like that, cracking jokes when it is inappropriate to do so. But, well, I admire that foolish quality. And women like it as well, American's foolishness."

"We won the war," I said. "Hiroshima."

"The war? That's all behind us. Businessmen are interested in the future."

"Cows," I said, "and horses. That's as far as I go."

He laughed. "A man should have a sense of humor," he said. "Women like to be humored. It leads to a happy marriage."

"What the fuck are you talking about, happy marriage?"

"Forgive me."

He looked at the .45 again.

I looked at it.

We looked at each other.

At about that time Shoko came back and sat down beside me and, under the table, put the palm of her delicate, warm hand against the inside of my thigh and rubbed it back and forth there until I got a hard-on. Then she laid her little hand on my stiff cock and said, "I think best for us."

Small head hard, big head soft.

Fashion plate flashed his gold molar.

The Leaky Faucet

Jesse Aaron

It was a little after two a.m. when my phone buzzed on the nightstand. I was in the middle of a dream in which I was trying to fix a leaky pipe under my kitchen sink. My old partner Mike was standing over me watching. Every time I would try to fix the leak the pliers would either be too big or too small, and each time I chose the wrong sized tool Mike would just shake his head and say,

"Nope, try again. You need the...."

But I could never hear exactly what he was saying, and the whole routine would start all over again as I switched to a different sized pair of pliers. The buzzing of my phone turned into the rush of water and then finally pulled me out of the dream. I woke up startled and it took me a full minute to realize where I was. I looked at the caller I.D. on my phone and knew I had to answer.

"Yeah, Mike, you okay?"

"Hey Sam. Yeah, I'm alright. Sorry to wake you, I'm parked out front. I need you buddy. Bring your Glock."

If anyone else had asked me to do this, I would have turned my phone off and gone back to the land of unfixable pipes, but for Mike I just answered:

"Give me five minutes, I'll be down."

As I groped my way into my clothes and attached the holster to my belt, I shook my head to clear away the dust that had settled there from too little sleep. I gulped some water and checked myself in the mirror. I smoothed down my long dark hair with some water and rubbed my dark eyes with the back of my hand. My slightly hooked nose looked red, and my eyes still looked like they were asleep, but I was at least somewhat presentable. I walked downstairs eight minutes later.

Mike was sitting in his red truck, parked at an angle so he could see me coming.

"Hey Sam, your late, you said five minutes."

Mike smirked as he said this and I got in the passenger side. I lifted my shirt to show him I was heeled.

"I was good and asleep when you called me you know. Having a nice dream about some pipe that was leaking."

Mike looked over at me and I could see his face light up in an eerie green color as the dashboard lights illuminated his features.

"You were fixing a leak? I wouldn't call that a regular dream. I would call that a nightmare."

Mike and I had a running joke about my poor home improvement skills.

"Ha ha, very funny. Where we going anyway?"

"Don't worry, you'll be back in bed by sunrise. Just need someone with me for show. You know how I'm always saying I'm going to start playing? Well, I won big on a college game, and I need to make a pickup of my winnings. If I waited until tomorrow he might stiff me. If I show up alone, there's the chance the bookie might not pay. He's not usually carrying, but just in case I need a witness. You're the only one I could trust. I've been chasing him down all day but I finally got him to agree to a meet up. He's holed up in a dirty tenement on the east side in the city. I just text you the address."

I snarled at Mike as I lay my head on the door for the hour-long ride into the city.

I wouldn't do this for anyone else, but I trusted Mike with my life. Not only had we been partners, but we were best friends. Since I left to start the agency we had drifted apart a bit, but we still spoke at least once a week.

Even though time and different jobs had pulled us apart, there was always a strong bond between us. The older I got the harder it was to make and keep friends like Mike, so I would do anything for him.

He leaned back a little as he drove, and his large bulk spread out on the seat like some kind of large bear. Mike was six two and as wide as a double door. His pale and round shaved head shone in the streetlights, and as he drove his glasses reflected the other car's headlights like passing train tracks in the same pattern, over and over. He knew I was tired, so he put on some of our favorite music and just drove.

We first met in the Academy, and the partnership was formed instantly when he covered for me in gym class. Anytime we had to partner up to practice the various impractical and painful come along holds he always went easy on me. If a gym instructor happened to be watching he would take the fall and make it look good.

In turn I helped him with the academics. Not that Mike was stupid — he actually had more street smarts than I could ever hope for, but I had four years of college and he had only one, so helping him with the book work just seemed natural.

As our trust for each other grew so did our friendship. After we got out of the Academy we asked for the same command and we partnered up right away. Everyone knew we were best friends, and even when the Sergeant put us on posts at opposite ends of the precinct we would somehow always end up together, but we made such good collars they could never complain.

We had both saved each other from physical harm so many times that we stopped counting. During our time on patrol together we had looked into the mouth of insanity and chaos so many times that we knew that we could never be closer to any other human being then we were to each other.

The other thing that bonded us like crazy glue was that we both tried to help people when we were able. A lot of cops walk around badge heavy and embrace the authority of the job, but Mike and I always had an understanding that our job was to help our fellow man, not show them how much collective muscle we had.

Neither of us enjoyed the punishment element of being a cop. We were not afraid to use our considerable combined strength when we had to, but we never used it unless it was absolutely necessary. I think this mutual respect for human suffering and the knowledge that we both felt the pain of others as if it was our own drew us together more than anything else.

It tore me apart when I had to leave, but I needed a different life, and Mike was ready to go too. He got hurt one night when I was off, and it was a golden ticket. He broke his hand while he was wrestling with some scumbag, and it happened to be his shooting hand and a ticket to a tax-free three quarters disability pension.

Since I had started the P.I. business we talked about him working with me, but he could only do office stuff because of his injury, and I knew it would kill him to be off the street, so we had mutually agreed that it was not a good idea. He got an offer to work a high-level security job at an investment firm and that was that. Lately we had grown a little distant, and it was starting to worry me. I was actually happy he had called me tonight. I was not ashamed of the fact that I missed him.

About an hour later I woke up to the bump of pothole and Mike's cursing as we pulled up in front of a dilapidated brown stone on the East side. I opened and closed my mouth a couple of times. It felt dry and sticky, like I had been chewing on cotton.

"So Mike, what's the story on this bookie, and since when do you bet on games?"

"Well, normally I don't, but this guy at work told me about it, and I figured what the hell. Not a regular thing, but they are paying me so much money, I figured why not, I got the money to lose. I know college ball pretty well from when I played."

Mike had played college football for a year before he had been kicked off the team. The coach had been picking on his teammate, and Mike hated bullies. He ended up throwing a chair through a window, and it cost him his scholarship and his first-string job as a defensive lineman. After that Mike worked construction for a while until the Academy called.

"Alright Mike, what do you need me to do?"

"I just got off the phone with this guy. Just wait in the truck. It's apartment one boy on the first floor. First apartment on the right-hand side when you go in. If I'm not out in ten minutes come in with the Glock ready, but it should be fine. And make sure I don't get a ticket."

Mike smiled his lopsided grin as he pulled his bulk from the truck by using the steering wheel as a balance to push himself out. As he walked away he gave me a small and casual wave.

I set the timer on my phone to nine minutes and played with the radio. I tried to remember what my dream had been about, but all I could remember was something about a leaky pipe. Seven minutes and forty-three seconds later I heard the pop of gunfire and Mike came staggering out of the building like he was drunk. I jumped out right away. He did not look right.

He dropped to the ground beside the truck and I picked him up and leaned his back against the side of the door. His eyes were glazed over and his shirt felt wet.

"Mike, Christ, what happened? What happened, oh God Mike…"

He mumbled out a few words that didn't make any sense.

"Leaking, water…on…the…floor…could be…."

His words faded into nothing and his head dropped onto his chest.

I pulled out my Glock and looked up at the door of the building. I saw a dark shape come running out and make a sharp left up the block. I was torn. Should I chase the dark shadow running up the street or stay with Mike? It did not take long to decide. I knew I could not leave him.

I leaned down to talk to him but his head was slumped over. In his hand was a crumpled betting slip. It was his winning bet written in code. At the bottom were two initials: R.W.

I leaned in closer and pulled open his jacket. I could see he had been shot at least once somewhere in the chest. It was difficult to tell exactly where with all the blood but it looked bad.

I grabbed both his phone and my own from the truck and called for an ambulance. When I heard the sirens getting close I ran up the block in the direction the dark form had gone. I knew the police would only slow me down and they would not follow up on this the same way I could.

As I ran up the side street, I felt the tears run and dry on my face creating a salty streaky trail that felt like war paint. Rage overtook me and I picked up speed as I rounded the corner. I didn't have much, but the betting slip, Mike's phone, and the building's location was a start.

When I got to the top of the block I looked around, and the only thing open was a twenty-four hour bodega. I stopped to get my breath back and then walked in. There was only one other customer in the back of the rectangle that made up the store's shelves and his back was towards me. All I could see was that he was wearing a grey pinstripe suit and a grey fedora.

I walked to the side and nodded at the dark-skinned short man behind the counter. I stared across the store and all of the bright colors of the food seemed to flash at me as they mixed in with the last of my tears. I pulled out Mike's phone and looked at the last number he had called. I did not recognize it so I dialed.

As soon as the call connected I heard a cell phone ring in the back of the store. The only other customer turned around to face me, and as he reached down into his pocket he shut off the call and Mike's cell phone went dead.

It could just be coincidence so I dialed again. I could hear the phone buzzing in his pocket and then he pressed a button through his grey suit pants and Mike's phone again went dead. As the man from the back of the store got closer I got a good look at his face on his way out. He had thin cheeks and a small round nose, and his eyebrows were plucked into two thin lines that gave him the appearance of some kind of large two-legged rodent.

As his thin form moved out into the street he picked up speed and I followed him out. He gave me one quick look and then began to run. I ran after him and quickly realized I would overtake him. He turned the corner and fell into a garbage pail and went down and I had him. He was already on his hands from the collision, so I dropped all my weight onto his back and he fell down flat on his face. I could hear something scrape the sidewalk and hoped I had broken off some of his rodent teeth.

He grunted and I kept my weight on him, then brought my knee up into the small of his back and pressed down. He squealed, so I let up my knee and flipped him over like a

Frisbee that had landed on the wrong side. I put my knee on his chest and my hand on his neck and squeezed a little to let out some of the fury I felt about Mike.

I knew I didn't have much time-two men laying in the street would not attract instant attention in this city, but the cops would eventually come. I let up some of the pressure on his neck but kept my knee on his chest to let him know we were not done. I grabbed the lapels of his jacket and got close to his face so he could smell my rage.

"Who shot Mike? Who did it? Tell me you piece of-"

He stuttered out his words so fast that I couldn't understand them, and then I saw the blood running from his mouth and happily realized the fall and my tackle must have taken out at least a couple of teeth.

"I, I don't know, I don't know, please let me up…"

"Cut the crap. You came running out of that apartment around the corner right after my friend and he comes out all shot up. Spill it, or I'll knock out the rest of your teeth!"

I tightened my grip on his collar and pulled back my fist behind my head and he winced and put his hands up.

"It wasn't me I swear! It was the toad, the toad, please mister please!"

"Gimmee a name! I want a name!"

"It's Rollie, Rollie the toad! That's all I know, please let me go!"

I could hear the sirens approaching and I knew I was out of time. I reached inside his jacket pocket and pulled out his wallet and put it inside my pocket.

"I know who you are, and if you are lying I'll find you and kill you."

I shoved him back down to the ground and landed one last swift left to his face and I felt something crunch. He screamed as I pushed myself up off him and ran the other way down the block.

I spent the next hour holed up in a dive bar several blocks away. When they closed at four a.m. I made my way over to a porno theatre and sat in the back with my arm over my face for a couple of hours, remembering all the parts of my life I spent with Mike that were now gone.

After that I went to a diner and had some breakfast. After the waitress brought me food and coffee I pulled out all of the items I had so far. I lay Mike's phone and the betting slip on one side and pulled out the Rat's wallet and laid it on the other side. I removed the I.D. It was a driver's license from Kentucky and the name said Salvatore Ignaccio.

It looked genuine but I'm not an expert on out of state driver's licenses. He had about two hundred bucks in small bills and three credit cards, all under different names. He also had a woman's handkerchief that smelled like strawberries. I shook the wallet out and searched it and found an inside hidden pocket that had an address. It was uptown on the East side and I knew my next destination.

Before I jumped in a cab uptown I went to the nearest post office and mailed all of the items from the wallet, Mike's phone, and the betting slip to my lawyer's office. They would show up in a day or two and might be needed.

I got out of the cab in front of a five-story walk up. It was sandwiched between two other buildings of exactly the same type and typical of the buildings in this neighborhood. The entire block was full of them. I rang the buzzer to apartment four E. I was buzzed in without any comment. As I clanked up the metal steps a sexy blonde passed me going down. She had all the right curves and she gave me a nod and a sultry smile on my way up.

I knocked on the door of four E and a large and round man opened the door. He was wearing a purple bathrobe and a stained white t-shirt. He had a large round head with a dimple on the top, and a fleshy neck that hung loosely over his chest. His skin looked shiny and wet, with either some kind of oil or sweat and he had bulgy eyes. His arms and legs dangled on his body and looked too long for his corpulent frame. Based on what I saw in front of me I gathered he must be the toad.

"Yeah, who are you? You want some action?"

I shoved my way in and pushed him up to the wall and put my elbow into the space between his large head and his slimy shoulder and pressed into his neck.

"I spoke to your rat little friend, and left some of his teeth on the sidewalk. Now talk and tell me why you killed my friend last night!"

The fat man sucked in air and tried to reach up and push my elbow off of him, so I pushed down until he gasped and his already bulging eyes looked ready to pop out of his head. He lifted his hands in surrender so I eased up the pressure on him.

"I didn't kill him, Sal did, and it was self-defense. Your friend tried to rob us out of a bigger payout than he deserved. He drew on us and we thought he was going to try and rip us off so Sal shot him."

I had no way to know if this was the truth, but he seemed scared enough that it might be.

I leaned back and moved my elbow back to my side and drew my gun. I motioned him over to the couch. His apartment was long and narrow and ran all the way from the front of the building to the back. We were somewhere in the back so I motioned him to a couch in the direction of the front of the building.

"Sit."

The toad sat down on the couch while I stood holding him at gunpoint.

"How do I know you are not lying? I should just kill you and then kill Sal and be done with both of you."

The toad gulped and rubbed the sagging skin of his throat.

"Mister, I did not kill your friend. I'm a businessman and I'm small time. You see where I live. Sal has a recording of everything-I can show you."

"Call Sal. Make him bring it here and we can watch it together. We'll have a little viewing party."

"Can I get my phone? It's over there on the night stand."

"Yeah, but reach slowly."

The toad made the call and after twenty minutes of the longest staring contest you have ever seen the door buzzed. I backed up to the door and buzzed in Sal. I could hear him limping up the metal steps and he gently knocked. I checked the peephole. No one but Sal.

I opened the door, and when he came in I searched him and found a knife, which I pocketed. I then shoved him onto the couch next to the toad. They looked at each other and shrugged.

"Okay Sal, where is the recording?"

He slowly reached into his pocket and pulled out a USB.

"Okay, now slowly you two are going to lead me to your computer and we can have our own little exclusive screening."

They led me to the next room and put the USB in the drive. When the video came up I could see Mike walk in and I gulped back as I realized I was watching his last living moment. He walked in and had a drink. They had a brief discussion about the slip. As Mike was talking I could see that he was staring at the opposite wall.

He seemed to be focusing hard on something on that wall, but I squinted at the video and I could not see anything. All that I could see in the video was a wall and some kind of picture on the floor in front of it. As he stared he asked them a question that did not seem to fit the situation.

"You guys got a leaky faucet or something?"

Suddenly Mike pulled his gun. Sal went down behind the desk in the corner as if he was retrieving the money and came up shooting. I could see Mike jerk with the shots and he dropped his gun and staggered out of the room. There was some whispered unintelligible panicked discussion between Sal and the toad and then Sal ran out.

That was it. I pulled out the USB and dropped it in my pocket. The toad looked up at me with his wet large round eyes for sympathy. I snarled at him and pointed my gun at his head. He winced and covered his face with his hands. I put my finger on the trigger and was seconds from spreading his head all over the wall, but I knew it would not bring Mike back.

Still, it would feel damn good to do this just once. Just one time I would like to just let someone have it without holding back. I was still turning the idea over in my mind when Sal made a break for it. He bolted towards the door, but I grabbed him as he tried to undo the locks and pistol-whipped him with the butt of my Glock right in the middle of his shoulder blades.

At that moment I heard an explosion by my ear that left a buzzing inside my head like there was a large bee trapped behind my eyes. I turned and saw the toad pointing a gun in my direction. Sal slowly crumpled to the floor crying and holding his chest.

"Now, sir, I missed you once but I won't a second time. Slowly drop your gun and – "

I did not let him finish. In one motion I ducked to the side, raised my gun, and let three rounds pop out in quick succession. I counted them, just like they taught me at the Academy. I had four more but did not need them. The toad dropped his gun and staggered back where he crashed into a chair and groped for the table as he went down. He let out a moan and then lay still on his back.

I walked over to him and stood over his body. His round eyes were glazed as they bulged out of his head and I could see he did not have much longer. He was rapidly sucking for air. Rather than help him I just looked down at him and watched as the last of his gluttonous life seeped out of him onto his cheap carpet.

I turned to check on Sal and saw he was crumpled against the door holding his chest and moaning. When he saw me he began weeping and moaned to me,

"Mister, please, get an ambulance. I need help, it hurts so

much, please, please....Oh God, I'm going to throw up."

I looked down at him with sharp eyes.

"You want help? Well, the best way to stop bleeding is direct pressure."

I put my foot right about where I thought it would hurt the most, on the center of the entry wound. Sal screamed, preceded to vomit on himself, and then he passed out. I pulled my foot back just in time and managed to keep my shoes clean.

Hours later, as I sat in the interrogation room sipping on the soda the detective had brought me I stared straight at the wall. I might come out of this without any jail time. They would probably slap some silly assault charge on me for my attack on Sal in the street, and I might even get indicted. But I knew they could indict a slice of toast and it still didn't mean anything. I had the USB and they would clearly get Sal for murder.

However, the toad-whose name turned out to be Roland Whitemore, was another matter. The only witness was Sal, who certainly would not take my side. My only hope was that the ballistics team would exonerate me based on the trajectory of the shots and the fact that the toad had shot Sal and that he had shot first.

I didn't trust Sal, and this might end my career. After sweating me for hours and trying to get me to change my story they finally released me, but they made it clear I should cancel any travel plans I might have made and they kept my gun.

I took the train home and fell asleep until my stop. When I got home I took a shower, and for the second time in twenty-four hours ate a couple of eggs and passed out. I was woken up by the blast of my landline's ring. I looked over first at my cell phone before I realized it was the old plastic phone I kept on my bedside.

I croaked into the phone as I tried to get my eyes to open all the way.

"Yeah, Sam Burden. Who's this?"

The voice sounded weak but I knew right away who it was.

"Sam, it's Mike. I'm alive."

He sounded miles away and I could barely hear him. I screamed through my sobs of joy into the phone.

"Mike? Really? Mike? My God, where are you? You're alive? "

I heard a voice but the words were unintelligible.

"Mike? Speak up! I can't hear you. Mike? You there?"

The words became fainter and quieter and then the phone went dead. I smashed the phone down and it dissolved in my hand like it was made of sand. I looked down at the multi-colored grains of sand left in my hand and woke up with a scream.

The room was dark and the clock on my nightstand said it was after ten p.m.

I turned on the T.V. and looked out the window to make sure it was not another dream. It wasn't, and Mike was still dead. I was in heaps of trouble with the cops, Mike was gone forever, and I might lose my agency. I turned off the T.V. lay back down and fell into a dark and deep dreamless sleep.

I woke up the next morning and after breakfast started to

come up with a plan. My lawyer, Dave Goldman, had left me a voicemail letting me know that I had a few days until the D.A. got everything together. He sounded desperate and requested an urgent meeting. The only good news he had was that Sal would probably die, which meant the D.A. would have no witness other than me to the shooting of the toad.

I would meet with him later. I realized my only hope was to go back to the apartment Mike and I had first visited. The address was still in my phone-I text it to myself just to be safe. I had memorized it anyway, just in case I needed it later. One of the first things I learned as a cop was to always know where you are in case you got into trouble.

This time I drove in myself and managed to find a spot a couple of blocks away. I had to be sure the cops were not sitting on the place, but when I walked up to the southeast corner to get a good look I could see that the building was not being watched.

I walked quickly across the street, and as I entered the vestibule I buzzed all of the apartments. It was an old trick Mike had taught me. In a building with twenty or so apartments, chances are at least one tenant was expecting somebody and would buzz you up without asking who you were.

It worked and I was buzzed in. I walked up to the side of apartment one B. I stood and listened for a while but it was quiet. I gently knocked on the door but there was no answer, so I knocked again, this time a little louder. Still there was no answer.

I tried the knob but the door was locked. I pulled out my favorite and most basic tool for picking locks-an old credit card. I slid it into the small slot between the edge of the door and the frame. In these old buildings a lot of the wood had warped and been chipped away over the years and this one was no exception. This often created a gap between the door and the frame.

The card slid right in and I worked it around until I found the inside of the lock plate, and in about thirty seconds I was in. I found myself in a one-room studio apartment. In front of me was a desk, a cheap sagging couch and a T.V. bolted to the far wall. Behind and to the side of the couch was a small hallway that led to the bathroom and a galley kitchen.

I recognized the room from the video and could see bloodstains from where Mike had been shot. My stomach tightened and I was filled with fury. The toad had not even bothered to wipe up the blood.

I searched the apartment and found nothing that could be useful to me. There was some old food, the carcasses of some dead roaches, and a few half-burned up betting slips in the oven. In the hallway there was a big picture of a tropical beach. The desk had some blank paper and some blank betting slips. The camera that had filmed Mike was bolted to the far wall facing the door, and I could see the wire that ran from it ended in a frayed end on the floor.

As I had done so many times already on my ride in, I played a rerun of the video of Mike's murder again in my brain. I didn't want to. Every time I thought about it I felt more and more pain and I missed Mike even more, but I had to. I was obsessed that I had missed something. Even in his last moment he must have left me some clue. The statement about the leaky faucet must mean something. There had to be something here that I had missed.

I sat on the sagging couch and that is when I heard the tiny whimper. It came from the direction of the hallway. As soon as I got up it stopped. It was so meek that at first I thought it might be a mouse, so I froze and just listened. Silence.

I went over to the small and narrow hallway. This was the same spot Mike had focused on in the video, but there was nothing there. Just before I was about to leave my foot made a slapping sound as it came down in a small puddle. I looked down and saw that the water was running out from under the wall. This was the same spot Mike was staring at when he made the comment about the leaky faucet!

It could just be a leaky pipe, but I didn't remember the water being there when I came in and I knew there should not be a water line opposite the sink and the bathroom.

I looked up at the picture on the wall and suddenly realized in the video the picture had been on the floor and not on hung on the wall the way it was now. I immediately noticed that the wall around it and behind it was not discolored. I removed the picture and could see the outline of a hidden door. I knocked on the door and heard a quick movement.

There was a small latch that held it closed with an open lock but no handle or knob, so I figured it opened out instead of in. I undid the latch but could not get a grip on the door to open it. I took out my credit card and pried open the edge of the door just enough so that I could get my fingers into it and then got it open.

On the other side was a crawl space, no bigger than the trunk of a large car. There was a small dark woman-maybe still a girl, curled up against the back of the wall studs on a dirty blanket. It smelled slightly of strawberries. Beside her was a bucket, some empty food wrappers, and some water bottles. I could see one of the water bottles had spilled and that it had provided the water I had seen running under the door.

I moved towards her and she whimpered and cowered as far back as she could. It was difficult to see, but even in the dim light I could see she was very thin and that she was terrified. I reached out my hand and spoke very softly.

"It's okay, I'm not going to hurt you. I'm here to help."

The girl's eyes looked up at me in supplication and she slowly started to creep out towards me. I stepped back into the light and called my lawyer Dave and then 911.

Three days later, as I sat behind my kitchen table, I slowly chewed my eggs and swallowed. It seemed like nowadays my entire diet consisted of breakfast food. I had today's paper spread out on the table in front of me. I liked my news from a real paper, not from a computer screen with some annoying pop-up ads. I liked the feel of real paper in my hands and the black smudges it left on my fingers, providing evidence that I existed and had at least accomplished one task for the day.

There was no story about the girl, but my lawyer had filled me in after I had found her. Apparently, in addition to running the gambling operation the toad had also been running a prostitution ring using kidnapped underage girls. When I heard that I was even happier I had killed him.

After the cops had finally convinced the girl to talk, she had told them all about it. She also told them that she had heard the entire incident with Mike and was willing to testify on my behalf for saving her.

As I sat there in the silence of the kitchen I realized how much I missed Mike. In the quiet of the kitchen I suddenly heard a dripping noise. I got up and leaned down under the kitchen sink. I could see that there was slow leak coming from the nut that connected the strainer to the bottom of the sink and that the water was slowly dripping onto the base of the cabinet.

I pulled out my toolbox from the pantry and dug around until I found my plumbers wrench. As I pulled it out the steel of the wrench reflected in the lights and I read the writing that was engraved on the side.

Remember Sam, righty tighty, lefty loosey! Your pal, Mike.

As I looked down at the wrench my eyes got wet, and I thought back to the moment Mike had handed me this wrench. It was one of his wedding gifts to me when I married my ex-wife.

We had a running joke about my poor repair skills. Late one night years ago when I was trying to put together a new desk, I had called Mike in a frustrated rage, as I could not get the pieces together. He calmly and gently had reminded me that to tighten the nuts I had to turn to the right. It had turned out that I was trying to tighten the pieces by turning the nuts the wrong way.

I went under the sink and tightened the locking nut under the strainer with the plumber's wrench and the dripping immediately stopped. I looked down at the wrench and mused that Mike was not completely gone.

The Leaky Faucet

His physical form might be somewhere else, but as long I was still walking around he would always be here. He was here in the wisdom he had passed on to me. He was here in the compassion and empathy I showed to all the victims of the world. He was here in the way in which I would help people by solving their cases, and he was here in this wrench in the words he had inscribed.

The leaky faucet had been stopped, and as I openly wept I finally began to accept that Mike was gone from the world but would never be forgotten.

Baby Mamma Blues
Julian Grant

Brittany stared into the cracked mirror already missing her Terence. She didn't usually. In the past, her step-outs were fast and meaningless, something to do, just quick sex in exchange for getting high or a few minutes tenderness. Richie never held her anymore. Sure, he had sex with her all the time — but it was always fast, late at night and when she was half asleep.

As a husband, Ritchie didn't understand her needs at all.

Why should he? Brittany thought as she clamped the iron down on her thin hair. *Ritchie gets everything he wants. He was working. Making real money. He got to call all the shots.*

He liked her to keep her hair flat for him and whatever Ritchie wanted he got. Brittany knew she was lucky. Out of all the girls in the Park, she at least still had a man that came home regular and provided.

Everything but care. Terence had been different.

Soft caramel skin, thick kissable lips and a sing-song voice with long, sensitive fingers that never failed to raise goosebumps on her own sallow skin. In all her short years of loving men and having her heart broken in return, she'd never once hooked up with a musician.

And now, Terence was gone.

He'd texted her and let her know that he'd joined up with a touring band and was going to be on the road for a while.

And that was that.

No more time together, parked off near the dump where no one could see them, taking the time with each other in ways that Ritchie never did.

The harsh cry of Jamal brought her back from her sweet memories, as she let the baby's cry continue. Her own Mamma had let her cry it out when she was young.

"Let 'em holler," her Mamma had said. "It's good for them. Builds up lung muscles and stuff."

Brittany scowled at the quicksilver memory, Mamma dead two years now, drunk driving taking her off the board. She'd only met her grandbaby once before she died.

She'd always liked her drink too much.

Brittany took a sip of the now-warm wine cooler sitting on the makeup table she'd got from Goodwill where she spread her girl stuff. It wasn't like she had a lot of it. Her makeup was there, of course, all care of the dollar store and some of the flashier bling pieces Ritchie had given her when he had 'courted' her. Including their 'wedding ring.'

She flicked the cubic zirconia her husband had claimed was a real rock across the scarred tabletop as it skittered off next to her ramshackle treasure box. She'd run it over to Estate Pawn, checking on the ring leaving Jamal in the car, once when Ritchie was out, just to see how generous her man was.

"…About thirty bucks, maybe. I'd go ten. Just cause I like you, sugar. We go back."

Brad, the guy who worked the counter had been one of her kinda-boyfriends back when she was still in school, his big belly now pooching out over his too-tight jeans. He'd slicked back his hair like the rest of the guys there and had draped himself in gold ropes just like Ritchie did. *Big Deal.*

"You sure it ain't real?" Brittany asked, her brow furrowing in concern. She'd heard all about how guys at pawn shops were lying sacks stealing rocks and stuff from people claiming they were fake.

"You wouldn't cheat me, would you?" Brittany leaned forward, pushing herself out towards Brad, giving him a little look-see. She'd at least inherited her Mamma's topside — and she was determined not to let it slide into the beer weight and fat her she'd packed on before she died. There was a difference between big boobs and fat boobs.

"It's a CZ. It ain't real… Hey, you still with Ritchie?" Brad asked, smiling at the free show Brittany was giving him. "You wanna hang out some time?"

She shut him down hard, stomping back to her car and slammed the door, which woke up baby Jamal as she stormed about her cheap-ass husband. *Bad enough he'd knocked me up fast enough, he'd also lied about my rock as well.*

Jamal's cries in the double-wide trailer chugged in wet frustration, a gurgling, choking sound snapping Brittany back to now.

"I'm coming, baby. Hold on. Mamma's coming"

She pushed herself away from the battered table wondering if she still had any apple juice left for the Cheerio's.

*****

After Jamal slurped down the last of the cereal, she took him outside to see if any of the other at-home Mamma's were at the playground. The one thing that Richie had sold her on, when he moved her in her to Camelot Park was that it was full of families.

"All kinds of kids and Mom's for you to hang out with," he'd smiled, passing her the smoke that she'd keep using to keep her weight in check. It had been nine hard months of not eating everything in the trailer and she was determined not to grow into one of the flabby cows she saw everywhere. *No wonder their men be stepping.*

Outside, the two-horseshoe array of trailers centered around a rusted jungle gym and slide combination that was covered in gang tags and littered with discarded and broken 40's of malt liquor. At first, she'd swept up, trying to keep back the broken glass and garbage from the play area — but she'd given up once she saw that no one here gave a rat's ass about the playground. As Jamal burbled in his stroller, Brittany stepped out into the bright summer sun, pushing back her freshly ironed hair into a thick wrap around her head. At least maybe she could bum a smoke from one of the other women and catch up on the gossip? Something was always happening at Camelot. She'd first heard about Bob losing first one leg and then the other to diabetes at the playground. The other moms would gather like crows around the bench by the busted ass play set, laughing loud and carrying on as their kids ran wild. Jamal was too little to play with them, but sometimes one of the older girls would be interested in playing mamma for a bit. "Don't be too ready to be in charge," Brittany muttered to herself as she counted back how quick she'd found herself in the role of mother that she'd was completely unqualified for. She'd only just started working up the street at one of the big-name burger places, happy to be making money at the drive through, relishing the freedom that even the little money she made gave her. She'd dreamt about her future, making a music video or being a phone star on one of the channels with her own makeup or hair shows and get millions of people to pay her for her advice and stories. *No chance of that now.*

All that disappeared once she met Richie, who'd swing by every day for a double-double patty and large diet soda. He'd smile and laugh with her, paying attention to what she had to say and making her feel really special.

Even more special than having the job.

She'd been hesitant at first to go out with him. He was older than her, of course, but her Mamma said that good men were hard to catch and if one was showing any interest, she might as well try and get him as soon as she could.

"Baby trap be best. Get yourself pregnant and he yours. He on the hook for child support even if he leaves you."

Brittany had barely listened to her own Mamma and had no interest in being a teenage mom but late-night drives and 'hanging out' had resulted in a positive test and her letting Ritchie know he was gonna be a daddy. She knew it could go either way. He'd be happy, shack up with her or even marry her, or he'd kick her to the curb. She could always get a procedure if she had to. Her own Mamma told her that she missed the scrape by a cat's whisker.

At seventeen, Brittany became a Mamma and by eighteen, she knew that Ritchie was probably already looking at others.

A wife knows. As Brittany shook her tightly-wrapped head, determined to chase away the black cloud that seemed to hover over her full-time these days, she passed by Bob's old trailer, where the new guy was just now unloading boxes from his truck.

It was the first time she got a real good look at Zak.

"You're a what?"

"I'm a G-Man. I pick up trash. I'm a garbage man," Zak laughed as he stretched in front of Brittany showing of the long, well corded muscles he had gained on the job.

She'd decided to introduce herself to him seeing as he lived across the lot, in old Bob's place. It turned out that Zak was related to Bob, a cousin or nephew and he'd ended up inheriting the rundown trailer when he'd passed. She'd made all the right noises when Zak told her about him dying as the air hung quiet in memory of the dead man. The last she'd seen of Bob was probably about a month ago when she'd gone over to rub oil on his stumps and pick up some extra money for a 'happy ending' massage that she kept to herself. He'd been a good neighbor and was too old to do anything other than appreciate the attention Brittany paid him — even if he paid her to do it.

"Get a good man, but don't depend on him for everything," her Mamma had shared. Another nugget of wisdom that Brittany had filed away as good need-to-know advice. Ritchie made good money, but she rarely saw any of it. He paid the lot fees all in one lump sum for the year and kept the fridge full of the food that he liked but Brittany had to do the actual shopping — the majority of the time they just ate fast food or free burgers that she'd bring home from the job.

She'd kept three shifts; all early morning runs from four until lunch that paid for the electricity and the TV bills while Ritchie handled the rent and the phones and gas money. He'd sleep with Jamal next to him while Brittany'd clamber out into the pre-dawn dark and make her house money sliding greasy meat into the night for long-distance truckers and late- night partiers.

"You miss him, Bob? I mean?" asked Brittany as she enjoyed the sight of Zak rubbing down his sore muscles with his sweat-soaked shirt. He had long hair and lots of different tattoos that Brittany imagined would taste salty to her tongue as she absently jostled the light-weight stroller keeping Jamal quiet. For now, her son was sleeping — but it wouldn't be long before she'd be up to her elbows again in a dirty diaper and his constant hunger yowls.

"Can't miss what you don't know. Surprised the hell outta me when I got the call from the lawyer. I thought for sure I was in shit for something."

Brittany smiled, dipping her head, a slight grin sliding across her face as she looked up at the sweating man under heavily lidded eyes. *Ain't no harm in flirting. I ain't dead.*

"You get in trouble a lot?"

Zak grinned at her, a crooked half-smile that lit up his bright blue eyes. "I'm a bad boy sometimes. That is true."

Brittany felt the pull, a little tug inside, that she liked to call her dinner bell.

"When the dinner bell sounds, you know you got something good on the hook." *Thank you again, Mamma.*

And just like, the bubble burst as Ritchie's white open top Camaro cut through the still morning air, the over-torqued engine louder than usual to Brittany's ears. She glanced down the street to see her husband's car turn the corner and bee-line towards their lot.

Zak watched the car pull in. "That your old man?"

Brittany nodded, spinning Jamal in his stroller back towards home as she hustled over to see what he was doing home so soon. "I gotta jet. See ya around."

"Catch up with you later, sometime?" Zak called as Brittany zipped across the road.

She spared him a last look, sleepy-eyed grinning at him again, hoping that he could read her expression well enough. It seemed that men were either gifted or ignorant of the ways of women and their signals.

Zak either got it or he didn't.

Judging from the swelling in the front of his jeans, he got her signals just fine.

The sound of the trailer door slamming open snapped Brittany's attention back to her husband as he stomped inside the house. *He's pissed. I sure hope it's not about me talking to Zak.*

*****

"Rondell's a bitch and I'm a gonna have to do something about him," Ritchie fumed as he gulped his large soda. He paced back and forth in the front room in front of the TV as Jamal played in his pen while Brittany hung back by the kitchen. She knew when he got worked up like this, it was best to be out of swinging range. They'd found the 'prison for babies' pen at the flea-market on Route 20 and after a good scrubbing and an almost new mattress, it had become their new favorite way to keep their son occupied when they either got busy or fought.

Brittany figured it was probably going to be the second scenario today.

"I always had the Flying J. Rondell's hustling my spot and I'm a gonna do something about it."

Ritchie pulled the Glock 18 handgun from the back of his overlarge baggy pants, tilting it sideways as he sized up his imaginary target. Brittany's voice, choking in her throat, was a thin whisper as she cautioned her husband to put down the gun.

"Ritchie. Remember, no guns in the house around Jamal…" Her husband span on her, his eyes bloodshot red. He'd been sampling more and more of his long distance 'go-go' product he'd been selling to the OTR and other long-distance truckers who pit-stopped at the Flying J truck stop for as long as she'd known him. She'd never imagined herself the wife of a drug dealer but the fact was that in this part of Gary,

Indiana you either worked the system for yourself or it worked you.

"Put the gun down, honey. We can work it out. K?"

Ritchie spat, *right on the floor of our own home*, and Brittany pushed over to Jamal pulling him out of the pen. The boy howled in frustration as his well-scuffed blocks dropped away as his mother drew the crying boy to her chest.

"I don't want you around us when you're acting crazy like this!" Brittany yelled, scaring Jamal who began to wail in protest as his mother hugged him hard. "You get out of here, Ritchie. You go calm down."

"Or what?" Ritchie sneered, raising the semi-auto handgun, sizing up his wife as she dared tell him what to do. The sour urine smell of Jamal's diaper wetting and the warmth of the child's pee flooded Brittany's shirt as she cocked her chin up, standing her ground as she stared Ritchie down.

"Never show them fear. They like dogs. They see you licked. They just keep on coming." Another Mom-ism. Another nugget of wisdom from the woman ground to chuck under the wheels of a big rig, probably driven by the same men Ritchie sold drugs to.

"YOU GET OUTTA HERE!" Brittany screamed as she walked over to the thin metal door of the trailer. Clutching her screaming child to her chest, she kicked open the battered door and pointed outside. "GO ON. GET!"

Ritchie, anger radiating off him in waves, snapped the gun behind himself, jamming it into his pants as he hustle-stomped out past his wife. "We ain't done," Ritchie spat as he pushed by her. "Not by a long shot."

"You go get right, Ritchie. Then you come home to your wife and child. You ain't no use to us like this. You go straighten yourself up."

The sound of the Camaro tearing out filled the near-empty park at this time of day as Brittany sunk down into the lumpy couch, stroking Jamal's head while she tried to sooth her baby. *At least nobody heard us fighting. Again.*

"Knock, knock, you alright in there?"

168

Brittany looked up, tears welling in her eyes, telling herself not to cry as Zak, now wearing his dirty shirt again, stuck his head inside the trailer, concern etched across his face. "Everything okay?"

Brittany burst into tears. *No, everything is not okay.*

*****

Zak actually listened as Brittany sobbed out a variation of the story once they got Jamal settled. *I'm not telling him jack about the gun. Or Ritchie's business.* He'd bundled them both in his truck, the baby cooing happily in Brittany's lap as he reached up to the dice dangling from the rearview mirror.

They headed over to Sonic where the three of them mowed down fruity drinks and cheddar fries and all the things that Brittany liked to eat but Ritchie never let her because they were too fattening.

"He ever hit you?" Zak asked, not looking at Brittany as he clutched the steering wheel.

Brittany shook her head.

"It's mostly threats with Ritchie, you know? He gets frustrated and I talk him down from doing something stupid. He gets mad really easy."

Jamal mushed happily on the French fries Brittany mashed up for him. Zak tousled the fine hair on his hair as the baby ate, his attention focused fully on the salty food.

"He's a cute one," Zak smiled. "I don't have any kids myself. That I know of."

Brittany smiled, flipping down the sun visor as she glanced at her makeup. It was a mess with raccoon tracks streaking down her face, her eyes puffy from crying.

"Why didn't you tell me I looked such a state? Here, take him..."

Brittany passed her son over to Zak as she started dabbing at her face with her napkin. Licking the corner of the paper serviette, she wiped away the errant streaks on her face as she rooted in her purse for more mascara.

"Baby want another fry? You want another fry?"

As she repaired the damage from her crying jag, Brittany watched as Zak played with Jamal, flying the snack into his mouth, buzzing his lips like an airplane.

"Ritchie doesn't take any time with him. I swear I don't know why we had him."

"Don't say that, Brit Honey. It's a sin," Zak whispered as he pushed his nose closed to Jamal, rubbing his face up against the boy carefully.

Brit Honey. I like how that sounds.

By the time they finished eating and got back to Camelot, it was time for Zak to head in for his shift.

"I'm working afternoons right now."

"I never knew 'G-Men' to work later in the day? I thought you guys only came by early and woke people up?"

Brittany smiled at Zak, Jamal balanced on her hip as she leaned into the truck.

"I'm at the depot. I run a back hoe mostly. Piling the stuff, you know. You'd be amazed at the things people throw away. Brittany darkened. She knew exactly what things people threw away. *Like their entire lives in a marriage that don't work. Stuck in a trailer park with no options.*

170

"You ever think about getting out of here?" Brittany asked.
"I just got here," Zak laughed, his eye's bright in amusement.
"Don't tell me you're sick of me already?"

Brittany smiled too. She couldn't help herself. There was something about Zak that reminded her of Terence. He was happy, not angry all the time like Ritchie. He was interested in Jamal and, judging from the side-eye she caught from him when he thought she didn't notice, he clearly had designs on her.

"Nah, I ain't sick of you. Not yet anyhow. I barely know you…"

"Well, I'm looking forward to getting to know you better, Brit Honey. I think we got a lot in common, you know?"

Brittany stood back from the truck, waving to Zak as he drove out of the park.

I do like how he calls me Honey.

*****

Tik Tok dragged Ritchie back after Jamal had finally gone down for the night. Brittany had spent the rest of the day picking up around the trailer not looking forward to when her husband came back. When Tik Tok carried him through the door, clearly dead drunk, Brittany breathed a sigh of relief.

"Where you want him?" Tik Tok asked as he staggered under Ritchie's weight.

"Couch is fine," Brittany said as she tracked the silver briefcase that Richie's guy juggled as he hauled her wasted husband over to the sofa. "What's in the case?"

Tik Tok plopped Ritchie onto the couch, setting the case at his feet as he stretched from the hard labor. From across the room, Brittany could hear the big man's body crack in response to all the heavy lifting. He tugged down his too- small t-shirt over the rolls of ebony blubber that spilled out as he waved a finger at Brittany.

"That's his business. Not yours. You leave that alone."

Brittany shrugged, turning to the counter, wiping up an imaginary spill on the surface just to keep her hands busy.

From over on the couch, Ritchie farted, a long trumpet that stank of stale beer as Tik Tok headed towards the door.

"Ritchie done good tonight. You be good to him when he wakes up."

Brittany moved to the man mountain as he ambled out the door wanting to know more. Outside, another car hovered, a road rat racer that Ritchie's crew favored, some kind of foreign car with neon accents across the bottom. Brittany didn't know cars but she did know trouble. The neon green hornet shadowed outside her trailer looked fast and vicious in the park's half-light.

"What's going on, Tik Tok? Did something happen?"

Laughter slipped out of the man as he popped open the screen door and waved to the car outside. Loud rap music could be heard booming inside the vehicle even with all the windows closed. The car's headlights slashed on in acknowledgement to the man's wave.

"Things are gonna be different around here from now on," Tik Tok smiled. From behind him, tucked in the fat folds of his back, he pulled out Ritchie's gun, passing it off to Brittany. "You wanna keep this safe for him. Make sure he gets it.

And dumps it."

Brittany held up her hands, stepping backwards as she eyed the semi-automatic warily. "Put it on the counter. I'm not touching that."

Tik Tok smiled, a thin whisper, as he wiped it down with his grimy t-shirt and slid it onto the kitchen island. "You ain't stupid, girl."

She eyed the gun, looking next to her husband and the suitcase sitting by his feet. *Something definitely happened.*

"Later."

The screen door slapped shut behind Tik Tok as he heaved himself down the steps over to his ride. Ritchie's Camaro was now parked in its usual spot — Tik Tok having driven it over for her dead-to-the-world husband. The man clambered into the small car, its suspension listing drastically as he slid inside, the music deafening and the car zipped off into the night with the echoing thunder of the music hanging in the air.

Inside, Ritchie continued to snore, as Brittany grabbed a dishtowel and picked up his gun carefully. She knew it was best to keep it hidden just in case anyone came by — *like Zak, maybe?* — and ducked down under the sink, pushing the weapon behind the few cleaning supplies she had under there.

Satisfied that the gun was at least safe for now, she crept over to Ritchie, checking that he was well and truly asleep. Drool slid out of his mouth onto the sofa as he continued to breathe deeply. From across the room she could smell the rich malt of the Old English 40's that he and his crew favored.

She'd come to hate the smell of the over proof beer.

Brittany slid in next to her near comatose husband, glancing at the case that she had never seen before. *Won't hurt*

*to take just a little look. For Jamal. In case there's something
dangerous in there.*

"Secrets be a thing," Momma had said. "We all got 'em.
Husbands. Wives. You wanna be smart? You know what your
man's up to. 'Cause he be stepping, or keeping a piece on the
side, it all be on his phone. Or in some secret hidey-hole. Like
a computer or a box." *Or a briefcase, maybe?*

Brittany popped the catches on the briefcase once she
pulled it onto her lap. The sharp snap of the metal tongues
surprised her and she whipped her attention to Ritchie in case
he heard her getting into his things.

He continued to snore, unaware of Brittany's spying.

Not spying. Checking.

Inside the case, the future beckoned.

*****

"I didn't know who else to tell. Or what to do. Do you know
what this is?"

Brittany slipped the small baggie full of blue crystal shards
across to Zack as they sipped coffee on the bench across from
the park's jungle gym. He'd been a little surprised when she
woke him up, knocking at his door just as the sun rose. All he
wore was a low-slung pair of gym shorts, showing off the
muscular torso she'd noticed before. Stitched across his left
pec was a woman's name — Gloria — that she asked about
once they settled at the empty play area.

"She was my Mom. She died a little while ago."

"Mine too," mumbled Brittany, hoping that Zack might be
able to help her decide.

The next few minutes would determine a lot.

"She was only forty-two," Zack continued, sipping at the go-cup that Brittany had prepared for him. She'd come prepared, asking Zack to help her with something and had pressed the instant coffee into his hand as he slid back inside to change. At the door, she couldn't help but admire him as she raced into the bedroom off the main room, dropping his shorts and sliding into the tight jeans he had worn yesterday.

"My Mamma too. Car crash," Brittany sighed, sipping at the lukewarm coffee. She'd left Jamal sleeping in his crib, hoping that it wouldn't take long for Zack to decide. When she passed him the blue package of drugs, she'd already made up her mind.

Perhaps he would too.

"It's Meth. Blue ice," Zack said, holding it up. "About a gram. Maybe two?"

He passed it back to her, a kiss of ugly sliding across his lips. "Is it yours?"

"Hell, no," Brittany said. "I'm not stupid. I'm a Mom. I don't do drugs like this."

"Good. That shit's no good for you. I should know."

Brittany tucked away the drugs away, her own lips tightening in worry.

Does he use? Shit. "You sure?"

Zack sighed, drinking his coffee as he looked out towards the dirty jungle gym. Old hamburger wrappers drifted across the ground as he ground his teeth in memory.

"Yep. That's what killed my Mom. So, yeah. I'm sure."

Brittany reached for Zack, sliding her hand down his toned arm.

"I'm sorry, Zack. I am."

Zack nodded, squeezing Brittany's thigh in thanks, his hand lingering on her leg as she slid closer to him. "Where'd it come from?"

Brittany looked about, her own trailer dark in the early morning hours as she tucked the baggie into the shorts she had slipped into for her meeting with Zack.

"I think Ritchie's up to something. I'm worried."

"Did he bring that stuff home? It's a killer, Brit Honey."

He still hasn't moved his hand.

Brittany's heart swelled at Zack's touch, still lingering on her leg as his kind words helped her do the math.

As the rising sun slid across the park, Brittany told Zack about the case, about Tik Tok and her husband's anger about Rondell.

"Is he a dealer?"

Tears slid across Brittany's face, thick and wet running the mascara that by now she should know not to trust.

"I didn't know any better at first. When I got pregnant with Jamal and we moved here, I was just happy to have a place to go to. With Mamma dead, and me unable to pay for the apartment, and what with being pregnant, I didn't look too careful at what he did for a living."

Zack nodded, listening to Brittany, his eyes on her. His hand slip up towards her hip, squeezing her to continue as she sobbed.

"He's got a gun and a whole briefcase full of this stuff. And a bunch of money."

Zack pulled Brittany close, wrapping his arm around her, comforting her as he leaned in and kissed the tears rolling down her chin.

They went back to his place.

*****

"Where you been?" Ritchie groused, Jamal propped awkwardly on his hip as he pulled the bottle out of the microwave. "Damn kid's been howling."

Brittany waved the bottle of cold sports drink at him, moving quickly to pluck her son from him as she took the too-hot formula away.

"I went to Brenda's and got you something for your head. Figured you'd be hungover." *He'll never know.*

Ritchie slapped Brittany's butt in thanks, snatching the drink from the counter as he shuffled back to the couch. The briefcase sat just where Brittany had left it after she had pulled the drug packet from inside — along with a handful of loose bills she'd already tucked away in her jewelry box.

"Where's my gun at?"

Brittany shushed her crying son, sliding him into the baby chair hanging off the worn Formica kitchen table.

"Hang on. I stashed it."

As Ritchie slumped down into the couch, he flipped the case up onto the coffee table, popping the locks.

Brittany grabbed a hand towel from the counter and pulled the Glock from below the sink. *No fingerprints.*

"Bring it, woman. I need it," Ritchie muttered as he stared inside the case.

"What'chu got there?" Brittany asked, feigning interest. She already knew that there were forty-four baggies similar to the one she had taken to Zack. Along with six stacks of banded cash, wrapped in rolls. She'd slid bills out of all of them, knowing full well that he'd miss a roll but not the loose fifties and twenties she'd stolen.

"My business. Don't you worry about it."

Jamal started to howl, giving Brittany an excuse to pour off half the bottle, filling it with tap water and giving it a shake as she handed it to her child. Jamal snatched at the lukewarm drink, gulping down the formula as Brittany watched Ritchie carefully. *He's not going to notice. He's not going to notice.*

"Hey, Brittany…"

She stopped fussing with Jamal, wiping at the stains on the table, her hands fluttering as her heart trip-hammered. "Yeah, Richie?"

He lifted up the sports drink, toasting her with the drink she'd lifted from Zack's fridge after they'd finished in his bed.

"Thanks for this. I need it. Had a helluva night."

Brittany breathed slowly, behind her Jamal slurped at the bottle, the sucking sounds drawing her back to the stolen kisses and taste of her G-man across the lot. Her thighs clenched as she smiled in memory of their time together.

Ritchie, of course, thought that the slow grin was for him. "Of course, baby. Anything for my man."

"You wanna come on over here? Maybe we get started on Jamal, Part 2. The sequel?"

Brittany struggled to keep the smile on her face as Ritchie slid his hand across his pants.

"It's my time," Brittany lied. "Plus, the baby's up."

Ritchie sucked his teeth, dragging a cold finger down Brittany's back as he sneered at her response.

"Well, maybe we don't then."

"I'll get you later, okay. Won't be much longer, baby." Brittany carefully walked towards her husband, giving him plenty of time to share what was in the case or closing the lid. She knew that if he closed the case, her mind was made up. "Whatever," Ritchie said, his eyes back down on the money and drugs inside the briefcase. He took one last look and slammed the lid down as Brittany dropped down next to him.

She placed his towel-wrapped handgun on top of the case. "Here's your gun. Can you please do something with it?"

Ritchie sucked his teeth again. "Shit, woman. Just a tool. Nothing wrong with a gun. Just the people who use 'em. They're the problem.

Brittany said nothing.

*****

"You think he's gonna know? I mean, if he finds out it's us, I don't know what he's gonna do. This could get really bad."

Zack took Brittany's soda from her lips, sucking softly on the straw as they both watched her husband walking the backline at the Flying J. Transport tractors and trailers were lined up against the back lot with a whole world working back here under the sodium lights.

In the back of Zak's truck, Jamal snored on the rear seat, Brittany having tucked him in with his favorite blanket as she and Zack watched Ritchie direct his runners out to the various cabs. All of them were clearly holding, shuffling from rig to rig, swapping what looks like everything from prescription pills to the now familiar baggies of the blue glass.

Sitting next to Ritchie on the hood of his Camaro was Tik Tok, arms folded, watching each runner as they hot-footed it from truck to truck.

"They have a system in place. They're fast," Zack said as he watched the dashboard clock in his truck. Brittany had never actually been in an F150, even a secondhand one like this on. Zack told her how he'd gotten this as his only inheritance when his Mom passed and it was all he had left to remember her by.

He pointed to an old Polaroid photo, a woman from the 80's with big hair and shoulder pads. You could see the resemblance easily as Zack gestured to the snapshot with the drink.

"She's pretty," Brittany said as she looked at the picture. "*Always compliment a man's Mamma. Ain't never met one that didn't hate their son-of-a-bitch father but loved their Moms. You say sweet things about them — and you're in good for life.*" Brittany smiled as her own Mom's advice kept her working the jackpot she'd devised once she knew what she — they — were going to do.

"You think you're gonna have any trouble taking him? There's a lot of guys here. And that Tik Tok's big. Ritchie told me once he killed someone."

Zack shrugged, passing the cold soda back to Brittany as he reached down beside his seat. *Look who else has a gun?*

"I'm not worried, Brit Honey. I got my own protection but I'm not gonna need to use it. Ritchie don't know me from Adam. He got nothing to worry about with me. That's why this is gonna work so well."

Brittany tracked Zack's gun nervously. Unlike Ritchie's, this one was a six-shot revolver, blue metal finish with a taped grip. It looked old.

"Where'd you get the gun?"

"Don't worry about where I got it. All you have to know is that I got everything covered. He'd not gonna know what hit him. And I'll be able to take him down."

"And you're sure about walking away — I mean, with me and Jamal.

Brittany reached back, squeezing her son's foot that had poked out from the short back seat of the large truck. She knew that she should use a kid seat when she drove with him — but it was late and no one was going to know. *Hell, we only live five minutes from here.*

"I came here, because of Bob's trailer and, to be honest, I figured, I'd just sell it or maybe live here for a bit. But it's all good. I can be a G-Man anywhere. They got trash all across the US and I won't need to work for a while once we get this score."

"And you know a guy, right, that'll take the drugs and stuff. Pay us for them?"

Zack cradled Brittany's cheek. "Trust me, Brittany Honey.

Everything's gonna work out just fine."

Brittany smiled. Maybe things were going to turn out okay for a change? *I'm due, right.*

*****

She waited twenty-four hours to call the cops and tell them that Ritchie was missing just like Zack had said. The officer on the other end of the phone was less than helpful once he found out that she and Ritchie lived at Camelot Estates.

"You sure he's not just off drunk somewhere?"

Brittany hung up on the police officer, itching to call or text Zack but he'd given her strict instructions not to.

"I don't want there to be any traceable phone connection between us at all. Make sure you delete all my texts and my number off your phone. I'm going to get a new number anyway. Just in case."

Brittany hated to get rid of the text messages she'd swamped with Zack. They'd been some pretty steamy chats swapped back and forth and she'd even sent over some sexy pix of herself for him when he asked. *Is he going to get rid of those too?*

She had no idea what Zack was going to do to Ritchie and what had happened.

"It's better that way, Babe. That way you can't tell anyone what happened if you don't know anything, right?"

Brittany spent the next two days wondering what exactly had gone on with Ritchie. She'd had to book off work since she couldn't bring her son in to the drive-through and she'd long worn out any welcome with the other Mom's in the park. They all had their own shit to handle and the last thing they needed was another kid before the sun was even up.

She sat, making the last of the food last, watching out the window for a sign of Zack.

The trailer across the way, his trailer, the one they'd first been together in, was still dark.

He hadn't been home since whatever he did happened.

It was on the fourth day the cops pulled up by the front door.

By this point, Brittany was anxious to hear anything — even if it was bad news, and since she'd done nothing, she figured she had nothing to worry about. *Right?*

Two cops, in a plain brown wrapper Crown Vic, heaved themselves out of the car dressed in light cotton suits, grey and black, and both of them needed shaves. The one out in front, the older one looked about the Park, his face hang-dog sad. The other, a younger version, forty pounds lighter, just looked pissed off at being stuck out here in Camelot.

Tell me something I don't know?

Brittany opened the door as the cops flipped open their wallets in unison displaying their cop ID.

"Mrs. Lewis? I'm Gates, this is Lane. Gary PD," the older cop said as he looked her up and down.

She juggled Jamal on her hip, making sure she kept her dumb face on. It was the one that Ritchie made fun of when she was trying to figure things out.

"Never let a man know what you're really thinking, honey. It pays to make 'em think you stupid. Even if you not. Let 'em tell you what they want, figuring you too stupid to understand."

Brittany's Mom's sage advice flitted across her memory as she cocked her head sideways at the men.

"Is this about Ritchie? He still hasn't come home yet. I called you guys about it a couple days ago. You find him?"

It was Gates and Lane's turn to look dumb as they glanced at each other. *News to them too, I guess.*

"Check on that, Lane. When did you call it in?"

Brittany shrugged. "What, today's Wednesday? So, Monday. No, Sunday. I called Sunday… 'bout six at night."

Lane nodded and headed back to the car as Gates stepped up onto the landing. "Can I come in?"

"You want to tell me why you're here then?"

"I'd rather we do this inside please, Mrs. Lewis. If you don't mind."

The old cop reached up to Jamal, chucking him under the chin as the baby erupted in a burst of happy gurgles at the attention. "Good looking boy you got there."

Brittany huffed, turning on her heel, not bothering to respond. "Place is a mess," she muttered under her breath as she pushed her away inside.

She plopped Jamal into the baby prison on the floor and headed into the kitchen. "I haven't got any coffee or tea or anything, Officer. We're kinda running on empty around here."

Gates, carefully checking the room, smiled at Brittany, as he stepped inside. Brittany watched as the old cop eyeballed her home, listening carefully.

"Be careful what you tell cops. You never know what they can use to trip you up. Let 'em say everything. You just stay hushed." *Yeah, Mom. I know.*

Brittany, a soft smile slowly kissing her, kept her back to the cop as she prepared for the bad news. *It's got to be bad news. Two cops. Coming here. Not uniforms? What had Zack done? Is Ritchie dead?*

Brittany turned, preparing for the acting performance of her life, as Gates crossed the space between them in a heartbeat.

She didn't even see the punch that knocked her lights out.

*****

The inside of the trunk smelled like gasoline and old junk food wrappers. Brittany couldn't see much; a thick t-shirt wrapped across her face and couldn't move her hands or feet. No matter how hard she tried, the cops had done a number on her, cinching tight whatever they'd use to tie her up.

Outside the car, she could hear her baby Jamal crying.

When the trunk opened, she was surprised to find it was dark out. And that she was at the dump.

Bright halogen work lights shined down on her from above, blinding her once they pulled the shirt off her face.

The young cop, Lane stood her up next to the cop car.

I gotta pee. I gotta pee.

"How stupid do you think I am?" Ritchie's voice came drifting out beyond the corona of light.

Brittany, peered through the brights, making out the silhouetted figures standing around Richie's Camaro. Her husband, pushed out into the yard, holding Jamal next to him as he glared at her.

"You was gonna rob me?"

She looked about frantically, her heart thundering in her chest as she searched for a way out.

Mountains of scrapped cars, engine parts and other metal trash reached up into the night, ringing her in a makeshift prison. She couldn't see anything other than the car in front of her and Ritchie's crew next to it.

"Ritchie, baby, I was worried, I had no idea where you were…" Brittany babbled.

"Always tell 'em what they want to hear. You lie, girl. You lie as much as you have to."

Shut up Mamma. Just shut up.

"Thanks, guys. I owe you," Ritchie said, slipping the old cop a folded collection of bills as the younger one slammed the trunk closed.

The cops walked over to their ride not saying a word, hopped inside without a second look and started the car up as Brittany stumbled forward, her feet tangling in the other t-shirts they used to tie her.

She fell down onto the oil-caked dirt, the wind bursting out of her in one hard bright burst.

Above her, baby Jamal reached out for his Mamma as Brittany began to panic. The dull pain from the fall meant nothing to her as she struggled with the bindings.

"Good luck getting out of those. Damn FIVE-OH know how to tie a bitch up. Ain't that right, Tik Tok?"

"Terence never got out. And he pulled hard," the man mountain laughed, moving to Ritchie, plucking Jamal from his father's arms.

"Don't you touch my baby!" Brittany howled from the ground, her arms straining at the knots holding her. "You let me outta here, Ritchie."

"Or you gonna do what? Go find another meal ticket like you tried with Terence. Or Bob? Or that Zack guy?"

Brittany gulped. *Terence. Bob. And Zack. Ritchie knew about all of them?*

Ritchie dropped down to Brittany on the sticky black ground, careful not to stain his oversized jeans as he knelt.

"You know why I married you?"

Brittany started to cry. Tears painting her face as she shrank inside. "Because you love me?"

Ritchie's laugher cut deep as he poked her belly.

"You got pregnant and my Mamma always told me to do right by any woman I got in a family way. I knocked you up with our son so I done the right thing."

"You did— you did— and I *love* you, Ritchie, I love… you."

Her husband stood, sucking his teeth, causing Brittany to cringe.

She couldn't help herself.

"You love me so much you went and had relations with that musician, and the old guy with no legs and then this guy?"

Ritchie stepped over Brittany as she craned her neck following him to a beat-to-shit LTD from the 1970's sticking out from the towering pile of car refuse.

He ripped open the trunk of the car. There was Zack, eyes open, clearly dead.

Despite the smell of the yard, the ripe banana scent of Zack's dead body drifted out to her on the floor.

"You never regret girl. You never be the first one to say you're sorry. Make sure he do it first. Anything you do, chances are good that he made you do it anyway."

I don't want to hear you anymore, Mamma. Be quiet.

"Get her in there with him," Ritchie spat as Tik Tok passed off her son to him.

"Who's a good boy? You a good boy? Who's your daddy?" Brittany howled in horror as Tik Tok picked her up and pushed her into the rusted car's trunk alongside Zack's body. "Damn fool thought he'd take me off after I took out Rondell," Ritchie whispered to Jamal as he ignored his wife screaming in the trunk of the car.

He turned, holding Jamal his arms, pointing at Brittany, smushed in next to her dead lover.

He pointed a long finger at Zack.

"That *fool* told me all about you, woman. How it was all your idea. You weren't content with embarrassing me with your goings-on. You turn Pro on me? You see my stash and figure you gonna take it? Get this fool to try a bump and rob with his big ass truck?"

The last thing Brittany saw before the trunk closed was her baby, smiling at her as the dark night fell.

Outside the sound of the car crusher thundering to life barely registered to Brittany.

All she could hear was her dead Mamma's voice.

You get a good man, you never let him go, Mamma said.

Brittany spooned in next to Zack's corpse hoping that it wouldn't take too long.

#27 – *The House Special*
E. James Wilson

In the *Elbow Room* sports bar, halfway down Main Street and alongside *The Golden Lotus* Chinese restaurant, there's a loud groan of disappointment from the bar crowd as someone on the big screen TVs fails to make a touchdown, or a basket, or whatever it is that's supposed to help the team win the game. Outside, the light rain is coming down mixed with some snow, so you know this isn't Miami, or Huston, or San Francisco for that matter.

As they settle back down to chug more beer and eat salty bar snacks, at a corner table off the main area, Perry says:

"It hasn't changed since the Romans organised it, wrapped the Coliseum around it, and called it sport."

Collville sips at a Manhattan, then puts the glass back down on the thin paper coaster.

"I'm not sure that Gladiatorial combat was a sport. I think it was more an early form of Reality TV entertainment."

Perry *sheesh*es, finishes his vodka rocks and waves to a passing waitress for a fresh one.

The noise in the bar ebbs and flows with the TV game and once he has another glass in front of him, Perry says:

"There's a bunch of guys coming down from Boston that I'd like to keep sweet. Billy Scofield, Mike Johansen and Lon Krantz. They're coming down here for a week. They wanted to stay at the Ramat, but I got them booked in at the LaBok. I told them it was more discrete. Plus I get a kickback from the local manager."

"So why are they coming all this way?"

"They want to evaluate the operation here, see if they can diversify and clean up some of their cash flow."

Collville looks over the rim of his glass. "You're not down for a performance review, are you?"

"No, nothing like that. They want to see what the lay of the land is."

Collville smiles. "If there's any truth in rumour then that would be Estelle, over at Recreational Escorts."

For a moment Perry gazes off into the distance, then:

"She sure can schtup and no mistake."

"Hey, you been tapping her out of watch?"

Perry looks Collville in the eye. "That's what I want to talk to you about."

"About fucking Estelle? Why? You want performance notes? A review or something?"

"No, I want you to whack Valerie."

"Sorry? You want me to whack Valerie?"

"Yes."

"Your wife of what 26, going on 27 years?"

"Yes."

"The mother of your two fine sons and your beautiful

192

woman of a daughter?"

"What is this, fucking Jeopardy or something? Yes, I want you to take Valerie somewhere and make sure she doesn't come back. Ideally while I'm entertaining the three stooges from Boston."

There's a roar of excitement from the bar crowd as a ball gets hit out of the park, or a runner breaks the race tape, or some other public orgasm moment.

When the ruckus dies down, Perry says:

"You want another one? I'm having another, and I don't want to drink alone. Makes me look like an alcoholic or something."

Collville just nods and finishes his drink as Perry waves the same waitress over and orders another Manhattan and a vodka rocks.

After she's sashayed over to the bar and clinked her way back, Collville says:

"What you're asking? I don't do that anymore."

"Seriously? You're Tony Carluchi's hammer man. You given all that up? Does Tony know?"

"I've not seen or heard from Tony for over six months now, so I don't think he's going to object. Besides, he gave me a great retirement present." Collville smiles wide, flashing a set of veneers and caps.

Perry looks down at his drink, the condensation off the side of the glass is slowly turning the thin paper coaster to mush. "So you won't consider a little freelance, for old times' sake?"

"No."

"Hey, I thought we were friends?"

"I told you, I'm retired. Tony's probably got some new guy, bucking for promotion, who'll do anything to keep in peoples' good books. If you ask him I'm sure he'll help out."

"Not even for fifty large?"

Perry pats his jacket pocket and Collville pauses, glass in hand, half way between the table and his mouth.

"Fifty?"

"Yes."

"To whack Valerie?"

"Christ, are we doing this again? Yes, to whack Valerie…. Hey, are you wearing a wire?"

Collville puts his Manhattan back down on the table, hard enough for the sound to be heard over the murmuring of the bar crowd, but not hard enough to slop his drink over the rim.

"Watch your mouth."

Then, glaring hot anger at Perry, he loosens his tie and unbuttons his shirt to the waist. Pulling the shirt open, he says:

"See?"

Perry leans in closer, all the while staring at Collville's exposed chest. Finally Collville says:

"What the hell do you think this is? Some freebie at a cheap titty bar?"

Perry leans back again. "These days it pays to be careful."

Collville buttons up his shirt and straightens his tie. "Do you know just how degrading that was?"

Perry picks up his vodka rocks. "I'm just saying, it pays to be careful."

"You want I should drop my pants so you can make sure I haven't anything extra inside my boxers? Or maybe check and see I don't have a microphone shoved up my ass?"

Two long minutes tick-tock by before Perry says:

"So for fifty large you're interested?"

Collville turns his glass round a couple of times, then says:

"So, maybe I might be. As a favour to you, because my regular is a straight 100 plus expenses."

"Christ, am I in the wrong business."

Collville looks across. "So how do you want it done?"

"Sorry?"

"The hit. How do you want it done? Do I just walk up to her and shoot her in the face? Beat her to death with a baseball bat? Drug her and toss her in the middle of the river with some scrap iron tied to her?"

Perry scrunches his face up in confusion. "I don't know. I mean, I never thought about it like that."

"What? Look, I'm an artiste. I'm not some gang-banger leaning out the window of a drive by indiscriminately letting loose with a 9mm machinegun."

Another thoughtful pause, then Perry says:

"Can you make it look like an accident?"

"Yeah I can make it look like an accident. It'll take a little longer, but it's possible. Does she ever take the subway? It'd be easy to make sure she goes under the train rather than steps onto it. Or, here's a thought, does Val still ride horses? She could have a riding accident. I haven't done one of those since Donny Necher."

"You did that?"

"Yeah he was one of mine." Collville leans back and smiles. "Last I heard it was still a cold case with no new leads."

Perry half shakes his head. "I don't think I care how you do it, just so long as she doesn't feel anything."

Collville runs his tongue over his new teeth. "I remember when the two of you first met. Gianni's Pizza Parlour. It was late, and it had been raining so heavy the water was getting backed up and filling the gutters – cars splashing it over onto the sidewalks. There was you, me, Ronnie Tectch, and that weird guy, Zach something-or-other – got himself shot dead holding up a gas station about six months after you got married."

Perry shrugs his shoulders, screws his face up in dismissal. "Hell if I remember."

"Sure you do. We were in one of the booths, smoking and generally beefing about anything and nothing. Then in walks Valerie with one of her girl friends."

Perry smiles. "Yeah, I remember now. She'd spent Saturday afternoon getting her hair fixed. It had been up in one of those beehive things. All very British, Mari Wilson kind of look. Except when she came out of the nightclub she got caught in the rain. I remember the whole fakakta thing ended up falling apart around her ears."

Collville stirs the ice in his Manhattan. "So, what's the problem? Why are you playing hide the salami with Estelle? I was there at your wedding. Hell, I was there when your first born came into the world. Val was gripping your hand in one of hers while the other beat the crap out of your arm. And all the while she kept saying that if you put another one of those inside her she'd personally rip your balls off…"

Perry nodded. "She's still looking to rip my balls off. She's thinking about a divorce."

"She tell you that?"

"Not in so many words. She's been to see Floyd Gillings. He doesn't take on anything other than divorce cases. That's how I know."

"You had her followed?"

Perry just nods, and the bar crowd cry out their disapproval as the call by the linesman is overruled by the referee, or umpire, or whoever has the final say in the matter.

"And you think whacking her is the answer?"

"Divorce and she gets half of what assets they can find. Dead and I get to keep everything."

Collville finishes his Manhattan, then checks his watch – a Breitling blue steel automatic. "Okay, I'm going to call it a night. I got a 6 a.m. to Chicago, then a red-eye to Fort Lauderdale straight after, so can we discuss this when I get back?"

"The fifty will still be here. The three stooges are not due down until the start of next month."

Perry swallows the last of his vodka. Looking over at the still crowded bar he says: "I'll come with you. But first I got to go to the john."

Collville nods and stands with him, both putting on their overcoats. Collville says:

"I'll pay the tab. Meet you by the fire exit – we can both go out the back. Save a lot of hassle trying to fight our way through the crowd."

Inside the restroom, Perry walks passed the customers at the urinals and goes into the stall farthest away from the main door. Throwing the lock, he unzips, urinates, shakes, then zips himself back up. For a moment he breathes out – long and heavy – and leans back against the stall door. For a sports bar the graffiti is pretty literate, considering the clientele.

He thinks about going home to Valerie – the indifferent reception, the even colder kingsize bed.

In their first apartment the double bed had been so close to the walls they had barely enough room for the two nightstands. They still managed to bang like rabbits though, until she became pregnant with Joseph. Then Teresa came along, and finally Michael.

By that time everything she'd originally had seemed stretched, or sagging, or just no longer appealing. He'd kept telling her, I'll get you a facelift. A boob job. A butt lift – or whatever the fuck it is they do to perk a woman's body back up and remove the Goddamn stretch marks.

Could you blame him for eventually looking elsewhere? Estelle was 20 years younger, 30 pounds lighter, and at least 2 grand cheaper a month as well. Plus, when she rode on top she could do this thing with her pussy without even moving. She said she could Kegel his brains out if she wanted to. And he often wanted her to.

Perry flushes, then wearing a smile and still semi-hard, unlatches the stall door, washes his hands, and leaves to find Collville waiting for him by the restroom door.

Collville points towards the fire escape doors at the end of the corridor. "I spoke to Michelle behind the bar. She's turned off the alarm so we can go out that way without any problem."

Perry nods and leads the way, not wanting to hang around even though there's nothing to go home to.

Through the doors and into the side alley – drizzle has replaced the rain-snow mix, but it's still slushy underfoot and grey sludge is around the base of several dumpsters.

As the door closes behind them, Collville says:

"What the fuck have you been up against?"

Perry stops and half turns. But Collville caries on.

"You got some crap on the back of your coat. Here, turn back around and I'll see if I can't brush it off."

Perry turns to face the alleyway entrance again and feels Collville's hands raising the collar of his overcoat. There's a second's pause as Collville pulls out a .22 with a small silencer attached and pushes the barrel up under Perry's raised collar.

Two dull thuds, and Perry's body is face down on the ground by the dumpster, blood oozing out from around the collar and pooling about his head.

The first one's from Billy Scofiled. He says there's a fine line between skimming and stealing, and you should have kept your fingers out of the honey pot. The second one's from Valerie. She says you should have kept your dick out of Estelle – and paying for a hit is going to be cheaper than getting gouged by some shyster like Floyd Gillings. And take it from me, she's still great in the sack.

He reaches inside Perry's overcoat and takes the fat brown envelope from Perry's jacket pocket.

#27 – The House Special

Both of them paid full rate, and with this contribution, that makes a quarter mil for the cost of a cheap piece and two bullets.

From his overcoat pocket Collville pulls out a brown and yellow hamburger takeaway paper bag. On the front is the name and logo of a drive-through on the far side of town. Carefully he puts the silenced automatic into the bag, then bends down to pick up the two spent cartridge cases. They go into the bag, along with the burner phone, then he turns and goes back into the Elbow Room via the fire exit door.

Down the corridor he stops and enters the men's restroom, takes out a small bottle of hand sanitiser, uses some of the liquid on his hands, washes them thoroughly with soap, dries, then re-applies more of the sanitiser. Gunshot residue taken care of, Collville picks up the hamburger bag and leaves. Heading back towards the bar, he stops by a painted door with the sign *Staff Only* screwed onto it. He knocks, turns the handle and walks straight in unannounced. Behind a desk computer screen the manager looks up as Collville puts the bag on the desk.

Collville nods. "Julius, Billy Scofield says could you clean up the garbage in the alley out back." Then pointing to the bag he adds, "And would you kindly make this disappear as well."

Julius ducks back behind the computer screen. "No problem. Give my best to Tony."

Collville runs the tip of his tongue over his front teeth. "No problem. I'll see what I can do."

But Julius is already putting the telephone handset to his ear and punching the number of his on-call lieutenant into the keypad.

Leaving the bar by the main exit this time, knowing full well that his overcoat will become covered in confusing anonymous trace fibres and hair, Collville steps out onto Main Street. He turns right, then right again and walks through the entrance to *The Golden Lotus*. There's still enough time for a House Special before he has to pack up his overnight bag and make for the 6 a.m. commuter flight to Chicago.

I Tried to Warn You

Brandon Barrows

It was an October morning when the telegram arrived.

DP SEEN IN HOOPER'S LANDING FL STOP NO DOUBT ITS HIM STOP

It was simply signed "JF" and told me, in ten words, more than I heard on the subject from any other avenue in almost three years, and not for lack of trying. David Parsons was in someplace called Hooper's Landing, fifteen hundred miles from home. I had no idea how much the postal orders I sent to "JF," and the dozen others like him across as many states, every month over the last few years added up to, just to keep their eyes and ears open, but whatever the amount, it was worth every penny if this tip proved true.

I slipped the note back into its little yellow envelope and dropped that into a drawer of my desk. I didn't need it anymore. There was no chance of forgetting. I stood, opened the door to the outer office and said, "Jeanie, come in here, will you?" I sat back down behind the desk, opening a different drawer as I did.

Jeanie, my secretary, the sole employee of my firm, appeared in the doorway. Petite, no more than an inch over five feet, she wore a muted-green dress that brought out the reddish highlights in her dark-honey hair and did nice things to an already-nice figure without being flashy about it. Framed by the doorway, she looked like a piece of art. She was more than just lovely, though – she was whip-smart and had no reservations about telling me things I needed to hear, whether I wanted to hear them or not. She was everything a private investigator's secretary was supposed to be according to Hollywood. Life imitates art.

"What's up, chief?" she asked.

I didn't look up or pause in what I was doing.

She'd handed me the telegram just minutes ago. Putting two and two together, she said, "It's him." It wasn't a question.

I tore the check from the book, waved it back and forth to dry the ink then flipped it to the edge of the desk. "Closing up shop for a couple weeks, Jeanie. That's three weeks' pay. If you don't hear from me after that, whatever's left in the account is yours, too."

Something flashed in the girl's eyes as she snatched up the piece of paper. She tore it into three pieces, shuffled them together and tore them three more times before dropping them into the visitors' ashtray on the corner of the desk.

"I know you don't like smoke, so I'll burn it after you're gone, Mr. Van Leuven."

I was no longer her friend, the "chief," I was "Mr. Van Leuven," her boss.

Still glaring, she added, "Don't worry. The office will be plenty aired out by the time you're back and I'll keep things ship-shape 'til then."

The look on her face told me not to argue.

I tried, anyway. "Damn it, Jeanie…"

It wasn't much of an argument.

There was a long, uncomfortable moment of silence.

Finally, she said, "I suppose this isn't the time to tell you how really stupid an idea this is, is it, Art?"

I nodded.

She sighed heavily. "Then I'd better get on the telephone and make the arrangements so you'll have time to pack a bag. Where to?"

"Miami, I guess." I stood up again. "I'll figure it out from there." I added, "You're the best, Jeannie."

"I know." She closed the office door behind her.

*****

The trip south, by train, took two days. A lot of time to think. My thoughts spiraled backwards as the train hurtled forward, putting distance between me and home, eating up the miles between me and David Parsons.

I went all the way back to the beginning, when my folks took in David Parsons, the son of a friend of my father's, after his own parents passed. I never knew just what happened to them. No one ever mentioned it. It was simply a matter of "David will be living with us from now on." I was eight years old. Who was I to argue?

And I had no cause to. I had two sisters, one older, one younger. Having David around was like getting the brother I always wanted without having to wait for him to grow up enough to play with. "Isn't it wonderful how the Van Leuvens took that poor Parsons boy in?" I once heard the Sunday church ladies say. "He's just like part of the family." And I agreed. For a few years, we were as close as real brothers.

But maybe it would have been better if nobody ever put the thought into words. If they just let the situation pass by without comment. Fat chance of that, of course. When we were kids, Dave himself never gave any hint of feeling like he didn't belong. Only later, when we were starting to become men, did the differences show. His restlessness, his risk-taking, and that streak of ruthlessness were things no Van Leuven I'd ever met possessed. As boys, maybe it didn't mean much. As young men, it was something else altogether. Everything became a competition with Dave. All I wanted was to be his friend, but all he seemed to want was to win, by any means.

At some point, Maggie came into our lives, bringing with her a light I never knew was missing. She caught Dave's eye first, but I was the one who caught hers. Without trying, we became inseparable. It was maybe the first time I won out over Dave. But as Maggie and I got closer, the distance between Dave and me grew. The bitterness in my foster brother became impossible to ignore.

When I turned eighteen, I announced I was going to become a cop. I'd never shared that dream with Dave before. He laughed when I did. "You're nuts, 'brother.' That's a dead-end life," he told me. Then he talked about his own big plans, his desire to be wealthy and important. It was all news to me. We'd both kept our dreams to ourselves. I began to feel as if maybe we never knew each other at all.

Not long after, I entered the academy. David Parsons left our family home, too. For two years, all I heard of him were rumors – and not the good kind. His name came up around the precinct often enough to make me worry.

Maggie and I had been married for a year when I next heard more than just rumors of Dave. I was late for dinner that night. Young policemen don't have much control over their working hours. I've always wondered if that saved my life or if it cost Maggie hers. I'll never know. I'd never have known it was David Parsons who killed her if she hadn't hung on just long enough to say so. I thought life was over, that I'd already reached that dead-end Dave warned me of. I couldn't imagine why he did it. The detectives who investigated had theories— I came to blows with the one who suggested an affair—but they never found my "brother" so they never knew for sure. For a few years there was a hint here, a clue there and then it became nothing more than an open file in someone's desk somewhere. It was infuriating, but not surprising. It's a big country, with a lot of places to get lost when you've got no roots. There was always Korea, too. More than one man had escaped a crime by enlisting.

My family never again spoke Dave's name, but he was all I ever thought of. Finding him, learning *why*, became my only purpose.

Eventually, I made detective, but I wasn't allowed to investigate. Too close to the case. Too hurt, too angry to be objective. I understood. But they couldn't stop me if I went private.

Now, I had almost six years with a private ticket instead of a badge. Three years since I had a whiff of my "brother." At times, it all seemed so unreal I half-expected to wake up in my childhood bed and find the whole thing was some horrific dream.

I Tried to Warn You

I woke to the rumbling of the braking train and knew it was no dream.

*****

In Miami, I rented a car from an agency. When the counterman asked where I was headed, he let out a low whistle and said, "That's a pretty desolate place, mister. What's out there, you don't mind my asking?" I told him I didn't know yet, thanked him for his help, and left him wondering.

It took a little time, but I found my way into the western swamp-country. Hooper's Landing was in Collier County, one of the smallest in the state. In the county seat, I found the sheriff's office and checked in as a courtesy. A sturdily-built, middle-aged deputy with a Stetson and a cowboy's mustache listened to my story about tracking a missing person—it was the truth, after a fashion—and when I was done told me, "Hooper's Landing's pretty close to the swamps, Mr. Van Leuven, and I'll tell you, it's almost impossible to find a man who wants to get lost in a swamp. Suppose a body has to come out sometime or other, but..." He shrugged.

David Parsons would come out of the swamps. If he was anything at all like the boy I once knew, he would want to be where there were people and whiskey, laughter and music.

I shook the deputy's hand. He wished me luck. I thanked him. I needed all I could get.

*****

I drove north and west from the county seat, traveling narrow roads hemmed in by water and vegetation, roads that ducked in and around and through denser jungle than I knew existed in this country. Though it was October, the air was heavy and hot and sticky. The lightest suit I owned was still too much clothing. In Boston, the chill wind was already promising the first snows, but here, the lushness of summer hadn't even begun to fade. Maybe it never would for all I knew. It felt like leaving the United States altogether for some strange, foreign land. I crawled the car through alien landscapes for a couple of hours, afraid of making a wrong turn and disappearing into the swamp myself. Signage was scarce and the maps I had were not very helpful, but somehow, I found the place.

Hooper's Landing was nestled on a spit of dry land in a crook of the Wacohatchee River, with swamp encroaching wherever it found an opening. It had probably grown up from some enterprising river-rat's trading-post and didn't look as if its purpose was much changed.

There was a filling station at the edge of the village. A diner called the Landing shared the lot. The boy who trotted out from the station filled up the tank then whisked a damp rag over the windshield, the whole time keeping his eyes on his work without looking at me. Strangers were suspicious, I supposed. That was good, in a way. Someone would remember Parsons.

The total for the fuel was less than two dollars. I handed the boy a five and said, "Keep the change."

His eyes finally came up and a tiny grin peeked through the distrust. "Thanks, mister!"

Maybe not all strangers were bad.

*****

The Landing Diner was the kind of place you can find in any town, coast to coast: a long, chrome counter with red-topped stools and four narrow booths to match. It was more run-down, maybe a little dirtier, than most, but it was air-conditioned, at least. A bored-looking, thirty-something waitress with an unlit cigarette crammed in the corner of her mouth glanced my way as I entered. "Sit anywhere. I'll be with ya shortly." It was after two o'clock. Except for an old-timer at the counter with coffee and pie, and a young couple talking in urgent-sounding whispers in the booth farthest from the door, the place was empty.

I slid onto a stool. The waitress appeared and placed a cup of coffee in front of me without being asked. "Haven't seen ya around before, have I?"

I shook my head.

"Passin' through? Must'a taken a wrong turn somewhere." She barked brittle laughter.

I gave her a smile the joke didn't rate. "Worried I would, but not quite. Looking for someone, actually. You get many folks passing through here?"

Whatever friendliness, or openness, the woman had in her disappeared. The look in her eyes changed like a switch was flipped. She could ask questions, but didn't like being questioned, even if it had nothing to do with her. It was an easy line to cross for strangers.

"What'll ya have?" she asked, all business.

I ordered ham and eggs, home-fries and toast. The food was sickly-greasy but I ate it and left a bigger tip than the waitress had probably seen in a long time. If I came back, maybe next time I'd get the benefit of the doubt.

*****

The Pinecrest Hotel was a two-story frame structure made of weather-greyed wood that looked ready to tumble down at any moment. But air-conditioners poked out of the windows and the sign out front said "vacancies" and those were the only things I cared about.

A sallow-faced man in denim traded me a room-key for a twenty-dollar bill, which bought me four nights' lodging. As I signed the register, I lifted a page, glanced up at the clerk and asked, "You mind? A friend recommended the place and I wanted to see when he was last here." The look on the man's face said he didn't believe me for a second, but also that he didn't give a damn. He just shrugged.

I flipped through the thick, musty pages looking for Parsons's signature. I didn't expect he'd use his right name, but I thought maybe I'd recognize his handwriting or the like. After several months' worth of pages, nothing jumped out at me and I gave up. If Parsons had really been in Hooper's Landing, he hadn't stayed at the Pinecrest.

I thanked the clerk, went up to my room and cranked the decrepit air-conditioner against the heat trapped in the room. Then I peeled off my sweat-soaked clothing, went down the hall and stood beneath the shower in the communal bathroom for ten minutes. When I got back to the room, the A/C hadn't made any difference. I hoped it wasn't an omen.

*****

Hooper's Landing seemed to only have one street, appropriately called Main Street. Aside from the filling station and diner, and the Pinecrest, there was a general store, a tiny clothing store, a barber-shop, a handful of residences and a bar called Rafferty's.

The bar was dim, the air cooler than outside but still damp and stuffy. Along one wall was a plank-board bar someone had once attempted to varnish. The rest of the room was given over to half a dozen mismatched tables and chairs and a small dance floor. There was a jukebox in one corner, but its lights were dark. Silence and closed-in heat blanketed the room.

There were only two people in the place when I entered. A man in bib overalls and calico shirt was draped over a table, dozing. Behind the bar was a long-faced, balding man with sleepy eyes, staring off into the distance.

As I approached, the bartender asked, "'S'yours, fella?"

"Rye, straight."

He produced a bottle and a relatively-clean-looking glass, poured off the liquor and pushed it towards me.

I sipped, expecting the worst, and found it pleasantly tolerable. I finished the rest in one go and asked for another. When the barman returned the glass, I placed a five-dollar bill on the counter and let my hand linger on it. Those sleepy eyes grew interested as they moved from the money to my face.

"I'm looking for someone," I said. "Maybe you can help me."

"Don' know 'bout that." He produced a rag from somewhere and began listlessly swiping at the bar-top.

"Just take a look. Maybe you've seen him."

I took from my jacket the only picture I had of David Parsons, a snap taken at our high-school graduation, the two of us in caps and gowns, grinning like mad. Maggie was to my right, my arm around her waist. She looked fresh and pretty and painfully young. She was only allowed to grow two years older. My heart flip-flopped, but I tamped it down and pushed the photo forward, tapping a finger against Dave's image.

"He'd be older now, about my age."

The man's eyes swept across the photo then back up to mine. "Friend of yours?"

"Yes."

He shrugged loose shoulders. "H'ain't seen nobody like that. Do better t'look down in Naples, mebbe. Gettin' be a big city now, y'know."

"Thanks. I'll keep that in mind."

I slid the photo back towards me and the money towards the barkeeper, who regarded it with both interest and distrust. I put the picture away then tossed back the rest of my whiskey and headed for the door.

It was clear that Parsons was here, or at least had been. The bartender was a little too anxious to head me off in another direction. If Parsons was just another passing stranger, there was no reason for him to care. That probably meant he'd be back. I just had to be patient.

*****

I knocked around the area for three days, renting a boat from a place on the north edge of the village and visiting as many of the homesteads up and down the river as I could find without getting too far from Hooper's Landing itself. I was still afraid of getting lost in that swamp and there was no one I could trust to guide me. There were places I could go on my own, but few people were willing to talk. I had more guns pointed at me in those three days than I had in all the years I was on the Boston PD.

Each night, I spent hours sitting in Rafferty's, nursing beers, watching the small crowd who gathered to drink and occasionally dance. It was the only place around to let off steam and I knew, sooner or later, I'd see just about everyone in Hooper's Landing, if I waited.

It was after midnight on the third evening, the start of my fourth day in Hooper's Landing, when a tall, lean man in a khaki sport-shirt with the collar turned up walked in. Electricity ran up my spine and my muscles stiffened. I couldn't see the man's face, but I'd know my "brother" anywhere.

Eamonn Rafferty, the sleepy-eyed owner of the place, was standing near the end of the bar when the door opened. Rafferty hurried towards the newcomer, grasped his arm and spoke hurriedly into his ear. The man's half-hidden face seemed to shrink deeper into the upturned collar. He hesitated a moment and then turned towards the door and disappeared.

I was already on my feet and moving, pushing past drinkers and dancers, but Parsons was gone before I got halfway across the room. Rafferty placed himself in front of the door. I shoved him aside and flung it open. The sound of rapid footsteps retreated into the thick, dark night.

A drunk was relieving himself against the side of the building. I let him finish, then grabbed his shoulder, turned him around and asked, "You see a man run past?"

"Oh, sho'," he agreed amiably.

"See where he went?"

He flung an arm out in the general direction of the swamp north of town. "Swamp. Where else?" he asked.

I ran towards the rental docks.

*****

Parsons might not have seen me, but he knew someone was looking for him. I probably wasn't the only one looking for

214

him. I doubted he'd taken up clean living after leaving Boston.

Pounding feet brought me to the docks in moments. A berth that was occupied when I returned earlier was now empty. It didn't necessarily mean Parsons took that boat, but…

Over the gurgle of the river, I told myself I could hear the faint sounds of a motor cutting the water. Whether I did or not is anyone's guess.

I hopped into the boat I'd been using, untied and pushed it away from the docks. A sliver of moon provided just enough light to work by. As I shipped the oars, Jeanie's voice shrieked inside my head, telling me how stupid this was. I didn't know the swamp. I was no boatman. Going into the swamp in the dead of night was suicide. But what choice did I have? I waited a very long time to see Parsons again.

*****

I relied on instinct, rage, three days' familiarity with the river and the wan moonlight. I didn't know how long Parsons had been in the area or how well he might know it. Better than I did, probably. But I had to try. All the while, my eyes and ears ached with the strain I put on them, trying to scan every atom of the swamp. Every sight and sound was amplified by fear and adrenaline.

Long hours passed. At some point, the silvered blackness of the night turned to gray and then the day began to come in sections, its red and orange light creeping through the trees and spilling over the water, shrinking the darkness until night went into full retreat. There was hope in the light, but little relief.

I was farther down the river than I'd ever been. At random,

I steered the boat down a side-channel. Minutes later, I spotted the rotting remains of an ancient quay and the flat-bottomed pole-boat tied to it. Huddled on a tiny hummock by the water was a shack with a thin column of smoke rising from the tilting chimney.

I tied up the boat, climbed ashore and shouted, "Hello in there! I need a little help, if you can spare a minute or two."

Silent moments passed, then the door of the shack flew open and a gnarled root of a man in a stained undershirt and ripped trousers stomped out, aiming an antique carbine at my chest. "Git away! Git off'n my prop'ty, god damn ya!"

"Hold on!" I shouted, hands over my head. "I don't mean any harm, I'm just looking for someone—"

"Git gone!" the man cried and raised the gun high, sending a shot whizzing over my head to disappear into the dense foliage across the river. The force of the blast and the man's own agitation caused him to lose his balance and stumble against the doorframe. I lunged forward and grabbed the rifle, tearing it from his grasp before he could hurt either of us. No sooner did I have my hands on it when a second shot rang out – from inside the shack.

A red blossom appeared in the old-timer's chest and spread across his undershirt. The look on his face went from surprise to horror before his eyes closed and he slumped backwards into the cabin.

"Damn!" Even with just one word, I recognized the voice. My stomach lurched. Somehow, I blundered my way through night and swamp and ended exactly where I needed to be to find David Parsons.

Parsons came barreling out of the cabin, shoulder lowered, knocking me aside. The carbine flew from my hand as I toppled and went down. In the moment it took me to regain my feet, he was already down to the water and in my boat, cranking the outboard.

"Dave!" I shouted.

He turned. For an instant, he looked like he was seeing a ghost. Then he shook his head, ripped the cord, setting the motor roaring, and aimed the boat towards the main channel, disappearing in seconds.

I ran to the quay, but it was useless. I'd never catch up to him in the pole-boat he left behind. He'd go back to Hooper's Landing and find a ride somewhere else or simply take the boat so deep into the swamp nobody'd ever find his trail.

Disappointment, frustration and a strange sense of relief warred inside me. For years, I'd been looking for a showdown with the man who killed my wife, while dreading the confrontation with the boy I grew up with.

I had my chance. I met David Parsons for the first time in almost fourteen years and I did nothing. I never even thought to draw my gun or pick up the old carbine or do anything else to stop him. I wondered, for a moment, if maybe part of me hadn't wanted to. If I caught him, it meant the chase was over and the chase, the search for Parsons, was the only thing that kept me going for a long, long time. Without it, what was left for me? What was Arthur Van Leuven without his vengeance?

I shook my head, wiped sweat from my brow and looked towards the man who died on the doorstep of his own home. I didn't know who he was or his relationship with Parsons. All

I could do was add his death to my "brother's" list of sins.

*****

Poling the boat was agony. I thought I was exhausted after a night in the motorboat, but pushing the pole-boat against the flow of the river was a nightmare. There was no way Parsons escaped me in this thing; I'd have caught up to him in moments. The boat must have belonged to the old man. How Parsons reached the shack remained a mystery.

After only minutes, I desperately needed a rest, but there was no possibility of stopping. Even a second would have meant losing what little progress I'd made. Minutes turned to hours and sometime around noon, I made it back to an area of the main channel I thought I recognized. My arms were limp and numb, but the sight gave me a little hope.

Then I turned a bend in the river and shock stopped me where exhaustion couldn't. Just past the bend, near a thick cluster of cypress along the river's edge, the rental boat lay half-submerged, kept just above the water by the waterlogged tree-trunk piercing its side. Leaning against the bole of a tree, knees pulled up to his chest, was David Parsons.

For a moment, I just stared, feeling the pull of the current, watching the sight before me grow further and further away. Something washed over me then and the agony, the exhaustion disappeared all at once. I slammed the pole into the riverbed and began to push towards the edge of the channel. I reached the mucky bank, climbed from the boat, looped its line around a protruding tree limb and scrambled up onto the higher ground.

Parsons hadn't moved from his spot against the tree, hadn't made any indication he even knew I was there. I pulled the .38

revolver from the holster beneath my arm and walked towards him, careful of my footing.

"Hello, Dave," I said.

My "brother" turned, looking over his shoulder at me. A brief, faded sort of smile passed across his lips. "Hiya, Artie. See the mess I made?" He swept a hand in the direction of the punctured boat. "Sorry 'bout your rig. Two wrecked boats in one night, would you believe it? Lost mine and only made it to that old swampbilly's place goin' overland." He paused. "Didn't mean to shoot him, you know. Was aiming for you. Promised him a double-sawbuck if he'd set you up for me." He chuckled, low in his throat. "Didn't know it was *you*, though, Artie. Lotta bad folk after me."

It was hard to believe the man in front of me was David Parsons. He was always beefy and hearty. Now he was lean and brown as a mahogany stick, with a whalebone kind of toughness to his skinny limbs. All the boyishness was gone from his face, replaced by the hard features of a stranger. There were many things I wanted to say, many things that *needed* saying. I'd practiced each of them a thousand times in my head. In that moment, though, I couldn't think of a single damned word for this man I didn't know.

Dave filled in the silence. "You're a long way from home, Artie. What brings a Boston boy into the swamp?"

"I could ask you the same, but we both know why we're here."

Emotion crawled across his face. "I'm sorry about that, Artie. It wasn't supposed to be like that. I never meant…"

"What did you mean, then?"

His gaze flicked from my face to the gun in my fist. He had a gun of his own back in the old man's shack. Where was it now? Lost in the river or just out of sight, waiting for his moment?

Parsons sighed and shook his head. "If you'd just let her alone, Artie. If only you'd…" His anger rose, but his voice went low. "I saw her first, damn you."

I shifted my grip on the gun, but never let the barrel stray from him. "That's not the way it works. Is that why you killed her?"

"No, damn it!" He stood and I backed up a step, keeping the gun between us. "I just wanted to talk to her, to try and see if… if we…"

"We'd been married a year, Dave. We loved each other very much. What did you think was going to happen? She'd throw away our life together and run off with you? You don't get to choose who someone else loves."

Parsons's jaw clenched and his eyes tried to bore a hole through me. "If you'd just—"

"All the ifs in the world won't bring Maggie back. And they won't change what you did, Dave. I'm bringing you home and you're going to answer for that."

"I almost did, back then. Almost turned myself in. But that wouldn't have brought her back, either, would it?" He sneered, his true self coming out at last. "Wanna bring me home? You're going to have to kill me first." His tone changed again and something sly peeked out through the hatred. "But you couldn't do that, Artie. We're just like brothers. Always have been."

"Turn around, Dave." My chest tightened as I reached into my pocket for the handcuffs I'd been carrying the last several days. "We're going."

"Kill me if you want me, Artie."

My fist tightened around the gun. I lifted it just a little higher, then let it drop. I couldn't do it. Not this way. Not with him asking for it.

Parson's tone become very soft. My childhood friend looked out of those eyes as he said, "I mean it, Artie. I've had enough. I've been running so long. I just wanted to get out, once and for all, go down to South America or somewhere and start over again. S'why I was hanging around this lousy swamp, waiting for a fella from 'round here to come along with my share of a big score we pulled a couple weeks back. I just needed some money to get started again." He forced a laugh. "Guess he pulled one over on me, though, huh?"

He seemed to shrink into himself. I couldn't help but see the small boy I first met so many years ago. My eyes felt hot and moist as I thought how tired, how weak he looked.

"Would you really kill me, Artie?"

I wouldn't. Even with all he'd done, all he took from me, I couldn't. I traveled across the country to bring him home, or kill him if I couldn't, and now it looked like I wouldn't be able to do either.

Somehow, the gun found its way back into the holster without my willing it.

"I knew you couldn't kill me." Dave showed me a sad smile. "Whatever else happened, we were always friends."

I rubbed grubby hands across my face, trying to hide the

tears. I couldn't think of anything to say or do. Nothing prepares you for that kind of situation.

"We were always friends," Dave said again.

And then there was a click.

It wasn't much of a sound, but it was enough to freeze my blood and make me forget everything else. I looked into the single black eye of a .45 automatic with the hammer drawn back beneath Parsons's thumb.

"I tried to warn you, Artie. I always knew you were headed for a dead-end. If only you hadn't come looking for me."

He pulled the trigger.

There was nothing but another click. We stared at each other over the top of the gun and the look on his face was horrible to see, twisted with hatred and jealousy and the fear created by years of desperation. And I knew then that I hadn't ever really known David Parsons, that I never really had a brother, after all.

He roared and pulled the trigger again, but I'd recovered enough to throw myself off to one side, falling to the ground just as the pistol exploded over my head.

There was no time for thinking or rationalizing or anything else now, but action. I flopped onto my back as I clawed the .38 from its holster. It exploded once, twice, three times and David Parsons flew backwards, slammed into the cypress tree, slid down to the ground and slumped silently in its shadow.

Shaking, nauseated, I pulled myself to my feet and inched my way over to where Parsons lay, still and bloody. I pressed a finger to his throat and found his pulse erratic but strong. A few minutes later, he was awake and sobbing, clutching his bloody, mangled arm, tightly wrapped in my jacket, and glaring hatefully at me.

"Get up," I said, in a voice I scarcely recognized. "We're going home."

*****

It took until nightfall to reach Hooper's Landing. The few people we saw acted as if we were invisible. I told Rafferty about the old swamp-rat, but he didn't seem to care. I tucked Parsons into my car and pointed it south towards the county seat, where I turned him over to the same Stetson-hatted deputy I spoke with earlier. He didn't act shocked or concerned when I told him Parsons was wanted for murder in Massachusetts, or about the old man in the swamp, just promised that he'd see the prisoner arrived safely home.

*****

I was at my desk the next Monday morning when Jeannie came into work. She didn't pretend to be surprised to see me, she didn't welcome me back. All she said was, "Is it over?"

I nodded. "Yeah."

"Do you want to talk about it?"

I shook my head.

She came around behind my desk, leaned down and kissed me softly on the cheek, surprising me. "When you want to talk, you know where to find me. I'm always here, Art." She smiled and retreated from the inner office.

Something clicked into place and a fog I didn't know I'd been living in began to lift. I realized all at once that vengeance wasn't the only thing I had these past years, that I wasn't alone in my quest or my sorrow. Suddenly, I wanted to talk to Jeannie very badly – not about David Parsons or death or violence, but about life and how much living I still had to do. She'd been so close for so long, but I was only just now seeing that.

"Jeanie, come in here, will you?"

She appeared in the doorway, framed like the work of art she was. A smile on her lips, she asked, "What's up, chief?"

The Li Fonti Job
Hollis Miller

I grew up in a rough neighborhood: a couple of blocks filled with nothing but pork and liquor stores, right smack in the middle of Queens. There wasn't a time when the police weren't lurking around the corner, waiting for some kids to make a mistake and rob a convenience store or snatch a lady's purse. That is, until Jackie Belluci came around.

Jackie was a high-ranking member in the Genovese family, and I'm talking *caporegime* high. Cocksucker had power like you wouldn't believe. He showed up, and the police started wearing shades so dark they might as well have gouged their eyes out. He had an olive oil smoothness about him. Tan, full head of jet black hair, a big nose but it worked for him. The neighborhood loved him, right down to the nuns and priests. He was nothing short of a superhero.

Jackie and I eventually became good friends. I was always a troubled kid—had a temper like the Tasmanian Devil—and was constantly in a pinch because of it. But this one time I really fucked up. I was about thirteen years old and had just saved up enough cash selling papers to buy a bike. To a kid in my neighborhood, a bike was like a brand-new Cadillac with white-leather seats. I was proud of that shit, and I earned it by my own doing. Until one day this kid, much younger than me, named Greg Bufano, took it right off the rack and rode the thing into the street. He bailed, but my bike got smacked by a two-ton delivery truck which turned it into spare parts. I beat the fuck out of the kid. He was only like six years old, but I thought he needed to be taught a lesson, so I did him good. Broke a few things, cracked a few more.

The next day I was having an ice cream with my friends when Mr. Bufano, who we called Big Boof, barged in the joint talking like he was gonna kill me. He was a thirty-something year-old guy, mind you. Lucky for me, Jackie Belluci was hanging around back and stepped in, told Bufano he lacked respect and I was just a kid and kids will do what they do. Jackie knew what had gone down the day before, so he took me under his arm and walked me to the bike shop a few neighborhoods over, a pleasant place so to speak. He took me inside and told me to point at whichever bike I liked best, and with a quick handoff of a few bills I had my Cadillac with white-leather seats back. Jackie told me if I stuck with him, there would be more of that coming, and that people like Greg Bufano's father would think twice about laying their hands on me, or maybe they wouldn't even think about it at all.

Fucking A did I stick around. At first, I did menial things, like grabbing coffees and sandwiches for Jackie and his friends. But as I got older I was upgraded to kicking Irish ass, and eventually taking out the trash for Jackie, if you know what I mean.

I never enjoyed taking anyone's life, but that was the only way to survive once you got involved. You were expected to obey orders, and *you'd* be the one chopped up in a few dumpsters if you didn't. That was the way things were, and without Jackie Belluci I probably woulda gotten pinched pushing heroin on a street corner. I owed him a lot. Like I said, I never liked it, but the way I saw it, we all signed a contract when we joined up. We knew what the deal was, that there would be risks. And even knowing that, we took them. That's how I made my peace with what I did. The life wasn't for everybody, but we had a good thing going, until one day, we didn't.

*****

I was about thirty-five at the time. 1988. I had risen through the ranks and had eventually become Jackie's number two. Our crew earned good. Really fucking good. Construction and unions were our bread and butter. I was bringing home envelopes that couldn't be sealed they were so full. So one day I'm sitting with an associate of mine named Jimmy De Marco in a bar called Bellissima's that was just another mob hangout. Everybody but Italians were afraid of this place, and that's how we liked it. I was sipping on something, I think it was scotch, and having a smoke when Jackie barged in looking like a case of the rabies.

"Oh," I said to him. "You look like shit."

"You break my balls," he responded.

A lot had changed since Jackie was young. He was the most Italian motherfucker you'd ever see. He might as well have had pasta sauce running through his veins. He was always a short guy, but now it really showed. About five-foot-seven, and rounder than a ball of mozzarella. He had these outdated glasses, thin as wire, with perfectly circular lenses resting on his beak. The top of his head was completely bald and whatever he had left was greased to the nines. Nobody woulda thought he was once the most eligible bachelor in Middle

Village. But to me, Jackie would always be the guy who took me to buy that bike.

"I've been up all night," he continued. "The Mangione construction job is completely fucked."

"What happened?" Jimmy asked. This job was big. My stomach sank to my knees.

Jackie took a seat. "This cocksucker Ralph Li Fonti and his crew jacked some equipment from the site. Mangione's pissed. Three-hundred thousand dollars of copper wiring. Gone."

"You're fucking kidding me," I said. "He knows that's our job. It's a four-million-dollar pay-day for us by the end. We gave him those no-shows too, in good fucking faith. Where'd he get the balls?"

"Quite frankly, I'm sick and tired of this guy. That's three times he's blatantly fucked us in the ass," Jackie said.

This guy Ralph Li Fonti was another captain in the family. He was a young guy, younger than me, and he only got the spot because of his will to push limits. Everyone else in the family thought that Frank "Father" Capriccio was passed up for the position, and for a while there was some bad blood, but it was resolved. Capriccio disappeared.

"I wanna send a message to the Li Fonti crew," Jackie said. "These games he's been playing have gone on for too fucking long. There are millions of dollars on the line here."

"What do you wanna do? Call a sit-down?" I asked.

"No, no, no. No more sit-downs. No more talks and resolutions. I want this guy gone."

"*Madone*! Let's slow down a minute here," Jimmy said, sitting up, pressing his cigar into the ash tray between us.

"Ralph Li Fonti's a captain, Jackie. This could start something big that we don't wanna follow through on. Those guys over there, they like him a lot. He makes them a lotta money."

"We call a sit-down, make him pay restitution to Mangione, we keep the no-show jobs for ourselves, and everybody's happy," I offered. "We let Bobby Manna arrange the thing and mediate. He's always a reasonable guy."

The first time Ralph's crew fucked with ours, we sat down with Bobby, the *consigliere*. The whole thing was a pretty heated ordeal. Some of Ralph's guys were posing as members of our crew and made collections on top of ones we *already* made on our routes, saying Jackie gave the order and nothing could be done. Ralph was a sneaky cocksucker, reminded me a lot of a Shylock money lender. I personally reached out to Bobby to set the sit-down in motion. He gave a location, some pizza place in Staten Island, and guaranteed everybody's safety. When things got sticky, I remember he put his finger down on the table and tapped twice. *We will decapitate both crews if need be,* he said. *There's plenty of guys itching to be a captain, and we're more than willing to put them there. We're a fucking family. Remember that.*

"And to boot," I said. "We can't whack this guy without consulting a higher power like that anyway. Nobody's hitting the mattresses. It's suicide, Jackie."

"It needs to be done, no more questions. We sat down with Bobby once and nothing's changed. Ralph's still playing games."

Jimmy and I glared at each other as we often did.

"Fine," I said. There was nothing I could do when Jackie

set his mind on something. It was a simple fact of life that I learned a long time ago, and I hated disobeying the guy. Jackie was a better role model than my alcoholic fuck of an old man. I wasn't even phased when he got cancer. "I'll get somebody on it. Maybe some *mulignons*."

Jackie shook his head. "It's gotta be you, Rich. Those blacks got big mouths. This needs to be tight-lipped."

"Me?" I said. It had been a while since I did somebody like this. I hadn't lost my edge, I knew that. But I was too high up for dirty work, and this ordeal was serious shit. "We can't have it trace back to our crew. A dirty cop pulls my fingerprint, you better believe they'll find me in a trunk somewheres stabbed to death."

Jackie just laughed. "Then wear gloves." He stood up and came behind me like a ghost. "I'll worry about the fall out," he told me, digging his fingers into my shoulders. That meant I was in. No way out. "You worry about putting a bullet in this guy's face."

*****

This Li Fonti *ciuccio* lived out in Mineola with the porkchops and all their unibrows and port wine. It wasn't a common place for connected guys to live. Rumor had it he lived away from everyone else because he had a thing for *mulignons*, or because he was a *fenucca*. I figured, if he liked *mulignons*, so what? I had a thing for Korean girls myself, had a *cumare* once named Hye-Young from Seoul. But other men? No way. That alone should get him whacked.

Now, I never liked Ralph one bit. In fact, I resented the cocksucker, but I knew him well. I got pinched when I was twenty-five on firearm possession and was in the can for a few years. Ralph Li Fonti was my cellmate. He got taken in pushing coke on some garbage routes, really routine shit in our thing. I never understood why they put two mafiosos in the same cell; all we did was scheme, smuggling in Cuban cigars and giving them out to the staff in exchange for more time in the yard or a hooker we could bang in the toolshed. I can't tell you how many rackets we had going. We didn't have quite the luxury like they show in the old mob movies, but it was something.

Ralph and I had a relationship like Jackie and me. Ralph was the captain, the shot-caller, and the idea man, while I was stuck with the dirty work. I had an aptitude for it. He sat in our cell with his legs crossed like the fucking Godfather, and all the while I was out beating on camel jockeys and chinamen who hadn't kicked up our cigarettes that week.

In my mind, Ralph and I had a mutual respect for each other. We knew our own strengths and we took advantage of them to make everything work. That made us partners. But one day I took a later shower than usual, right before lock up. I was drying off in front of the sinks when I hear Ralph on the other side of the wall telling some spic that I was his loyal dog, and whenever he threw a bone, I'd blindly chase it. Fuck that guy. Without me, he woulda been nothing in the can. He didn't have the balls to be his own muscle. I never was the type that expected much, but at least give credit where it's due.

Until the Li Fonti job, I thought my foot soldier days were over, and quite honestly, I missed them. I was never the stone-cold killer type. I remember my hands always trembled on the steering wheel, the tips of my fingers would freeze up, and no matter the weather I always had the heat absolutely blasting. I was constantly shaky until the last moment, and then it was like I was a different person. I never misplaced a bullet, never batted an eye when the knife hit a rib and felt nothing when I buried them. Like I said, they signed up for this life just like I did. They cut their palm open, held a burning saint just like I did. They took *Omerta*. They devoted their life to the family and all it entailed. If they died, it was business, never personal.

I merged on Grand Central Parkway towards Mineola at 3:00 AM sharp.

It was the middle of summer, already seventy-eight degrees. I wore a thick Rangers jersey, looking like a real New Yorker over here. I even had Timbs to complete the fit. I didn't want to look like a mobster and raise some eyebrows unnecessarily.

A little more than half an hour went by and I was barely halfway there. Construction holdups. But I had time to break everything down. Ralph lived in a six-story apartment complex, fifth floor. I would have to pick the lock, but no worries, it was a skill I acquired in the neighborhood; we all did.

The Belluci crew always used a tan Buick that we stole out of Harlem for our hits. The tags were fake, untraceable, the tires worn to flat tread, and the seats were covered in blankets that we constantly replaced and dry-cleaned. We took no chances since the RICOs hit back in the seventies. I was born after the 'Golden Era' of the mob as they say, but it never felt like we were weakened at all. We just chose to operate in the shadows instead. They may arrest a hundred or so guys every ten years, but everyone's replaceable. The FBI flaunts their arrests like fucking peacocks, but they don't do shit.

4:01. Finally pulled up to the place. I was expecting some kind of beach resort with palm trees and white, stone walkways, and it was pretty much that. Ralph wore nothing but Tom Ford and Cavalli, drove a Rover, and refused to drink anything younger than twenty. I was more of a tracksuit type of guy, the occasional button down with slacks, and I didn't give a shit how old something was as long as it tasted good. I liked classy shit, but *va fungool* if you think I'd ever live in a pretentious place like this.

"*Madone*," I mumbled.

I took my piece from under the seat, an M9A3 Berreta, good quality, Italian-made hardware, and screwed a silencer on. This is suburbia we're talking about. Gunshots go in one ear and out the other in the city, but here, forget about it. I unzipped my jacket and slid the piece down into the coat pocket. I could feel my hands trembling like Michael J. Fox. My pulse felt heavy in my neck. It *was* a good thing feeling that again. My watch read 4:05. The complex was dead, but the sun was about to check in and rouse everybody from here to Montauk. If I didn't get a move on, this prick would wake up and my day would be a whole lot harder.

I took a deep breath, slipped on a black ballcap, pulled it down as far as it would go, and got out.

The place had tight security, but we were ready for that. Jackie somehow got ahold of a punch code, so we didn't have to be buzzed in as guests. There was a security guard too but the fat fuck was knocked out. I walked in ready to make him a corpse if need be.

The inside of the complex was pristine. The carpets were a deep garnet, the walls beige and decorated with paintings of

European landscapes, and there were no pets or cigarettes allowed so it smelled like a hospital. There was a nice little sitting area in the lobby complete with a fireplace. You would never find something like that in the city.

This was a message job, nice and easy. Usually, there were a dozen steps you had to take post-mortem. Dicing up the body, cleaning up the mess, discreetly placing some trash bags into your trunk, and sinking them to the bottom of the harbor with some chains and cinderblocks.

This time, we wanted Ralph Li Fonti to be found. It was a message, like I said. I just had to deliver it. Pull the trigger and get the fuck out of there.

I took the stairs up five flights and found Ralph's crib. 514. I reached into my pocket, feeling for a tiny, titanium lock pick that was one of the best things I ever bought. Getting my numb fingers to separate the denim felt like surgery, but as soon as they met the metal, the shaking stopped.

I picked the lock and let myself in. Ralph's place was classy; open floorplan, warm colors, fine china, a beautiful wet bar, and a sleek plasma tv set into the wall just above a fake fireplace. Every wall had a picture of a famous Italian slapped on it. Frank Sinatra, Frankie Valli, Sophia Loren, Brando, and even some of the guys from the old school. Capone, Lucky, Joe Bananas, Vito Genovese. It suddenly didn't feel like I was alone.

The apartment only had two rooms, so there was only one place this prick could be.

I reached for the knob of Ralph's bedroom and carefully twisted it. The bed sat against the opposite wall, facing me. I silently unzipped my jacket, took my piece from the pocket like I had done so many times before, and flipped the light switch.

Ralph stirred, clenched his eyes. I stood there watching him. I could have ended it right there, painlessly, but I wanted him to look at me first. I wanted him to see that he was right about me. I was a dog, but he wasn't my only master. He finally opened up his peepers and craned his neck to see what the fuck was going on.

"Rich?"

I put a bullet right between his eyes. His head jolted backwards onto the pillow as his brains splattered all over the shiny Mahogany headboard. The chunks were so thick I could hear them sliding down the wood.

"Cocksucker," I said, even though I knew Ralph couldn't hear me.

I slid the Berreta back into my coat, and my stomach started twisting. I felt everything I ate that day erupting from my guts like a geyser, so I rushed to the pot. I didn't know why it happened at the time. I had never gotten sick over anything like this before, nothing. But I know now. Prior to Li Fonti, I had the support of the king of kings, Vincent Gigante, *our* godfather, and thus the family in its entirety. Bobby Manna, Sammy Santora, the other captains. Here, we were operating in the unknown, unsanctioned, no permission, and I was frightened.

I cleaned up my chunks, wiped everything down for prints, and fled into the morning.

*****

After about a week of looking over my shoulder and peaking

between the blinds before I stepped outside, things were going good. Mangione Construction stuck with our union workers, and I had just pulled down more scratch than I ever had in a week. Twenty large, from the construction job alone.

Life was so good I decided to take a day off and soak in my Jacuzzi for a while, just to celebrate. Come the afternoon the sun was shining, and I was steadily sipping on a nice Long Island iced tea, wearing nothing but a robe and swim shorts, when my phone chimed.

"Hello?"

"Rich. It's John. I—"

"John who? I know like thirty Johns."

I heard a sigh. "Calvano."

"Oh! Detective Calvano! Johnny C, how you been? *Come stai?*"

John was once a raging alcoholic and a degenerate gambler who owed about fifty large to the wrong people. I don't know if you know, but being a cop pays for shit, so this guy was in deep, but Jackie and I had been probing for a cop we could flip. John was the perfect guy. I personally stepped in on his behalf and paid his debts and sent him off to get rehabilitated or whatever. When he got out, I made sure he knew who to thank and who he now belonged to.

"No time for small talk. Look, kid. There's some scary shit going around that I think you might wanna know about," he said. "Some violence is about to go down in your part of the world and the department wants us to let it happen. You might wanna consider getting out of town for a while."

I sat up. "What did you say?"

"Ralph Li Fonti's murder was called in a few days ago—"

"So what? What are you talking about?"

"Your crew's a target. You were spotted on camera at Li Fonti's place, Rich."

My forehead creased up like a layer cake. "You're losing me. What's this have to do with me getting out of town? Is there a warrant out for me or something?"

John sighed. "Listen, that info got leaked to your friends. You're in fucking danger. Leave town."

"Leaked?" It didn't take me long to realize. "You're the fucking rat, aren't you? You crooked motherfucker."

"I didn't say anything about that—"

"After all I've done for you, you sell me out? This is how you repay me for getting you sober, and saving your ass from getting chopped up into little pieces? Are you fucking serious?"

"Just get out of town, Rich. I'm trying to help here."

"Take your help and shove it up your ass! If I ever catch wind of you again, I'll—" He hung up.

I looked at the phone and shouted, "Cocksucking piece of shit!"

I stood up, fuming like never before. I rarely let my emotions get the best of me, but I was a dead man. I ripped the phone off its side table and tossed it into the Jacuzzi and slapped my glass of iced tea to the ground.

"Fuck," I said, pacing. My time in La Cosa Nostra was up. The bell had finally tolled. It happened to everybody.

I went inside, threw on some clothes, and started packing.

Money, jewelry, guns, a few changes of clothes, everything. I would never see this place again, and I had cash laced in every inch of the walls, the mattress, you name it. We wise guys run a cash business, strictly. I couldn't just slip a few credit cards into my wallet and go. I ended up filling about three duffle bags. It was barely half, made me sick.

Then, the phone on my bedside table started ringing. I went over and sat on the bed but was hesitant to answer. If the wrong people knew I was at home, I'd never step foot in the sunlight again. There'd be a car just out front at all times, and the second I tried to flee, everything would go black. But then again, what if the call was something I needed to hear?

I picked up the thing and brought it to my ear.

"Who is this?" I asked.

"It's Jackie."

"*Madone* am I glad to hear your fucking voice."

"They got Jimmy," is all he said. My heart started thumping. It all seemed more real now. Jimmy was gone, and we were next in line, no doubt about it. "Word is the order's coming down from Gigante, that stumbling prick."

"What the fuck are we gonna do?"

"I'm sending some friends of ours to your place. Vin Sigler and Danny Boy. You know them, they're good kids, loyal. They'll look out for you. In the meantime, pack your shit. I have a safehouse down in Apalachicola where we can lay low for a bit."

"Florida?"

"What? You wanna test our luck here? The whole fucking family after us?"

"I told you this was gonna bite us in the ass, Jackie!"

"*A fa Nabila*. Let's let bygones be bygones for now—"

I sucked my teeth. I had poured my whole being into La Cosa Nostra, and it was all over just like that. I'd be looking over my shoulder the rest of my life. The mob has connections everywhere. *Everywhere.*

"—I'll be over in thirty."

*****

Jackie pulled up in his frost white Lincoln, a brand new 1987 Continental. He wasn't driving, of course, most captains had one of the younger guys in the crew take them everywhere, usually a relative of some kind, blood or not. Jackie's was his nephew, Anthony Barese, who was just a kid, no older than sixteen. That fat piece of *baccala* dragged a kid into this shit. I couldn't believe it.

Vin and Danny Boy had arrived a few minutes earlier packing heat in case of a shitstorm. From what we could tell, Gigante hadn't sent anybody to my place just yet. They were probably looking for a hit on Jackie first and foremost.

I could see Jackie was on edge, and no fucking wonder. The whole family was after us, every crew, not just the Li Fontis. I couldn't imagine how big that contract musta been. I mean, we were way outta line. Being a made man means you're an untouchable without the say-so of the boss, and Li Fonti was a good earner. We whacked him without consulting a soul, and to be quite honest I was a little upset about it. I fucking told Jackie what would happen if we got made out and look who was right? And just look where my loyalty got me.

Jackie plopped down in my living room sweating and

huffing like a sick dog. "We gotta make a stop at Donatello's before we head south," he said.

"That's thirty minutes backtracking with good traffic. We need to get the fuck out of the city before they lay us out on the street."

"We need the money from the freezers," he told me. "There's too much to leave behind. I worked too hard over the years for that shit to go to waste."

"Whatever."

I didn't wanna argue too much. With Jackie in a state like this, pissing him off could put me six feet under in a Jersey cornfield on our way down to Florida. We were both out of the picture, dead men, so the prick could whack anybody at this point. The rules didn't apply to him no more. I was careful.

"Alright," I said. "Let's do it."

Vin and Danny Boy packed my bags, threw them in the trunk of my Cadillac, and posted up as Jackie and I stepped down to the sidewalk and into our cars. I felt like John Gotti minus the cameras and fangirls. I took one last look at my place, the culmination of all the shit I had done, the dream of every poor Italian kid, and drove off.

The streets were fucking packed. We were sitting at lights for twenty minutes sometimes before moving an inch. I always hated how big delivery trucks would park in the middle of the street, not giving a fuck what's going on around them, and that day they came out in droves. But it gave me a lotta time to think.

I wondered why I even agreed to kill Ralph, knowing *con*

certezza it was the wrong thing to do. Whacking a guy over copper wiring, looking back, seemed extreme. A sit-down was all we fucking needed, for Gigante to set the record straight and tell Ralph to back off. Jackie was sharp as a razor back in the day, but I guess being sixty-two made him go *ubatz*, fucking smooth-brained or something.

I remembered when Ralph became a capo too, youngest capo in family history. He had "Father" Capriccio whacked to cement his place and nothing was ever done about that, by Gigante or anybody. The thing was, Capriccio wasn't an earner. He was living solely on respect for being an old timer and having connections in Buffalo and Philly. But Ralph brought in boatloads of money for the family through a tax evasion scheme in Connecticut convenience stores. Capriccio was shot five times in his home. It was no mistake who was responsible, but Ralph made too much money for Gigante and management to act.

That was when I realized that our code was a load of bullshit. Honor and loyalty meant nothing when money was involved. Made guys got clipped all the time, but as long as the money flow wasn't fucked up, it didn't matter. La Cosa Nostra was just a bunch of guys bound by rules that were bent and broken by anyone and everyone. Fucking Jackie was godfather to this kid Anthony Barese, and he dragged him into this mess and made him move down to Florida with him, where he'd be constantly paranoid about getting buried beside his uncle in a grave they dug for themselves. Jackie mighta been the worst godfather I ever saw, clearly showing his loyalty, his pledges under God, didn't mean nothing. I wasn't dying for this guy, nor tucking tail in some backwoods safehouse in swampy, mosquito-infested, fucking Florida. No way.

I floored it to get beside Jackie's Lincoln, nearly killing some Hindi cabman in the process. We rolled our windows down. "I've gotta make some arrangements with my ma," I told him. "I need to make some calls."

He glared at me. I was surprised he didn't put a bullet in my eye right there and then.

"You know my pop's got cancer, Jackie. Fucking chemo. My ma can't afford that shit on her own. She needs to know where to find some money. That's all."

He nodded and rolled the window up, and I made my way over to the street side, relieved. I spotted a payphone just a few blocks up and put the caddy in park, grabbing a few quarters before hopping out. I made sure I had my piece tucked tightly in my waist band. For all I knew, we were being followed. My eyes moved around to every face that passed. I didn't wanna live the rest of my life like that.

I put a quarter in the thing and dialed 0. "Operator," said a woman's voice.

"Patch me through to a Louis Manna. Bricktown, New Jersey."

Louis Manna, or Bobby Manna as I called him earlier, was *consigliere* for the family. *Consigliere* was the last and only liaison to the boss. If you had a beef, you talked to them.

"Just a moment, please."

It didn't take long for the call to go through. "Speak," he said. I didn't respond right away. I wasn't sure what I was about to do was what I wanted. Jackie was all I had growing up, he and the life, but he broke the rules, fucked up big time and was dragging people down along with him.

"It's Rich, your friend from the security tapes," I started. I put my tongue in the corner of my lip and sighed. There was just silence for a moment. "I can give you a location on Belluci. Otherwise you'll never get him, he'll disappear."

"And?"

I swallowed. "I want immunity in exchange for the information. Jackie was the shot-caller on that thing the other day. He's the one you want. I don't expect anything out of this, just a guarantee of my safety. I'll make restitutions of any kind, you name it."

There was a long pause. I heard some muffled chatter in the background. I couldn't believe I was going through with it, couldn't believe there'd be a day in my life without Jackie in it, especially by my doing. No doubt his nephew and the other two guys would go down with him. They didn't deserve that, but Jackie started this shit, not me. We shoulda never been in a spot like this. We coulda had a sit-down.

My heart was beating like a drum while I waited for the response. I even started biting at my nails. I knew that Bobby's word didn't mean I was totally safe. They could fucking lie, bring me in for a meeting and blow my brains all over the place, but it was a chance I was willing to take.

"We'll get the word on the street to leave you be," Bobby finally told me. "Now, where is he?"

"Do I have an absolute guarantee?"

"Absolutely."

I looked up the street at Jackie's car. I remember the heat was radiating off the roads that day like I'd never seen.

Standing there, I thought back to what Ralph had said about me. How I was nothing more than a loyal dog. Fuck him. No way was I going to do somebody else's bidding ever again. I wasn't putting my life at risk for any cocksucker other than myself. It felt, enriching, I think is the word.

"He'll be at Donatello's Pork Store in twenty minutes. 3471 30th Ave, Queens."

I hung up and found a bench nearby, stretching my legs out like I'd just finished a few rounds with a hooker. I pulled out a pack of Marlboros and lit one up. I never drew it into my lungs, just let it burn between my lips as I sat there. I was waiting for the sirens. I wanted to know when it happened. Jackie was going to hell, no doubt about that, and I was sending him there.

And for once I didn't know how to feel.

Voice Over

Joe Giordano

A raging female voice in my head insisted I commit murder. I'd resolved to drown the bitch in a fifth of Scotch when I bumped into Maxey inside the Dead Rabbit, an Irish pub that often served as a way station for cops contemplating eating their guns. I'm Bragg, and I'm a gold-shield homicide detective out of Brooklyn South.

Nicknamed the Dog of Flatbush, Maxey dressed like a cover model for *GQ*, and enjoyed a sex life that would've exhausted Casanova.

"You look like shit," was his opening pleasantry.

"It's the howling banshee in my head."

"You hear voices?"

"Just one."

His face clouded. "Sounds serious."

"An occupational hazard."

He placed a hand on my shoulder. "You should see someone."

I sighed. "After I'm drunk."

"No. Really." He produced his iPhone. While scrolling his contacts, he said, "I know a psychiatrist with an office in the

West Village. I'll call her if you like."

The voice in my brain screamed an objection, so the potential stigma about a cop consulting with a shrink caused me only a moment's hesitation before I nodded.

From his tone speaking with her on the phone, Maxey had a personal rather than a professional relationship with the woman. He said, "You'll recognize him by his baby blue eyes." He chuckled at her response, then turned to me. "She's still in her office and will see you now."

I left the Dead Rabbit with her address in my pocket and arrived at a brownstone displaying a plaque, "Dr. Beverly Lange,"

Dr. Lange, in her late thirties, was shapely, wearing a designer gray suit and only a trace of makeup. Her hand felt like cashmere when we introduced ourselves, and she directed me toward an expensive couch.

"Am I supposed to lie down?" I asked with a tinge of discomfort. Now that I was in a psychiatrist's office, my imagination wandered to how my boss Lieutenant Dixon would skewer me if he found out. A grizzled African American, and not the touchy-feely type, Dixon would probably declare that his suspicions about my lack of sanity were confirmed.

"Make yourself comfortable," she said, her tongue touching her upper lip when she smiled.

I sat and she sunk into a plush armchair opposite me, poising a gold pen over a notebook.

"What are you feeling?" Dr. Lange asked.

"I have a voice in my head, and I'm never comfortable. She

speaks and I lose focus."

She crossed long legs and jotted something, staying silent.

I used the same technique in interrogations to keep the suspect talking, so I complied. "I feel like a Picasso painting, deconstructed, at oblique angles. The voice plagues me even when I'm asleep. Am I possessed?"

Dr. Lange spoke in a soothing tone. "You're experiencing 'auditory hallucination.' About 4% of the population suffers from this condition, which society unfortunately stigmatizes. When did the voice start?"

"During a murder case."

"You must've been going through a stressful time."

"Sounds like my job description. I want to rip off my head. That's why I'm here."

"When you react to the voice, you give it power."

"What do you mean?"

"If your voice loses its audience, it'll get bored and go away."

I sat back. "That's easier said than done."

"I could prescribe tranquilizers, the standard medical practice. The voice would be muted, but drugs only deal with the symptom, not the root cause."

"I want relief, but I can't sleepwalk and do my job."

"Your recovery begins when you recognize *you* have the power. The voice can control only with your tacit permission."

I blinked. "That sounds so logical."

"You need something to take your mind off work." Dr. Lange sighed and approached the couch close enough that our knees were almost touching. "Now, you lie down," she said bending to me.

For the remainder of the hour, Dr. Lange administered horizontal therapy.

I was out of her office and almost back in my car when I realized that my voice had left me. The harpy must've gotten jealous and split.

Although relieved, on the drive back to my apartment, I wondered about Dr. Lange's credentials and if Maxey had hooked me into some sort of Tinder, exotic role-playing spinoff. The next day, salvaging the tatters of Maxey's integrity, I received an email invoice from the good doctor. About the cost of an expensive dinner for two in Manhattan. I resolved that if my voice ever returned, I'd revisit Dr. Lange for another repast.

*****

The next morning, Lieutenant Dixon called me into his office and assigned me a case. I sat across his desk as he read from the scene cop's report.

"Edward Castin, white, thirty-three, shot three times in the back on a quiet street in Gerritsen Beach not far from the apartment complex where he lived. He was still alive when the EMTs arrived, but he died in the ER without regaining consciousness. No surveillance cameras were on the street and the shell casings had been retrieved by the murderer." He grimaced and tossed the report in my direction.

"Not exactly a neon flashing arrow pointing at the killer," I said.

"Or killers."

"Forensics will tell us how many guns were used." I observed. "He still had his wallet and an expensive watch."

"A robbery gone wrong or perhaps money wasn't the motive," Dixon said. "While you wait for the coroner to complete the autopsy, talk to Castin's family, friends, neighbors, and coworkers. You know the drill."

"As Edison might have put it," I said, folding the report into my jacket pocket, "cracking cases is 1% inspiration and 99% perspiration."

Dixon chuckled and said, "Don't let me keep you," which was my invitation to get to work.

*****

Dixon had described the street where Castin was murdered as quiet. He could've put all of Gerritsen Beach in that category, a section of Brooklyn that suffered one murder per year. Gangs and drugs were elsewhere. Castin's parents were deceased, he had no siblings, and an uncle in California hadn't seen him in years. He worked at Bastar and Holmes, an investment firm in Lower Manhattan, but I started with his neighbors. A bleach blonde in her forties, Veronica Supple in 5G lived next to Castin and seemed anxious to talk. She dressed to emphasize her cleavage and looked me up and down when I asked about him and flashed my credentials.

"I'm guessing you're a Scotch man," she said in a suggestive tone as she escorted me into her small living room, obviously not taking the death of her neighbor hard.

"Not on duty." I grabbed an armchair so she couldn't sit next to me. She took the couch opposite, crossing her legs and allowing her skirt to ride up her thigh.

My line of defense in these circumstances was to keep my eyes on my notebook and maintain a businesslike tone. "What can you tell me about Edward Castin?"

"Good looking. Stylish dresser. He entertained women. Lots of them," she said. "All ages. All hours." She took a moment before saying in a conspiratorial tone, "I saw a few wedding rings."

Sounded like another Maxey with a bevy of jealous husbands and boyfriends wanting his ass.

As I jotted in my notebook, I asked, "No men?"

"Not that I noticed," she said, her forefinger outlining her blouse's V-neck. "You're not wearing a ring."

I pretended not to hear. "Did you get any names?"

"Never introduced," she said stifling a yawn.

I hoped my tech guy could unlock Castin's phone, and I'd have a look at his photos and contacts.

She stretched her arms. "I'm so tired, I could go to bed."

I gulped. "What kind of guy was he?"

"Friendly," and added, "in case you're wondering, I batted my eyelashes at him a few times, but I never saw the inside of his apartment. Even with all the female visitors, I wondered if he was gay."

Probably, I thought, Castin decided to avoid creating the jealous neighbor from hell.

"You really have beautiful blue eyes," she said, stretching languidly.

End of interview. I cleared my throat and stood.

She spoke quickly. "You should talk to Ivan Gorky in 6F.

He could be Edward Castin's evil twin. Rumors say he's connected with the Russian mob."

"I'll do that," I said making haste toward the door. I half expected to be tackled and let out a relieved breath when I was safely outside. I phoned the precinct and learned that Ivan Gorky had been picked up a couple of times in red-mob Brighton Beach hangouts but never charged. Miss Supple's comments had opened two lines of investigation. Castin could've been done in by a jealous husband or fallen victim to some sort of gang-hit mistaken identity. I walked up a floor to Ivan Gorky's apartment.

He was home, answering through a closed door and only opening a crack when he saw my badge through a peep hole.

"Were you expecting a hostile visitor?" I asked.

"No," he said without conviction. He opened the door wider, his eyes scanning the hallway but didn't invite me in. Over his shoulder, I spotted a half-empty gallon of vodka on a cocktail table. Miss Supple's description of him as Castin's twin was excessive, but they had the same blond hair, size, and build, and on a dark street Castin could've been mistaken for Gorky.

"I'm investigating the murder of Edward Castin who lived in 5G."

"Didn't know him," Gorky responded in a gruff, Russian accented voice.

"Had you heard he'd been killed?"

"Saw it on the TV news."

"You two have a rough resemblance. If someone was after

you, they could've shot him thinking you were the target?"

He seemed unfazed by my suggestion. "Everything is possible."

"So, someone is after you?"

"Nobody still alive," he said in a dismissive tone. "Anything else, officer?"

"Not now," I said and walked away.

*****

Back at the precinct, I got a call from Agent Maxwell at the FBI. We'd worked a case together and developed a mutual respect.

"Your victim Castin was a person of interest in an insider trading securities fraud investigation. Someone tipped him on the success of a biotech's phase 3 cancer drug trial, and we believe he collected a fat commission when he profited a Russian mobster, Yuri Sharov's account. We'd confronted Castin and although he made no admission of wrongdoing, we were negotiating for his testimony against the Russian. His boss, Rich Bastar may have been in on the scheme. I wanted you to know before you inquired about Castin at the firm."

"Do you know who gave him the inside information?"

"That would've been part of our deal. None of the company executives traded before the news became public."

"You think Castin was silenced?"

"Can't rule it out."

*****

When I was ushered into the cavernous office of Rich Bastar of Bastar and Holmes, he was dressed in a thousand-dollar suit and didn't stand, merely raising his eyes from a desk the size of an Olympic pool.

"I'm investigating the murder of Edward Castin," I said.

"Terrible tragedy. Our top performer, he was our youngest vice president and would've been a named partner before much longer. I hope you find who killed him."

I took a seat opposite him and gazed around at the paintings and expensive furnishings. The only thing missing was a golden idol.

"Will this take long?" he asked with a tone of impatience.

Oh, boy. Much longer than it would have, I thought, putting all my actions into slow motion.

As I removed my notepad from my jacket inside pocket, and flipped pages, I repeatedly clicked the ballpoint for maximum annoyance.

His darkened expression reminded me of a smoking volcano.

"What can you tell me about Edward Castin?"

"A master of the straddle, swap, derivative, and hedge. A foreign language, I suppose, to you, Detective."

I loved meeting condescending assholes who believed they were the smartest person in the room. I chose to ignore his disrespect. "Did he take drugs?"

Bastar stiffened. "Not in my presence."

Not a denial. I'd wait for the toxicology report. "Tell me about his clients?"

Bastar raised his arms. "The crème de la crème of Manhattan's elite. Our firm develops a personal relationship with our customers. Edward consulted with them about their plans, hopes, and dreams, then designed and executed a financial plan to exceed their expectations. We insist on a minimum of ten million dollars to invest, but Edward was in such demand that we contemplated raising that to twenty million."

"You never heard a complaint?"

He answered with a dismissive wave. "We received a few death threats after the crash in 2008, but these days," he chuckled at his cleverness, "the market is heaven with foie gras."

The guy was wearing on me, so I hit him with a zinger. "Had Castin gotten a bit too close to any client wives?"

Bastar blinked a few times before answering, perhaps wondering what I knew. "That would've violated our ethics code."

"I'm sure he'd never do that," I said with a trace of sarcasm. "Anyone cancel their relationship with your firm recently?"

"I couldn't reveal that."

"I'd like a list of your investors so I can speak with them."

Bastar fidgeted uncomfortably. "I'm afraid you'll need a subpoena. Our clients have an expectation of confidentiality."

"With Castin gone, how are you handling his clients?"

"I'm taking them."

"They'll soon learn that their association with your firm has involved them in a murder investigation." I stood. "I'll be in touch." When I got to the door, I turned. "Were any of Castin's clients connected with the Russian mob?"

Bastar gulped before croaking out, "Confidential."

I smiled and when I left, I called Maxwell.

"Get anything?" he asked.

"More suspicions. I didn't mention Sharov's name, but when I asked if they had a red-mob client, Bastar almost shit in his silk drawers."

*****

Inside the autopsy room, the razor thin coroner stood aside Castin's body. I never got used to the smell and wondered how anyone could, but the ME acted like we stood in a floral field.

"What have you got?" I asked, hoping he'd be succinct.

He ticked off the details in a dry tone. "Three gunshot wounds in the back. 9 mm. Single weapon. No DNA from his assailant on the body, no skin under the fingernails. Traces of cocaine were in his system." He sighed. "Sorry, Mr. Castin didn't provide me with any clues as to who shot him."

I thanked him and left, heading for Johnny Digital, my nickname for our thirty-year old reclusive tech expert with black stud earrings, who I could imagine hacking into banks if he left our employ.

"Do you know how difficult these phones are to unlock?" he asked.

Johnny obviously needed some strokes, so I laid it on thick. "You're a genius. I don't know how we'd solve cases without you."

A narcissist, with no complement seeming excessive, he puffed up like a happy parakeet, and excitedly showed me what he had. Scrolling through Castin's pictures of women in various states of undress, he stopped at one, beaming like he'd discovered a lost treasure map.

"Recognize her?" he asked expectantly.

The fortyish woman knelt on a bed, holding her arms overhead like a posing *Sports Illustrated* swimsuit model, sans the bathing suit.

I could tell from his face that my hesitation disappointed him.

"I bet you don't subscribe to *People Magazine*," he said glumly.

I asked with some exasperation. "Want to tell me who she is?"

He shot me a snide look and kept me in suspense while he searched the internet for a picture of Darcy Warren, the leading candidate for New York mayor in the next election. The caption identified the person next to him as Sylvia Warren, his wife, and the woman in Castin's photo.

"Holy shit," I said.

"Yeah," Johnny said, "Castin was porking the next mayor's wife. *People Magazine* would pay plenty for that story."

I stared hard at him. "Don't you dare."

"Hey," he said in a defensive tone, "I was kidding."

"I'm taking this to Lieutenant Dixon. Not a word to anyone."

"Yeah. Okay."

*****

I closed Dixon's door before slumping into a chair opposite him. "Would you care for a hot potato?"

His eyes went from me to the photo of Sylvia Warren I slid over to him, saying, "We found this on Castin's phone."

"Christ."

"You recognized her. I'm impressed."

"We met at a fundraiser. He lifted the picture for a closer look. "This woman is in shape."

I teased. "Want a wallet-sized copy?"

He slid the photo back to me. "Who has seen this?"

"Johnny Digital and the two of us. I think I scared him into keeping quiet."

Dixon leaned his chair back, sticking his thumbs under his belt. "Would Darcy Warren kill a guy because he slept with his wife?"

"Perhaps not him personally, but a loyalist could've done him a favor."

Dixon blew out a frustrated breath. "What else have you got on the case?"

"Castin boffed a slew of women, probably enraging more boyfriends and husbands than just Darcy Warren. And the FBI was investigating him for insider trading in a conspiracy with a Russian mobster, Yuri Sharov. Castin also snorted cocaine."

"Talk about a guy living on the edge…" Dixon shook his head.

"Motives for his murder range from being killed trying to score drugs, a robbery gone wrong, jealousy, a gang hit, or a case of mistaken identity. The more I dig, the more options I find. The only thing I know for sure is that he didn't commit suicide."

"But your best hypothesis is that he was assassinated by the Russian?"

I frowned. "A double tap to the skull rather than three shots in the back would be more like a professional hit. And although Castin never regained consciousness, leaving him alive on the street was amateurish."

"You'd agree that the murderer collecting his brass suggests a presence of mind."

"He didn't panic, but a cop show could've taught him to clean up after the shooting."

Dixon scratched his chin. "I suppose you'll need to approach Darcy Warren."

"If he knew about his wife's infidelity, he's a suspect."

"If the scandal gets out, he'll be damaged as a candidate, but if he wins in November, he'll remember that the NYPD, particularly you and I, almost killed his chances."

"Vengeance is mine, sayeth the politician."

"Exactly."

"Are you telling me to stay clear of him?"

"I'm advising you to tread so lightly that walking on eggshells would seem like stomping."

Dixon looked as depressed as I felt when he waved me out of his office.

I was contemplating how I'd approach Warren when my phone buzzed with a call from Agent Maxwell.

"I hope you have good news because I definitely need some cheering up," I said.

"Remember the insider trading case and Yuri Sharov?"

"How can I forget?"

"Turns out he used the proceeds to funnel political donations through multiple Russians he later reimbursed, a scheme to circumvent campaign contribution limits."

"Tell me he spread the money widely," I said, dreading his response.

"No. Just to Darcy Warren."

My shoulders slumped.

Maxwell was upbeat. "He'll be the next mayor. Big deal. Huh?"

I blew out a breath.

"Wait, I have more," he said.

I took a seat. "Go ahead."

"Warren has a regular golfing foursome at a Westchester club every Saturday. One of the players is the CEO of the biotech firm of the insider trading scheme. I think I've found my leak."

"So, Warren gets a tip on a stock he passes to Castin, who makes a ton of money for a Russian thug, who donates cash surreptitiously to Warren's mayoral campaign guaranteeing the Russian that he'll have a guy in Gracie Mansion who owes him big time?"

"Bingo."

"What are you going to do about it?"

"With Castin dead, the link to prove Sharov traded on a tip is gone. He'll claim he followed his broker's advice and was lucky. Warren will disavow knowledge of campaign contributors. The most Sharov gets is a slap on the wrist. To put them away, pin the murder of Castin on them."

*****

How do I question a murder suspect with the finesse of handling a snowflake, so the interrogation doesn't boomerang and take me out at the knees? The only way I knew how to proceed was straightforwardly. If Warren was guilty of Castin's murder, I'd nail his ass.

Handsome, physically fit, wearing a blue tie, white shirt, and gray suit with an American flag lapel pin, I found Warren in his campaign headquarters, and he invited me into his office.

"I'm always happy to speak to members of law enforcement. You guys are heroes."

I smiled politely at the confetti he'd thrown at me. "Did you know Edward Castin?" I asked in an innocent tone.

"You're investigating his murder? Of course. Terrible shame. Such a bright young man. My wife and I invest with Bastar and Holmes and he handled our finances."

I watched Warren for a sign of discomfort in discussing his wife's lover. "What did you think of him?"

"Capable," Warren said without a change in facial expression. "He knew his job and we did well financially."

I skated closer to the nub. "I've been told that he was quite a ladies' man. Did you ever see him in the company of women?"

"He handled himself professionally, and we had no personal interactions."

"Neither you nor your wife?"

260

He stiffened. "What are you implying?"

He knows about the affair, I thought, but he's not sure if I do.

"I hate to break this news to you, but we found evidence on Castin's phone that he had a close relationship with your wife."

Warren grimaced, but he remained silent.

I returned to my innocent tone. "Do you have any idea who might have killed him?"

His tone was brusque. "If I did, I would've come directly to the police."

"Of course, but sometimes we have suspicions we might not wish to volunteer. I assure you anything you tell me will be completely confidential."

"Like speaking to a priest."

"You could say that."

"You want to hear my confession?"

"If there's something you wish to get off your chest."

Warren had recovered his composure. "If Edward Castin stole blossoms from other men's gardens, why should anyone be surprised he got a dose of DDT." He stood. "I have nothing else to say, Detective, and I have other appointments." His tone became threatening. "By the way, if that picture you say you have becomes public, I'll be deeply disappointed in the police."

I left his office convinced that he was involved in Castin's murder.

*****

Tatiana's Restaurant in Brighton Beach was abuzz with the clatter of plates and Russian conversation. Before I arrived, I looked up asshole in Russian, *mudak*, in case it would come in handy. When I approached a tattooed hulk the size of a sequoia, I could smell his sweat and acrid breath. He blocked the doorway to a private dining room where a wiry, tattooed, pasty white Sharov and two young women were having lunch. I flashed my badge, and the goon glanced over his shoulder toward his boss, got a nod, and let me in.

The two dark-haired women wore plunging dresses. Sharov said, "Get lost," and they hurriedly left the room.

On a lintel behind him sat a horizontal line of Russian *matryoshka* nesting dolls, lions with mouths open ready to gobble their smaller neighbor.

Sharov displayed a disturbing smirk.

I remained standing and leaned my knuckles on the table. "I'm investigating the murder of Edward Castin."

"Do I know him?" Sharov asked with mock surprise.

"You were his client."

"Maybe." He shrugged. "So what?"

"If you know who murdered him, now would be the time to tell me."

Sharov leaned back. "Detective, you waltz in here and expect me to be a police informant?"

"I will find who killed him."

"Of course you will," he said in a sarcastic tone and added, "have a drink on me. That's all I have for you."

I left muttering *mudak*, certain that Sharov had probably

ordered the killing for his mayor friend.

*****

Johnny Digital tried to avoid me, but I cornered him in the men's room.

"Something terrible happened."

"Spill it," I demanded.

"I must've plugged in the wrong password too many times and Castin's phone wiped its memory. The picture's gone."

"Bullshit," I said, "destroying evidence is obstruction of justice."

"It was a mistake. I swear."

I left him and stormed into Dixon's office.

As I entered, he said, "I heard."

My voice was loud. "Are you going to fire that twerp?"

"Sit down."

I began to speak, and he held up a palm. "Calm down."

I slammed my butt into a chair.

He took a few beats before he said, "The photograph was toxic. Do you think the brass want the next mayor to put a target on NYPD's back?"

"Warren is complicit in Castin's murder."

Dixon's eyebrows rose. "You have proof?"

"Sharov ordered the hit on Warren's behalf."

"Let's see your evidence."

I puffed out an angry breath and crossed my arms.

"What do I always say?" Dixon asked.

I reluctantly responded. "Detectives without evidence are loudmouths with an opinion."

He raised his arms in shrugged agreement, pausing before saying, "Get me proof of Warren's guilt, and we'll bring the evidence together to the Commissioner, but not a salacious photo that simply damages a woman's reputation."

*****

I was back in my office when a rumpled bed of a detective shuffled into my office with a self-satisfied grin on his face. "Late last night, Ivan Gorky received a double tap to the head on the same street as Castin."

I sat up straight.

He waved a paper in my face. "I just received forensics on the 9mm found on him." He paused dramatically. "The gun matches the slugs found in Castin. I solved your murder."

I stared at him, and his face morphed into a pissed-off frown.

"I don't know what's eating you, Bragg, but the least you could do is thank me," he said before lumbering out of my office.

When he was gone, the female voice in my skull screamed. "You worthless slab of protoplasm. Warren and Sharov got the better of you. Kill them both or you'll never rest."

I pulled out my phone like drawing a six shooter. I dialed and got voice mail. "Beverly, I need to see you."

I ran to my car and sped to the West Village, zigzagging through traffic, horns blaring around me.

The voice wouldn't stop.

I parked illegally and left my shield on the dash, hoping I wouldn't get towed.

The raging in my head continued.

I arrived at Beverly's office breathing hard, ignored her receptionist, and burst into a session.

The woman on the couch looked startled.

Beverly frowned at first but then must've read the expression on my face.

"Helen, I have an emergency. I'm sorry. I'll make up the time next week. Thanks for understanding."

I stood trembling in the center of the room as Beverly closed the door.

She neared me.

"The harpy's back." I begged. "Can't we skip the psychiatry chitchat today?"

Beverly ran a soothing hand through my hair. "Psychiatry chitchat is my favorite foreplay," she giggled, as she melted into my arms.

The voice huffed but stayed silent.

The Usual Unusual Suspects

Laurence Raphael Brothers is a writer and a technologist with 5 patents and a background in AI and Internet R&D. He has published over 35 short stories in such magazines as Nature, PodCastle, and the New Haven Review. He is most proud of his romantic noir urban fantasy novellas The Demons of Wall Street and The Demons of the Square Mile (Mirror World Publishing, 2020 and 2021). Follow Laurence on twitter: @lbrothers or visit https://laurencebrothers.com/bibliography for more stories that can be read or listened to online.

With degrees in Crime Scene Technology and Physical Anthropology, Florida author *Shannon Hollinger* hasn't just seen the dark side of humanity - she's been elbow deep inside of it! To see where you can find more of her work, check out www.shannonhollinger.com.

Lillie Franks is an author and teacher who lives in Chicago, Illinois with the best cats. You can read her work at places like *Always Crashing*, *Poemeleon*, and *Drunk Monkeys* or follow her on Twitter at @onyxaminedlife. She loves anything that is not the way it should be.

H.E. Vogl is a retired professor who has turned to writing fiction. His stories, occasionally dark but always absurd, explore the quirks in the fabric of everyday life. Vogl's work has appeared in *Fiction on the Web*, *Bewildering Stories*, *Every Day Fiction*, and *Fabula Argentea*.

Allison Whittenberg is a Philly native who has a global perspective. If she wasn't an author she'd be a private detective or a jazz singer. She loves reading about history and true crime. Her other novels include *Sweet Thang*, *Hollywood and Maine*, *Life is Fine*, *Tutored*, *The Carnival of Reality* and *The Sane Asylum*.

Bruce Harris writes Crime, Mystery, and Western stories. He is the author of *Sherlock Holmes and Doctor Watson: About Type* (2006) and *Anticipations* in D. Martin Dakin's *A Sherlock Holmes Commentary* (2021).
His *Murder at Bullet Pass* appeared in *CRIMEUCOPIA – Dead Man's Hand*.

Robert J. Mendenhall is a retired police officer, retired Air National Guardsman, and former Broadcast Journalist for the American Forces Network, Europe. A member of Science Fiction and Fantasy Writers of America and Mystery Writers of America, he writes in multiple genres including science fiction, historical fiction, crime and suspense, horror, and pulp adventure. He holds a Master of Fine Arts in Writing from Lindenwood University, St. Charles, Missouri.
He has had short stories published at Saturday Evening Post.com and in three *Star Trek: Strange New Worlds* anthologies by Pocket Books. He has also been published in

anthologies from Kayelle Press, Dark Quest Books, Fey Publishing, Dreadful Café Press, Chaosium Publishing, Zimbell House Publishing, Local Hero Press, Nomadic Delirium Press, Rogue Star Press, Airship 27 Productions, and Dark Alley Press, as well as various print and web magazines. Visit his web site: RobertJMendenhall.com, follow him on Twitter: @robtjmendenhall, or send him an email at: robert@robertjmendenhall.com.

Shawn Kobb is an American diplomat who has lived, worked, and traveled the world. He uses this experience to fuel his writing. He has numerous writing credits in mystery, horror, sci-fi, and fantasy. You can find out more about his writing at shawnkobb.com. He is currently living in Budapest, Hungary.

Dan Meyers sadly passed away in 2018 after becoming the victim of a massive stroke, from which he never recovered. We first made contact in a writer's forum in 2015, where he asked questions, then asked if I would become his beta reader. The pieces were not quick in coming – he owned and worked a farm in the US, but wrote during the winter periods when he had a fraction more spare time to do so. The two that were completed were originally destined for a proper anthology of his work, to be titled *Tales from the Travelling Carnival*. Dan's *First Person Singular* appeared in *CRIMEUCOPIA – We're All Animals Under The Skin*.

James Roth is an American who likes to say he was "Made in Japan" during the U.S. occupation of that country. He lived there for many years. China as well. But now he divides his time between Zimbabwe, South Africa, and the U.S., places where it never snows. He writes fiction and nonfiction in a variety of genres and recently completed a historical mystery/noir novel set in Meiji era Yokohama.

His *A Career Killing* appeared in *CRIMEUCOPIA – Careless Love*.

Jesse Aaron served as a police officer in New York City and Connecticut for over five years and also worked in the field of private security/investigations. His first novel, *Shafer City Stories* is available on Amazon.com and he is currently working on a compilation of *Sam Burden* stories for future publication. Jesse's style is dark and gritty and his stories focus on the underside of the police and private detective worlds. Jesse has a love of all things Noir, Science Fiction, and Fantasy.

Julian Grant is a filmmaker, educator, and author of strange short stories plus full-length novels/non-fiction texts and comics. A tenured Associate Professor at Columbia College Chicago, his work has been published by **Quail Bell, Avalon Literary Review, Crepe & Penn, The Chamber Magazine, Clever Magazine, Peeking Cat Literary Journal, Danse Macabre, Fiction on the Web, CafeLit, Horla, Bond Street Review, Free Bundle, Filth Magazine & The Adelaide Literary Magazine**. Find out more about him at www.juliangrant.com.

E. James Wilson is a 20-something 70-year-old, born in Brazil to English and American parents. At the age of 15 he taught himself to type because most of his school teachers stated that his handwriting was, at best, atrocious. From that point on it was a rapid descent into cheap cigarettes and lurid prose, to the point where his parents bought him a book tutorial on Pitman Shorthand and told him to become a journalist.

Fifty-five years later he is still writing fiction, but it's no longer printed in newspapers as fact.

At present he is living on a small farm in Patagonia, with some chickens and half a dozen goats.

Brandon Barrows is the author of the novels *Burn Me Out, This Rough Old World, Nervosa*, and has had over seventy published stories, a selection of which are collected in the books *The Alter In The Hills* and *The Castle-Town Tragedy*. He is an active member of Private Eye Writers of America and International Thriller Writers, and lives in Vermont by a big lake with a patient wife and two impatient cats.

His short story, *Don't You See?* appeared in *Crimeucopia – As In Funny Ha-Ha, Or Just Peculiar* – and *Night After Night* appeared in the *Crimeucopia – Careless Love* anthology.

He can be found at http://www.brandonbarrowscomics.com
On Twitter @Brandon Barrows

Hollis Miller is a first-year high school English teacher and recent creative writing alumnus of Lenoir-Rhyne University. During his tenure as a student, he began to explore what it meant to write good fiction, especially the gritty kind. He was awarded the Edythe Beam Mayes Award for exceptional talent in creative writing by the university, which he received in both 2020 and 2021. He is only twenty-two years old, and this is his first publication.

Joe Giordano was born in Brooklyn. He and his wife Jane now live in Texas.

Joe's stories have appeared in more than one hundred magazines including *The Saturday Evening Post, and Shenandoah*. His novels, *Birds of Passage, An Italian Immigrant Coming of Age Story* (2015), and *Appointment with ISIL, an Anthony Provati Thriller* (2017) were published by Harvard Square Editions. Rogue Phoenix Press published *Drone Strike* (2019) and his short story collection, *Stories and Places I Remember* (2020).

Joe's *Prophetic Justice* appeared in *CRIMEUCOPIA – The I's Have It (MIP 2021)*

Joe was among one hundred Italian American authors honored by Barnes & Noble to march in Manhattan's 2017 Columbus Day Parade. Read the first chapter of Joe's novels and sign up for his blog at http://joe-giordano.com/

16 stories ranging from the 14th to the 21st Century, all from women authors whose forte is crime.

Featuring *Karen Skinner, Hilary Davidson, Pauline Gostling, Linda Kerr, Kate Miller, Tiffany Lindfield, Lena Ng, Ginny Swart, Sandrine Bergèss, Michelle Ann King, Amanda Steel, Kelly Lewis, Paulene Turner, Claire Leng, Madeleine McDonald and Joan Hall Hovey.*

Paperback Edition ISBN:
9781909498198
eBook Edition ISBN:
9781909498204

CRIMEUCOPIA

We're All Animals Under The Skin

Featuring: John Gerard Fagan, Nick Boldock,
Weldon Burge, Chris Phillips, Dan Meyers,
Jeff Dosser, Eve Fisher, Emilian Wojnowski,
Fabiyas M V, Lamont A. Turner, Edward Ahern,
Robert Petyo, Al Hagan, Caroline Tuohey,
Steve Carr, Bobby Mathews, Michael Bracken,
and June Lorraine Roberts

18 authors take time to look under the skin of the people who sometimes inhabit their heads, and put what they find down on paper.

Featuring John Gerard Fagan, Nick Boldock, Weldon Burge, Chris Phillips, Dan Meyers, Jeff Dosser, Eve Fisher, Emilian Wojnowski, Fabiyas M V, Lamont A. Turner, Edward Ahern, Robert Petyo, Al Hagan, Caroline Tuohey, Steve Carr, Bobby Mathews, Michael Bracken, and June Lorraine Roberts.

Paperback Edition ISBN:
9781909498235
eBook Edition ISBN:
9781909498228

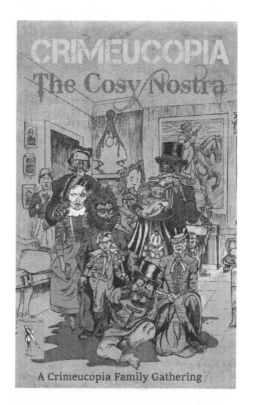

A Crimeucopia Family Gathering

17 writers take us on Cosy journeys - some more traditional, while others are very much up to date.

Eve Fisher, Alexander Frew, Tom Johnstone, John M.Floyd, Andrew Humphrey, Joan Leotta, Gary Thomson, Eamonn Murphey, Matias Travieso-Diaz, Madeline McEwen, Lyn Fraser, Ella Moon, Gina L. Grandi, Louise Taylor, Judy Penz Sheluk, Joan Hall Hovey and Judy Upton.

Paperback Edition ISBN: 9781909498242
eBook Edition ISBN: 9781909498259

CRIMEUCOPIA

As In Funny Ha-Ha

Or Just Peculiar

Putting the Outré back into OMG are

*Jesse Hilson, Gabriel Stevenson,
Maddi Davidson, Brandon Barrows,
Robb T. White, Regina Clarke,
Martin Zeigler, K. G. Anderson,
Andrew Hook, Ed Nobody,
Jody Smith, Michael Grimala,
W. T. Paterson, James Blakey,
Emilian Wojnowski,
Andrew Darlington,
Lawrence Allan, Ricky Sprague,
Bethany Maines, John M. Floyd and
Julie Richards*

**Paperback Edition ISBN:
9781909498266
eBook Edition ISBN:
9781909498273**

*The five writers here have very
respectable track records in the
Western genre, and are old
hands when it comes to telling
compelling stories.*

*So join
John M. Floyd
Alexander Frew
Jim Doherty
Bruce Harris
and
Brandon Barrows*

*and let them take you back to a
time of six-guns an' whiskey,
an' wild, wild fiction.*

*Paperback Edition ISBN:
9781909498266
eBook Edition ISBN:
9781909498273*

You're driving me crazy
You're making me mad
'Cos the only way of lovin' you
Is with a good love gone bad...
(Vicky LaPerso – The 1956 Ventura Tapes)

Oh Baby, Baby, How Was I Supposed To Know...

Is Love ever perfect? Or is it an obsession that remains rather than just a passing phase? And who's to say that Revenge isn't, in fact, a dish best served hot from the flames of passion?

Fifteen writers tell us about affairs of the heart – some with humour, some with a darker intent, and others that are never quite exactly what they seem. Is it all about manipulation? Can there be more than one agenda? And does Love really conquer all, even when it's supposedly blind? Or maybe Love is just an old Devil, looking for mischief?

Steve Sneyd, Ange Morrissey, James Roth, Michael Wiley, Gustavo Bondoni, Matthew Wilson, Peter W. J. Hayes, Wil A. Emerson, Brandon Barrows, Bern Sy Moss, Michael Anthony Dioguardi, Russell Richardson, Robert Petyo, Sam Westcott, Bryn Fortey and *Vicky LaPerso* – all of whom take us on roller coaster rides through a fictional Tunnel of Love.

Paperback Edition ISBN: 9781909498303
eBook Edition ISBN: 9781909498310

CRIMEUCOPIA
The 👁's Have It

*Featuring: Mike Job, Jill Hand,
Joe Giordano, Michael Thomét,
Michele Bazan Reed, Paul R. Paradise,
M. C. Tuggle, Edward Lodi, Lynn Hesse,
Kelly Zimmer, John M. Floyd
and Shannon Lawrence*

It Was 3:15 in the A.M...

Investigators and investigations are the mainstay of most Crime fiction sub-genres. Everything from the original *Golden Age* of country houses and the amateur sleuth, through to the high tech ultra-modern 21st Century – a place where the cyber investigators sometimes appear to be baffled by old-fashioned motivations of power and greed, and human foibles such as love and revenge.

So is there any real difference between the Private and the Public Sector investigators? Not much, if writers are to be believed, and the two can often be found straddling both sides of the 'what's legal procedure?' fence.

Of the twelve authors contained within, eleven are voices new to the world of Crimeucopia - and although the theme is *Investigators*, the material ranges from Cosy, through to not too Hardboiled - and most are touched with a vein of humour, be it light or dark. Rather like a box of chocolates...

Featuring: Mike Job, Jill Hand, Joe Giordano, Michael Thomét, Michele Bazan Reed, Paul R. Paradise, M. C. Tuggle, Edward Lodi, Lynn Hesse, Kelly Zimmer, John M. Floyd and Shannon Lawrence.

Paperback Edition ISBN: 9781909498327
eBook Edition ISBN: 9781909498334

Made in the USA
Coppell, TX
11 May 2022

77684490R00169